DREAMS AND DESIRES

Her lover lowered himself to the edge of her bed, his black velvet dressing gown a shocking contrast against her lace coverlet. He reached across the expanse between them and stroked her loose hair. Down his fingers slid, letting her tangled locks fall across the back of his strong fingers, down still farther until they came to her shoulder. His warm hand curved around her neck and slipped under her loose bed gown, then across her back and around her shoulder, forcing the gown to give way in his direction.

He smiled at her as her breathing quickened, and without freeing her gaze from his, his clever fingers pulled at the ties that held the front of her gown together, and his hand resumed its exploring.

Elizabeth awoke with a start, crossing her arms protectively across her bosom. "Oh no," she cried, "not again."

Again Elizabeth had been visited in her sleep by this stranger who seemed so familiar yet whom she could not recognize. She knew only one thing. Her dreams always came true. But how she wanted this one to end, she was not sure and trembled at the thought of finding out . . . .

Elizabeth's Gift

Elizabeth's Gift

by

Donna Davidson

A SIGNET BOOK

SIGNET
Published by the Penguin Group
Penguin Books USA Inc., 375 Hudson Street,
New York, New York 10014, U.S.A.
Penguin Books Ltd, 27 Wrights Lane,
London W8 5TZ, England
Penguin Books Australia Ltd, Ringwood,
Victoria, Australia
Penguin Books Canada Ltd, 10 Alcorn Avenue,
Toronto, Ontario, Canada M4V 3B2
Penguin Books (N.Z.) Ltd, 182–190 Wairau Road,
Auckland 10, New Zealand

Penguin Books Ltd, Registered Offices:
Harmondsworth, Middlesex, England

First published by Signet,
an imprint of Dutton Signet,
a division of Penguin Books USA Inc.

First Printing, April, 1994
10 9 8 7 6 5 4 3 2 1

Thanks to those whose skilled assistance
nudged Hawksley and Elizabeth to a happy ending:
Karyl Barnett—critique partner and friend;
Greg Alt and David Trottier—screenwriters and mentors;
Orange County RWA—friends and teachers;
Pat Teal—agent extraordinnaire and
Allan—historian

Dedicated to
Allan, husband and lifelong sweetheart

Chapter One

Paxton, England, June 1809

NATHAN DUNBAR, Marquess of Hawksley, heaved his tall frame from the bath, delivering a careless spray into the roaring fire. Angry hot spits of steam mirrored his black mood and two large puddles of water soaked into the carpet at his feet.

"Sent like a damned errand boy," he muttered, "to spy on Elizabeth, an impudent young chit of sixteen summers with no manners and even less looks."

He raked the toweling roughly over his arms and chest, swearing in disgust as the elegant, embroidered scrap of linen crumpled soddenly in his hand. "Damned henhouse!"

His charcoal eyes swept around the room, tallying crocheted doilies, dainty lamps, and even turned-down bed sheets bearing the offending feminine touches of tatting and lace. A deep longing swept through him for the rough, masculine comfort of home at Standbridge with Grandfather roaring at old retainers, dogs sprawled underfoot, and some uncensored, meaningful conversation.

Making arrangements for Elizabeth's debut in London was not a task for the heir to a dukedom, two full years past his majority, but Grandfather, the wily old devil, had added a mystery that he knew would ensure Hawksley's compliance. *"Get to know the gel again now she's grown. She's the last twig on your grandmother's family branch, and if my suspicions are not playing me false, she'll liven up your visit and present a puzzle to satisfy even your inquisitive mind."*

He tossed the useless wet cloth into the cooling bathwater and stepped back toward the fire, his powerful back and leg muscles shuddering in pleasure as cold, wet skin heated and dried. He closed his eyes and rolled his head backward from side to side, his mouth relaxing in a moment of self-mockery. Despite his grandfather's finest-sprung carriage and most skilled and sober coachmen, the English summer rain and highway potholes had, as always, prevailed. He should have spent the last three days on the back of a surefooted, intelligent horse, and to the devil with the weather; he'd choose a soft rain over bruised bones every time.

He shuddered again as he recalled the twittering reception he'd endured tonight.

He'd arrived just as the dinner gong sounded, putting paid to his most fervent wish, to be pointed toward any horizontal surface, preferably a well-warmed bed, where his frozen body could thaw comfortably while his mind remained happily unconscious during the process. Several devious strategies for evading the dinner table strutted out for selection, but none could outshine the pride and anticipation of his welcoming committee. Nor could he, or any gentleman in the kingdom, be less than gracious to Elizabeth's aunt, the kind and gentle Eunice Wydner. Resigned, he assured her it was a small matter to erase his travel dirt, and was quickly shown to his chamber.

Presentable at last, he'd hurried to the cozy dining room, smiled and complimented through each dainty remove, and carefully observed Elizabeth, his prey. Surprised that it was Elizabeth who unobtrusively directed the serving girls, he'd almost missed the probing examination she conducted of him in return. He raised a dark eyebrow, daunting to any but the most foolhardy, but she lifted her chin and stared back, while her fingers trembled and fumbled for her water glass.

Then, almost as if startled, the fluttering fingers stilled and she'd gasped, leaned forward, and looked deeply into his eyes. Oblivious to his questioning expression, she fell back against her chair and a pleased little sigh floated into the air. Without the courtesy of an explanation for the tiny drama, she smiled pleasantly and signaled the serving girl to refill his plate.

His irritation grew as the ladies' attention enveloped him like a snug tea cozy. As each lady pressed upon him a hearty portion of her favorite food, the muscles in his legs twitched with exhaustion and he fought against the enticing urge to clear the table with a mighty sweep of his arm. Overfed and overcosseted, he was dangerously near the brink of some unforgivable breach of manners.

He begged to be excused from the table, pleading travel fatigue. They immediately fussed and clucked anew—he thought for a moment they were going to follow him to bed and tuck him in. He bowed and kissed each hand, determined to ferret out some reasonable male servant and order a steaming bath for his aching body.

Before he could escape from the room and articulate his bone-weary needs to anyone, Elizabeth smoothly intervened, affectionately shooing her aunt and cousin into the parlor, briskly dispatching a hot bath to his room, and bidding him wait for her return. She reappeared moments later with a tray bearing a perfect hot toddy, concocted exactly as he liked it. With a few soft words, she had provided the secret cravings of his imagination.

He'd tried to pull back the reins of his runaway annoyance and express the proper appreciation, but as he opened his mouth to bestow a fitting word of gratitude, she looked directly into his eyes, without a touch of proper feminine respect, and smiled a *knowing* little smile. Gad, he would liked to have smacked the impertinent expression off that plain little freckled face, but the lightest blow would have left nothing but a pile of skinny broken bones and no triumph at all.

Now, contentedly alone, his aching muscles soothed by the warm bath and his admittedly unreasonable temper appeased by Elizabeth's intuitive knowledge of just what comforts a man needed, he could certainly overlook the fact that, although she was nothing like the sweet, biddable child he remembered, her forward behavior did in the end rescue him.

He would arrange the financial particulars for Elizabeth's season with Eunice Wydner early in the morning and be on his way before noon. As for his report to Grandfather, he could tell him with perfect honesty that his precious ward was unique, an original—

A hesitant scratching at the door alerted him to servants returning to remove the bath. He snatched his dressing gown from the foot of the bed, quickly slipped it on, and roared. "Come!"

Her again, he thought, as Elizabeth's distinctive, surprisingly low voice floated through the open door, calmly giving directions. The servants hurried into the bedchamber, nervously darting glances at the barefooted, barely clad young guest. He had no need to check his reflection in the tall pier glass to know what they saw; he'd overheard more than one whispered remark to describe society's view of him. "A great hulk of a man, my dear, not unlike the bear at Astley's Circus, but rich and a duke someday . . . so smile when he makes his bows."

The servants finished and began to leave. He waited to see if she would enter, curiously eager for their next encounter, if only to ask her about her strange behavior at dinner. Very properly, she remained out of sight.

He stepped out into the hall. She stood quietly a few feet from the doorway, overseeing the cumbersome tub's ungainly journey down the back stairway. She still wore the simple faded muslin gown he had been annoyed to see at dinner, so unlike the ice-blue confection adorning her elegant, flirting cousin, Mariane, or her Aunt Eunice's softly draped gown and scarves. All this infuriating girl needed was an encompassing apron to complete the costume of a country servant.

"Did you need something, my lord?" she asked, turning to face him. Her solemn expression instantly disintegrated, her wide eyes blinking rapidly, her mouth open, gawking like a startled bird. He realized the cause at once—he had carelessly presented himself before her covered only with the hastily donned dressing gown. Manners dictated a contrite apology and speedy retreat. But, fascinated, he watched her expression, transparent for once, as her curiosity took over. She took a deep breath, then swiftly inspected him, gulping a little at bare, heavily muscled legs, her eyes growing wider as she continued slowly upward to his broad chest. Yet she carried on with a thorough, studious absorption, amusing him with how closely she resembled his last tutor as that worthy scholar had plowed doggedly through the library, soaking up book after book, tucking information away like a squirrel storing nuts for winter.

He took advantage of her distraction and quickly returned the appraisal. She was thin, but clearly a female, with slight, immature breasts, but no man-stirring feminine appeal. Her finely boned face was all eyes, deep-water green, framed with light auburn brows and lashes. Her mouth was too wide when she smiled, and too small in repose. He could have rested his hand on top of her head without raising his arm more than shoulder-high. Her fragrance evoked an almost forgotten memory of his mother . . . lavender . . . brisk, sweet lavender. But then, he never dwelt on maudlin thoughts. Never.

"Does my grandfather not support this family properly," he mocked, "that a child must order the household?" Ah, that stiff-

ened her spine and brought her back to attention. Her hair flew as
her head snapped up to face him, the carroty frizz standing up like
a hissing kitten. Her eyes flashed, bright green now, like blinding
sunshine on new spring leaves. He watched the peach flush of
temper move up her neck and face as she struggled to regain control. Why so much pride for a female only ten years and six, and
why these uncommonly managing ways? She had ever been a
sweet, agreeable child in her nursery days.

No *lady* in his family had ever been forced to toil beneath her
station and, although Elizabeth's family connection was not inti-
mate, she was the sole grandchild of his grandmother's cousin.
Her parents and his had perished together when the family yacht
was lost at sea, and the duke had placed Elizabeth in the care of
her father's sister. In exchange, the duke had embraced the small
family as his own, providing funds and a dowry for Eunice's
daughter as well as for Elizabeth. The duke visited the family occasionally to see how they went on, but had never involved
Nathan in their affairs until now.

Just as well that Grandfather had not accompanied him, Nathan
reflected with a trace of contrition. No gentleman would have
rudely alluded to the household's dependency, nor should he have
taunted Elizabeth, disparaging her youth and intimating a lack of
the housewifely skills she seemed to have assumed.

She looked like a child playing grownup, he thought. How
would she ever fare in London next year? The thought made him
smile.

She glared at him, then, as if thinking of some deliciously
wicked thought, she returned his mocking grin with an impish one
of her own.

"Get dressed," she ordered briskly, "I'm going to need your
help after the household retires."

"Wha—" Before he could marshal a single argument, she had
disappeared down the stairs.

Never, he vowed silently, the only task he had left on his plate
was to drag his tired body beneath the counterpane of that very
tempting bed. He had come to carry out Grandfather's orders, not
those of a haughty little baggage like Elizabeth. No mystery was
so tempting that it could not wait until tomorrow!

He sat sprawled in the chair, fully dressed, wishing he had another splendid drink to pass the time and cool his temper while he

waited for Elizabeth to return with more of her imperious directives. How his friends would howl to see him brought so low, dressing on command and awaiting further orders.

In deference to his position as heir, he was accustomed to a measure of respect from society at large and dignity was a garment he wore with confidence. Since his parents' death, the duke had personally directed his education, gradually handing over estate issues to explore and allowing him to make decisions without interference. In essence, he already held dominion over family concerns.

Grandfather denied Nathan's allegation of ulterior motives in bestowing such authority and responsibility upon his youthful grandson, claiming an old man deserved a rest, never mind that he interspersed his periods of rusticating at Standbridge with trips to London to counsel with his War Office colleagues. It had not escaped Nathan's notice, however, that Grandfather's eagerness to hand down his governing reins increased in direct proportion to his own appeals to join his friends in the skirmish against Napoleon.

Nevertheless, the result was the same—Nathan's authority was unquestioned as was his consequence.

And now the old fox had set him down in the middle of a checkmated situation, compelled by his mysterious instructions to study the tyrannical little *puzzle* herself. She, in turn, blithely treated him with a lack of deference no one had attempted since he had been in leading strings.

The trick here, he thought, was to play the game and outsmart the old fox, and for that he would need a clear head, unclouded with emotions and bad humor. So, be fair, Nathan, he chided himself, why this unusual reaction to Elizabeth? Was he so accustomed to shy, tongue-tied, completely forgettable ingenues that a candid stare from a little miss barely out of the nursery provoked him?

In London he wagered with seasoned gamblers without a telltale twitch or blink, and on the road he maneuvered his high perched phaeton around the tightest corner without raising a heartbeat . . . so why did a little nonentity like Elizabeth have him hopping like a performing monkey?

He could hear what the old man would be saying now, *"Patience, boy, a child jumps on another's provocation; a man reasons logically and seldom jumps at all."* Very well, his first logical thought was that Grandfather was probably planning Elizabeth's future betrothal to some worthy fellow—some poor sot who needed a halter to lead him.

The next logical thought . . . why waste his heir's energies in such an insignificant decision? The old man's motives and actions were far from frivolous, and his brand of humor hadn't the finesse to set this trip up as a mere prank. Moreover, the old rascal would have wanted to be in on any joke at the finish, to laugh uproariously at his own cleverness.

Nathan's exhausted body was begging for rest, not riddles; a tightening at the back of his neck and a throbbing pain over his left eyebrow signaled the onset of a headache. He was just drifting into the welcome escape of sleep when the door quietly opened.

"Ah, poor tired fellow," she whispered. The door clicked shut behind her, and her soft footsteps signaled her departure.

He had heard her, of course, but he didn't care, suddenly hating the whole situation. Nothing was so important that he must jump hoops to help her. He stood and stretched; the room was so blasted hot now that he was dressed, typical of female abodes. Of course, if they wore sensible clothing instead of those ridiculously thin muslins, a man wouldn't always feel like escaping to the cool outdoors. He crossed to the window, pushed it open, and took a deep breath. Wonderful, he thought, wonderful and fresh and head-clearing. He loved the smell that followed a cleansing rain. He watched the low floating clouds, now silhouetting themselves against the full moon, and then moving on, granting him a panoramic view of the buffeted elms resting quietly after the storm. He eavesdropped on night sounds drifting clearly through the air, identifying owls and crickets and . . . *what the devil?* . . . his eyes narrowed as a slight figure moved purposefully across the graveled walkway toward the nearby stables. Elizabeth, he thought, determined to plague him with yet another eccentricity. She carried a lantern in one hand and a long-handled harvesting basket in the other, which she dropped to the ground in order to open the heavy stable door. She slipped inside, and after a moment reappeared carrying a large object, something awkward and heavy by the way she hefted it and struggled to stuff it into the basket. She walked awkwardly back toward the house, the heavy basket banging against her leg with each step. She stopped directly beneath his window.

"Well," she hissed, looking directly up at him, "are you coming to help or not? Use the kitchen door, it's open."

He had no choice but to go and see what was afoot. Not only would his blasted curiosity plague him if he let her go alone, but it would give him great satisfaction to return to Grandfather with the solution in hand. He hurried soundlessly from the room, down the back stairs which would surely lead to the kitchen, and soon found his way out into the yard.

Without another word she handed him the basket, which more or less confined a heavy length of rope. He followed as she hurried away from the house, attired suspiciously like a stable boy with worn boots and a bulky workman's coat. She was certainly a curious character, he thought, grinning more in sympathy now that action was at hand. He followed her swaying lantern as she marched past the small pasture and fast-stepped down a steep incline toward a dark outline of trees. She stopped finally beneath a sprawling ancient oak and directed him. "Climb up on this heavy limb and tie the rope securely out near the end where it hangs over the stream."

"Tie the rope on a branch," he sputtered. "In the middle of the night?" Was the girl addled? She wanted him to climb out on a branch that would probably break under his weight and drop him into the stream? With the intermittent clouds hiding the moon, he couldn't even see the end of the branch, let alone any water; it probably hung over a deep ravine!

He should follow his first impulse and dispatch her home to bed where she belonged. Ah, but the lure of deciphering Grandfather's riddle was too enticing; if there was some genuine mystery here to unravel, mayhap this midnight adventure was part of it. Let her play it to the end as if it all made complete sense.

"Can you show me the stream?" he queried with exaggerated politeness, peering into the darkness.

"Over here." she said, leading the way to a low arched bridge that spanned a widened pool in a rain-swollen stream. She dropped the basket at their feet and held the light out over the water, revealing a huge tree limb washed halfway under the bridge with bits of debris beginning to pile up around it. She balanced the lantern on the railing and turned to capture his attention. "Tomorrow, Mariane will be displaying you to all her friends and you'll probably be maneuvered into going out in the boat."

He arched a dark eyebrow, clearly refuting anyone's ability to "maneuver" him into anything.

"You'll have to ape the manners of a gentleman," she taunted, answering that insolent eyebrow. "You remember how—the ladies strike a pose in their flowered hats and frilly dresses, and you shower compliments and grant their every request—" She stopped. "You can swim, can't you?"

"Yes," he answered automatically, trying to follow this swift change of direction, "but—"

"Good," she interrupted, "if Mariane should fall in, she might be pulled down under this wood, and you can see how her hair might get tangled and stuck." She tentatively touched his forearm, her small fingers tightening with unexpected strength. "Go after her. Don't waste time searching in the water near the boat, the stream runs strongly as you go deeper, and she will drift more quickly than you think. Swim down with the rope and tie it around her and then pull her hair free. She's excitable, she'll fight you and might swallow water and choke. When you get her out, just grab her tight around the middle and shake her good."

She snatched her hand back from his arm and turned to lean against the railing, staring at the white ripples of water beating against the trapped branch. Her voice was unsteady now. "Maybe it won't happen, please God it won't, but we can't take any chances, can we?"

Was the little imp crazy? He studied the child, the taut, vibrating presence of her moving him to an intense awareness. No, she was not crazy, although he was beginning to feel deranged himself. Elizabeth was more like a brilliant firefly, sparkling and flitting around too fast to catch. Evil? No, he didn't think so; her motives weren't self-serving or malicious. Untruthful or too-highly imaginative? Possibly, but ignoring her scenario for tomorrow's excursion was unthinkable, just as giving it credit was.

Blast! Now he was trapped into spending tomorrow doing the pretty with a swarm of giggling girls, but *not*, he vowed, suffering a dunking in the rain-chilled water. There had to be some other solution.

He lifted her chin firmly with his fingertips and turned her face toward him. "Elizabeth, why are you doing this? Whatever gave you the idea that Mariane would fall into the water tomorrow?"

She bit her lip, holding back an answer.

He pursued, "Is this some silly female plan of Mariane's to gain attention?"

"No, of course not," she murmured, then cleverly drawing his thoughts along lighter lines: "Can you imagine Mariane, or any young lady, willing to spoil her gown or appear to such disadvantage?"

Try again, he thought, give her some diplomatic way to admit she has a too-busy imagination. He offered, "You've explained that the girls wouldn't intentionally fall overboard, and I assure you that I'll be very careful, so shall we agree that we have nothing to worry about tomorrow? Let's just forget about all these dramatic precautions and return to the house. I'm sure we're both anxious for our beds, and . . . "

"Nooo," she moaned, pulling away in visible distress, "please, you have to believe me . . . I'm not a child who requires humoring."

A trickle of suspicion forced his next question. "And, where exactly will you be tomorrow?"

She cast him a scathing look. She was a quick little thing, he'd have to give her that, but he held his ground and insisted. "Well?"

She took a deep, calming breath, brushing away the insulting question with a brisk answer, "Mariane has her own friends, I shan't be asked."

He ran his hand impatiently through his hair, trying to follow a direct train of thought and fit the scrambled pieces of information into a recognizable mosaic. Elizabeth was plainly too earnest about this to have any part in tricking him, and he found himself beginning to trust her. That left one last piece to fit into place, the bit of the puzzle he had no desire to decipher.

If she was right, *how* did she know what was going to happen tomorrow? Logic? Impossible, everyone knew that female brains were incapable of complex reasoning, thus the educational system was structured to send boys to school to study mathematics and languages and history so they could manage their holdings and govern the world. Girls were taught embroidery and music, how to walk and bow properly and how to hold their fans and flirt, so they could grace their husbands' homes.

So, she was only a girl. Just ask the girl a simple question, the answer couldn't bite. Perchance she was privy to someone else's mischief. "Elizabeth," he said firmly, "no more evasive games, you *will* answer me and I *will* know why we're out here in the middle of the night preparing for a completely unlikely disaster."

She lowered her head and said reluctantly, "I can see it happening."

He exploded, "You put me through all this on the rare chance that you *think* it might happen?" He grabbed her without thinking, appalled as his fingers dug into her delicate shoulders, only just stopping himself from shaking her violently. He carefully softened his grip as she looked up and faced him squarely, speaking with utter seriousness. "No, I mean, I *know* it will happen, I have *seen* it in my mind, just as I have seen other things happen, and these pictures are never wrong."

"Pictures, what pictures? What do you mean you see it in your mind? Lord, Elizabeth, don't say things like this."

She continued, her face pinched, choosing her words with care, "I seldom see important things like this, or as clearly as this. Sometimes I don't understand the pictures or even the thoughts I hear, but I'm not *trying* to see or hear anything."

"You *hear thoughts?*" he challenged, focusing on the new, even more appalling aspect of this whole nightmare. An irrelevant memory flashed through his mind of a gypsy fortune-teller he once saw at a fair. Is that where Elizabeth got her eccentric notions, from some hag crooning mysterious warnings over a dirty glass ball?

She shrugged loose from his grasp and said in a cold, biting voice, "Pay attention, Lord Hawksley, Mariane's life is in your hands. Just now you were wondering if I was playing at being a gypsy fortune-teller." She nodded grimly at his stunned expression. "How would you like to know things you can't share with anyone? How do you think I knew you were aching for a hot bath or how to prepare your drink?

"You heard my thoughts at dinner," he mused out loud. "And what was that happy little sigh for?"

"I'd just discovered you were the man I saw in the boat with Mariane. You were only a shadow, but few men match your size."

"You pictured me rescuing her?"

"No, I saw her drowning."

He stared at her in absolute horror as the truth settled heavily on his shoulders and shivered down his back. She was no hysterical child concocting a wild story, she was truly afraid. And the unpalatable truth that she had been so delicately stepping around was that she knew *exactly* what she was saying, and that tomorrow would unroll *exactly* as she had described. And, God help him, he believed her. Question after question crashed through his brain, but before he could voice any of them, the full enormity of possible consequences to her, to the family, to the entire village, struck him like a blow.

"Does anyone else know you do this? Aren't you afraid someone might lock you up in the family attic?"

"I never do any harm, sometimes harm happens, but I always do what I can for good." Tears filled her eyes, delicate glistening drops that somehow had him swallowing to ease his own aching throat.

He closed his eyes and rubbed the bridge of his nose. "So you can eavesdrop on someone's thoughts, anyone's thoughts?" . . . then a white, savage light exploded in his brain. "*All* my thoughts? You've been listening to *all* my thoughts?" he growled, sending all traces of sympathy straight to perdition.

"No, not *all*," she replied with a returning touch of humor. "Your thoughts are very strong and sometimes I heard them before I could block them out. I really don't pry," she said primly, "it's a matter of honor . . . and good manners."

"Honor and good manners be damned, this is not a drawing room game!"

She flinched and stepped back, visibly withdrawing. He took a deep breath and willed himself to be calm. It annoyed him to see her standing so motionless, bracing herself against his rough anger with a fragile strength; she was so young, so obviously practiced in restraining emotions that must be frightening. Why had no one eased her life, comforted her? He said softly, "Honor and good manners won't protect you if anyone, *anyone* learns about your . . . "

"Affliction?" she offered with a tired dignity.

Before he realized what he was about, he awkwardly drew her small frame into an embrace he needed more than she, and as she burrowed her head into his chest, he felt in his soul that these last few moments had linked them with a warm, almost tangible flow of *something* between them. Unwillingly, he could see into her intrepid little spirit, he could feel her despair, he could experience the conflict between fear of discovery and the absolute necessity to act on her knowledge. What an enormous burden she carried. No wonder she chose to act as chatelaine and caretaker when she should be wavering between doll parties and party dresses.

No matter, he thought, the specter of lifelong responsibility falling heavily on his shoulders, it was no longer her burden to carry alone. *This* is why Grandfather had sent him, to hold one more rein in the passing down of family obligations. But what solution could there be? It was not comparable to draining a field or roofing a cottage, or even the more delicate prospect of retiring a no-longer useful servant. This was like starting a war, or even more seriously, putting down a beloved faithful animal.

He ventured another question, dreading the answer. "Who else knows about this?"

She leaned back a little and looked up with a peaceful, untroubled expression. "I have never actually told anyone." She shrugged and grinned. "Of course when I was little, I was often accused of eavesdropping and punished, which was a great deterrent, I assure you. Then when I realized no one else was popping into other people's heads, I was ashamed and tried to stop it. It's very distracting, so I am schooling myself to keep it muffled." Her smile widened and she rested her head against his shoulder. "I feel safer with you knowing, though."

He smiled in the darkness, absently caressing her unruly hair, surprised at how easily one comforted a child. With a need to clarify every point, he asked, "How does my grandfather know?"

She raised her head, her eyes wide and startled. "Your grandfather knows?" She hesitated, watching him closely. She chose her words carefully, as though moving through a breakable assortment. "There is a reason why he might have guessed. Grandfather—he asked me to call him that even though it isn't precisely correct—knew my grandmother, of course, since she was cousin to your grandmother."

She drew a shaky breath and continued. "My grandmother was like me, she saw pictures too. I have her diaries and it seems—"

He groaned like a man in pain. She anticipated his next question, which was just as well since he was incapable of speech.

"It's like freckles or crooked teeth, it runs in the family, and what's more—"

"My God," he breathed, cutting through the cheerful clutter of words, "your grandmother?" He searched his memory for revealing clues or incidents, but could only recall a warm, loving woman with . . . ah, yes, with an audacious sense of humor.

"But your grandfather seemed so happy with her," he protested. "How could he stand it, no privacy, no control over her whatsoever? What could be worse than a wife who could read your mind?"

She stiffened in his arms, and he could feel her quivering like a doe sensing danger. What the devil was wrong with her now? She stepped back out of his arms, isolating herself once more, and said in that managing voice he detested, "Promise me about tomorrow."

Wondering why her detachment felt like a betrayal, he said, "I promise, I have no choice." He picked up the basket and marched back to the tree. She followed closely behind with the lantern and held it high as he snatched up the rope and climbed out to tie it securely. When he was satisfied that the other end trailed freely in the water, he dropped back to the ground, impatient to concentrate on a plan for her.

"Lord," he mused, rubbing his neck as the lurking headache returned in full force, "I will have to do something to safeguard her, which is exactly why that old rogue sent me into this bramble broth. He will just have to live with my decisions, then, and maybe choke on them.

"The first thing we need to do is put a tight rein on you. No more of this sticking your nose in where it doesn't belong, Elizabeth. Keep your mind to yourself, and out of other people's thoughts. You can just bumble along with the rest of humanity, my girl, no telling what nonsense you might hear."

No telling, indeed, he'd hate to have her inside the brains of most of his cronies, and the thoughts of half the male population of this little village would probably frighten her, if she wasn't a mere child. And that won't last very long, another few years and she'll be marriageable age. Maybe *that's* the answer, marry her early to some country gentleman who will keep her busy minding a dozen babies.

His thoughts came to an abrupt halt as she bowed her head and covered her face with her hands. He felt the veriest bully, dismaying her with such harsh directives, commanding her to prevent something she had no control over. He had probably terrified the child.

"Elizabeth?" he said softly, expecting tears and pleas, or even a childish tantrum.

She lifted her delicate face, tipped her head to one side, flashed the most enchanting grin, and teased, "A *dozen* babies?"

Chapter Two

TEARS tickled and itched their way down over Elizabeth's freckled cheeks, breaking into her sleep as the dream began. The dreams always sent the emotions ahead first, like cowards, then the pictures floated in behind, just as if they had been invited.

She tried to stop the dream, pulling her knees up and wrapping the soft quilt over her head tight as she could. She squeezed her eyes closed and hummed, trying to close it out.

She recognized the recurring dream from her childhood and panicked. She gasped, trying to stop the terror, but her heart was already beating too quickly and she couldn't breathe as it drew her into the whirlpool.

The swirling colors made her feel sick—all the dark shades of night and the red of dying roses, turning black around the edges. The colors poured across the deck of a boat, swirling around her sleeping mother and father and Nathan's parents too.

"Get up, get up," she whispered in the dream, *"oh, please get up and come home."*

A tall man stood on the deck, shaking with a glowing red anger, his head thrown back, howling silently as his rage made the veins on his face and neck swell like worms. Finally, his shuddering slowed and he opened his eyes. He examined the scene before him and smiled.

His head lifted and turned, his smile slowly stiffening into a snarl like a wary animal. Searching. Elizabeth's heart thudded with fear.

Don't look this way, she thought, and held her breath. But his glance drifted slowly to the place where she cowered behind Nathan in the dark. The monster paused, then he began searching again. A snarling sound came out of that empty face and echoed into the salt air—he was searching for her and Nathan but couldn't find them.

Angrily, he turned back to the sleeping people and smiled again. He pulled a long shiny knife from his pocket. The golden dragon on the blade came alive as he pointed it at their parents and started the colors swirling faster and faster. They covered Nathan's parents, then moved to her own beloved mother and father, swirling so fast she could no longer see their sleeping faces. The colors spread until they began to flow over the side of the boat and into the lapping waves.

"No!" She cried out and started forward to stop him, to push him over the side into the cold water instead, to stop the hot, glowing evil, but she couldn't move fast enough no matter how hard she tried.

She sobbed in frustration, knowing how this dream ended. The white wind was coming, freezing everything as it blew into the picture, mixing the colors softer and softer until they were gone, and her parents would never come home again.

The first time she had the dream Nanny heard her screams and came in and told her that if anyone knew about the dreams they would think she was a witch and no one would love her if she didn't stop. Sobbing, she promised not to tell anyone, but she vowed with all the fervor of her broken heart that someday she would be faster and stronger and she would stop the dreams from happening.

She wanted to wake up. She didn't want to be frozen in place and watch the wind approach.

Then she realized something was wrong—this time the white wind stopped, hovering, waiting. Confused, she hesitated, then turned back to look at the gleeful monster.

A jolt of pure rage tore through her and she lunged forward.

He turned, surprised at the attack. He quickly raised the shiny instrument of death at her, but she didn't care, she wanted only enough time to stop the evil man. Nothing else mattered.

She felt the wind moving again, accelerating toward her, howling over her face and into her ears, slowing her down. She screamed in frustration as she struggled forward to destroy her enemy.

Then she heard Nathan's voice behind her, yelling her name over and over again. She had forgotten him! He would help her; he was huge and not afraid of anything.

"Nathan, help me, help me . . . "

She felt his warm hands on her shoulders, shaking her.

Furious that Nathan was keeping her from attacking the monster, she wailed out loud and began pounding him with her fists. He let her vent her anger, then stopped her useless attack by simply holding her wrists together with one large hand.

With the other hand, he patted her hair awkwardly and crooned, "It's all over now, Elizabeth. I'm here and you're safe. Quiet now, quiet, quiet . . . "

The dream vanished and she instantly awoke. Oh, no, she was in her sunlit bedroom, and Nathan was real. Breathing slowly, she willed herself to grow calm. How humiliating to have Nathan see her in this state. Must she always make a fool of herself before him—just as she had after the death of their parents?

After the tragedy, relatives and friends had filled Standbridge, Nathan's family home, but she would accept comfort from none of them. She had followed Nathan from room to room, afraid to let him out of her sight. Like a miniature guard dog, her childish motive was to safeguard him, but he had soon grown concerned about his bedraggled, tearful shadow and sent for her nanny.

Now, each time the duke sent word of his impending visit to Paxton, she would launch mighty prayers that his grandson would not accompany him. She had planned that somehow, before that uncomfortable moment occurred, to be transformed into a mature, irresistible beauty. And here she was, everything she didn't want to be, waking noisily in the middle of a recurring childhood nightmare. How charming.

She drew a ragged breath and said in a tired voice, "Let me go, Nathan."

He held her a few inches away from him and lowered his head to look into her eyes. "Sure?" he said with a teasing grin.

Refusing to return his look, she turned away, immediately wishing the looking glass over her dressing table did not reflect the embarrassing scene so clearly.

"I don't think I shall let her go," he said, laughter rolling through his voice. "Such a little tiger, she might hurt me if I do."

He released her hands and leaned back. His laughter faded, and she dreaded the inquisition she knew would follow. Nathan was ever one for questions.

She scrambled back under the covers, pulling them up under

her chin, and assumed an indignant pose. A gentleman would certainly take the hint and leave.

The wretch only grinned at her posturing and made no move to leave. "What was wrong, Elizabeth? A bad dream? Were you worried about Mariane?"

Resigned, she abandoned the pose and fell back against the pillow. "No, it was an old dream I sometimes have when I am upset."

"And am *I* in the dream, Elizabeth? You were calling me to help you, I heard you as I passed your door."

She looked into his face, wishing those dark eyes were not so compelling, so full of authority, knowing he would never let her refuse an answer. "Yes," she said with a trace of bravado and a twist of the truth, "usually you are cowering behind me, hiding from the monster I am trying to kill, but this time I was trying to get you to help me and—"

"What?" he shouted. "I was cowering . . . hiding behind you?"

"Shhh, you dolt! You'll wake the entire house. You cannot stay here. I am not a child anymore, and I hate to think what anyone would say to see you sitting on my bed."

He promptly stood and folded his arms across his chest. "Is this better, Miss Propriety?" It wasn't, but she couldn't think of a way to remove him, so she simply glared daggers at him. He ignored her lethal expression and demanded, "Tell me about the dream."

"You are like a dog with a bone, Nathan. It is not important, it's an old dream about our parents." She hoped that would satisfy him, but his face remained unchanged and he motioned with his hand for her to continue. She felt her temper rising and opened her mouth to put an end to the conversation, when the door flew open and Mariane rushed in, her white muslin dressing gown flapping around her dainty bare feet.

"Elizabeth," she began, "I heard voices and—Lord Hawksley, what are you doing in Elizabeth's bedroom?"

Nathan ignored the interruption and continued to frown at Elizabeth. Finally, he grinned and said, "Reprieve, little tiger."

Elizabeth answered, her voice free from tension for the first time since awakening, "No, Nathan, *finis*."

Hawksley merely grinned, an expression she was beginning to detest. He strode to Mariane, lifted her hand, and planted a quick kiss in the air above it, saying, "Good day, ladies."

Elizabeth grimaced as he slammed the door behind him, like the great oaf that he was.

"Oh," Mariane sighed, "did you see that? That is what all the gentlemen will be doing in London, Elizabeth. Are you not excited to be going to London next season? Oh, can I not go with you? I will be sixteen then and many girls do come out at that age. Oh," she cooed, "I know while Lord Hawksley is here he will see I am really very mature for my age and will let me come with you."

"Yes, that would be a wonderful idea," Elizabeth said, her thoughts scrambling through the conversation, looking for a way to use it to keep her cousin away from the stream. "You must be very dignified while he is here and display all the social skills you have. Perhaps your friends might take tea with you this afternoon and he will see how well you comport yourself. I am sure he would be impressed."

Mariane's face glowed. Elizabeth knew her younger cousin would take London society by storm with her golden beauty. She had drawn compliments from the cradle and had only grown more lovely as the years passed.

Mariane sighed again and pressed the almost-kissed hand against her cheek. "Perhaps Lord Hawksley will fall in love with me."

Elizabeth ignored the flutter of pain in her chest and latched feverishly onto Mariane's gesture. "Perhaps he will, if he thinks you could behave as a future marchioness."

Mariane surprised Elizabeth by saying, "Marry him? I never said I wanted to marry him. He is so *big*, Elizabeth. Imagine gliding through a doorway wearing a court dress with him by my side, we would become stuck and have to be pulled through. Even the dining room chairs squeak when he sits on them, have you not noticed?"

She dropped her hand and added, "I want a slim, blue-eyed gentleman with blond hair. Someone graceful who would look wonderful dancing with me."

Elizabeth snapped. "There is nothing wrong with Lord Hawksley, he is strong and handsome and—"

"Handsome? Really, Elizabeth, he takes up so much *space*. He doesn't walk, he prowls. Even when he is carrying on a polite conversation, he is abrupt and he has no idea how to flirt or share *on dits* that are interesting."

She pouted. "When I lisped, did he think it was darling like my other beaux? No, he just leaned over and asked me what I had said."

Elizabeth bit her lip to stifle a giggle. "And?"

Mariane's lovely face flushed. "I couldn't remember."

Elizabeth strangled back the laughter that was threatening to erupt and ruin all her plans for keeping Mariane busy and out of the boat, but she was losing ground fast. She pictured Hawksley and said, "He is like the squire's stallion, he simply needs to be harnessed."

Mariane sat down at Elizabeth's dressing table and proceeded to brush the tangles from her silky hair. "If we must use farm animals for description, Elizabeth, Nathan far more resembles a plow horse."

Desperate, Elizabeth offered, "He is heir to a dukedom, do you not want to be a duchess?"

That brought on another pout, followed by a thoughtful pursing of her lovely lips. "You may have a point. As my Aunt Sylvia says, if I were a duchess, everyone would have to give over to me, would they not? I would be first going into dinner and whatever I said would be important." She admired herself, turning sideways to see the glowing tresses falling to her waist. "Rich," she mused, "I would be rich, which Aunt Sylvia says is almost as important as having a title."

She shook her hair and turned to face Elizabeth. "Perhaps I shall marry him, but not until I am ready to settle down. First I want to attend balls and ride in the park and dance at Almack's."

Her eyes narrowed in speculation. "I suppose he would be suitable for practice, as long as he is here." She walked toward the door, saying grandly, "I must dress and present myself at breakfast." She made a childish face, reminding Elizabeth that whatever she said, her cousin was only fifteen and barely out of the schoolroom.

"Uggg," Mariane said with loathing, "breakfast at this hour."

"Good morning, ladies," Hawksley said, entering the sunny breakfast room.

Elizabeth glanced up quickly, suppressing a smile at the contrast he presented. His linen, while immaculately white, gave a resting place to bits of tree bark, his gleaming Hessians carried a fringe of wet grass, and his thick curly hair was surely the inspiration for the term "windswept."

Hawksley smelled of fresh air and the peaches he carried into the room. He deposited them on the damask tablecloth and enthused, "Just beginning to ripen, they smell wonderful." He proceeded to rub one on a napkin and then thrust it between his white teeth. Elizabeth watched him devour it in a few quick bites, fascinated as he caught the warm juice with his tongue before it could escape. He sat on the cushioned seat of the deeply curved bow window, leaned back, and studied her in return with no pretense of doing anything else whatsoever.

"Breakfast is ready on the sideboard," she croaked, marveling at how she lost her composure whenever he directed that penetrating glance at her. No wonder Mariane felt more comfortable with her slim, graceful swains than this mannerless giant.

"Shall I serve you?" Why had she said that when she had no intention of waiting on him? She was grateful Aunt Eunice was late this morning since that gentle lady expected the girls to behave with excellent manners at all times, and she knew hers were strained to the breaking point.

"Yes, please. Just pile on whatever you see there, I'm not particular." He sat up and amended. "Except kidneys. I hate kidneys, don't like to smell them and don't like to eat them."

Elizabeth lifted the cover from that particular dish and set it aside, allowing the pungent aroma to drift through the room. She glanced over her shoulder for confirmation that she had scored a direct hit.

She knew in an instant she had gone too far when she heard his thoughts fly across the room.

"Nathan, don't you dare," she protested. She could see what he planned like a little play in her mind. As he rose, she turned to place herself firmly in front of the sideboard.

He reached her in a few short strides. Easily reaching around her, he picked up the offending dish, walked to the window, and opened it. He dropped the bowl into the bushes below, and closed the window again. "I don't like cats either, but they serve a useful purpose, so I like to do them a good turn now and then." He smiled that mocking smile and said to her, "Are you an animal lover, Elizabeth?"

Mariane broke into the duel with an innocent offering of

humor, "She likes horses, Nathan, especially stallions. She says you remind her of one."

"Mariane," she said quickly before her cousin could elaborate further," what plans have you made for Lord Hawksley today? I am sure he is looking forward to being entertained by such charming girls."

She did look at him then, amused at the picture she saw in his mind, a vision of his picking her up by the nape of the neck and shaking her.

Before she could respond, Mariane sat primly at the table and began picking daintily at her food. "We could entertain at home. Melinda and Patience are both excellent musicians and we might enjoy learning some of the London dances from you, Nathan."

It was Nathan's turn to claw at his neckcloth and look hunted, but Mariane continued, musing between bites, "Or we thought we might have a picnic down by the stream while the weather is still fair and the flowers are blooming on the hills."

"Dancing." Nathan's voice grew faint. "Dancing is a particular favorite of mine." He looked at Elizabeth for assistance, but she raised her fingers to her twitching lips and waited wide-eyed for his answer.

"Elizabeth will accompany us, of course," Nathan said finally, to which she firmly nodded her agreement. She had no intention of letting Mariane out of her sight until Nathan was safely on his way back to London.

Mariane looked confused at his insistence and Elizabeth's agreement, but one look at Nathan's firm jaw stopped any protest she intended to make. She recouped her control of the conversation and added, "I would like to go for a ride first, Nathan. In your carriage. Through the village to pick up Melinda and Patience and back again. We have been planning it ever since your note arrived."

Mariane looked pleadingly at him and Elizabeth saw a glimmer of the power she was sure the younger girl would wield when she reached her full potential. In any case, Nathan succumbed with no protest at all.

The house erupted into a flurry of preparations. Tea with all the elegancies Cook could create. Orders for another dusting of the pianoforte and fresh flowers in the parlor. At least a half dozen changes of clothing for Mariane, which Elizabeth had no intention of witnessing.

She escaped to the stables to view the week-old colt. The seclusion, she discovered to her unpleasant surprise, gave Hawksley the opportunity to follow and grill her further. When motivated, he could orchestrate a conversation quite skillfully.

"Perhaps we could tie Mariane to her bedpost, Elizabeth."

"Perhaps you could lock her in the nursery."

He chuckled. "She seems much younger than you, Elizabeth."

"Aunt Eunice and I have spoiled her, I suppose," Elizabeth said in defense of her cousin, "but she has always been a sweet child and has made me feel welcome from the very first."

"You are barely out of the nursery yourself." At the indignant look she leveled at him, he laughed again. She started to turn away and he quickly apologized. "I was not laughing at you, Elizabeth. I was thinking about children and how charming they can be. I believe I have missed a marvelous source of amusement." Before she could protest, he inserted smoothly, "Of course, I am realizing very quickly that you are really a wizened old lady in disguise. So, before you lose all your faculties, tell me, when did you first have the dream, Elizabeth? You mentioned it concerned our parents."

His dogged intensity irritated her. Dreams were private and he had no business making her drag them out for his inspection, especially this one. She knew there was no escape, however, since she had already told him it involved his parents. She answered him briefly. "I first saw the picture when our parents were on the yacht, when they died."

"And I was in the dream?"

"The first time was not a dream, it was a picture that woke me up. Afterwards I kept dreaming about it. There is a difference." Perhaps he would chase that clue and forget about the details of the dream altogether. But, no, he persisted in the same direction as only Nathan could.

"And our parents, yours and mine, they were there?"

She turned around to face him, leaning against the stall door. She nodded once, wishing he would finish and leave her alone. Knowing he never would, she told him the entire dream, detail by detail. Even then, he had still more questions.

"And the monster, who was he?"

Tears came to her eyes. She was angry now, desperately thinking of how to stop him. "He was death, I suppose. A tall man with no face who took our parents and then went hunting for you and me."

That took him by surprise, but he pursued the original thought. "Think, Elizabeth, he must have had a face. You were upset and probably forgot . . . you were only a child then and were not paying attention."

The tears were falling then. Furious, she attacked. "I was a child, Lord Hawksley. True, I had just seen my parents' death, but I tell you, he had no face."

He frowned at her tears and said brusquely, "I am sorry, little tiger, it's true I am an insensitive brute and I forget myself when I get hold of an idea. I cannot resist a puzzle and have to pursue it until I find an answer."

Not at all appeased, she quickly wiped her cheeks and composed herself before exiting the stable. They reached the front of the house to find Hawksley's coachman waiting with the carriage.

The front door opened and Mariane rushed out and pirouetted at the top of the stairs, a Reynolds painting come to life in a yellow sprigged muslin with matching yellow kid slippers and the most frivolous bonnet ever created, complete with daisies being wooed by an imitation butterfly.

Neither was surprised when she delivered the first disruption to their careful plans for the day. Mariane's words rushed out in one breath. "Elizabeth, Mother is in need of some assistance. I would attend her myself, but she has one of her beastly headaches and you are the only one who knows what to do for her."

At their silence, she looked at them each in turn, then assured her cousin, "We will be back before you know it, Elizabeth. You don't mind, do you?"

Chapter Three

SHE couldn't find the words to answer Mariane's question aloud. She didn't mind? She wanted to scream her objections. She wanted to tie Mariane to her bedpost until she was old and gray, safe from the stream and the picture in her mind. Instead, what she must do was outsmart that picture. Stalling for time while she gathered her thoughts, she walked slowly up the stairs to where Mariane waited for her answer.

Those few seconds moved like a feather falling slowly from a nest high in a tree . . . Nathan stood tall and strong beside the carriage, not grinning now or teasing . . . but waiting for her decision. Could she give her trust to him?

Looking into Nathan's eyes, she answered Mariane. "Of course I don't mind helping your mother, Mariane. Go along with Nathan."

She nodded briefly to Nathan and watched helplessly as Mariane skipped down the stairs, then remembering her resolve to impress Hawksley with her maturity, strolled the rest of the way to the carriage with the aplomb of a grand dame.

Elizabeth walked into the house without looking back, holding her fear in limbo until she heard the cadence of the departing horses' hooves change as they left the gravel of the driveway and turned down the dirt road toward the village. She stopped in the middle of the entry hall and covered her eyes with a shaking hand.

Mariane, leaving her watchful protection. Eunice, upstairs in unspeakable agony, unable to even care for herself. Nathan, still not entirely convinced that Mariane was in danger.

She wanted to run wailing through the house, warning everyone what was going to happen, but the servants would either believe she was possessed, or they would feel protective toward an hysterical young female and humor her. No one would believe her.

Think. Slow down and think. This wasn't a picture coming in the night, something seen by a child. This was something in the future, something she intended to stop at any cost.

Nathan would drive Mariane to her friends' home and back again. That would give her ample time to attend to Eunice. She lifted her skirt and petticoats and ran up the stairs. She stopped in her room where she kept the laudanum hidden. Once Eunice's pain started, she would lose all sense of time and take too many drops in a wild attempt to find some surcease from the agony.

Elizabeth hurried to her aunt's room and opened the door. Slipping quietly into the dark room, she pulled the door behind her almost closed, leaving only a sliver of light from the hallway to guide her to the bed. She walked softly across the room, careful to glide without vibrating the floor.

She carefully poured a glass of water then measured the elixir of opium into a spoon. She helped her aunt to sit, lifting the pillow along with her head and shoulders in one smooth motion, careful not to touch her sensitive neck or jar the bed. Eunice smiled her thanks as Elizabeth administered the laudanum and water.

Carefully, Elizabeth lowered the pillow and her patient to their original position and hurried to the wash basin to pour a bit of cool water onto a dainty towel. She twisted the excess water from it into the bowl and returned to place it across Eunice's forehead and temples. A sigh escaped the older woman's lips as the cold began the pain-reducing process.

The medicine would take longer to work since Eunice had delayed asking for help. Normally Eunice would have arisen early and they would have enjoyed their early breakfast together, and had the morning been less eventful, she would have grown concerned for Eunice and gone up to see for herself instead of being grateful for her absence.

Anxiety twisted like a knot inside Elizabeth. How much time would pass before Mariane would return to upset their established plans? How fast would Mariane insist Nathan drive his cattle? Would she want to impress her neighbors with speed or would she choose the elegance of driving slowly in a duke's equipage?

She pictured the maze of country lanes and winding paths that connected them. Where would Mariane direct the unsuspecting

Hawksley? Certainly through the village—but most certainly not just the simple trip she promised him. After fetching the girls, every cottage that overlooked a road would have the privilege of seeing Mariane and her friends tooling along with the Marquess of Hawksley in his crested carriage behind perfectly matched horses. Pressed to "spring 'em" he would insist on a safe stretch of road, which could only be reached by a circuitous navigation around Botts Hill. If Mariane's wishes triumphed, they might not be back for an hour.

Elizabeth wanted to put the troublesome girl over her knee—not an unfamiliar urge. On the other hand, she must assume a portion of the blame herself. Knowing Mariane was Eunice's heart's delight, she had spoiled her as much as anyone, playing maid to Mariane to keep her temper sweet, keeping peace in the house in an effort to please Aunt Eunice, and assuming a liaison role with the household staff to free Eunice from the painful job of making decisions.

She refreshed the cold cloth and sat once more to watch over her aunt. She owed this dear lady more than she could ever repay.

During her stay at Standbridge after her parents' death, she had remained stalwart as long as she had been allowed to stay close to Nathan, watching carefully to make sure the monster from her vision didn't find him. Eventually, life resumed a natural pattern and she was sent to the nursery. She spent her days there curled in a ball, reliving the nightmare picture, speculating how she could have changed the outcome and brought her parents back home. She tried to remain awake as long as possible each night, dreading the return of the vision. In a few weeks she no longer had the strength to arise each morning, but lay wide-eyed, staring at the ceiling.

Eventually, news reached the duke that Elizabeth was no longer speaking or eating and that she ignored the coaxing of the frightened girl pressed into nursery service.

The duke turned his attention to her immediately, but that was worse. How could she respond to his entreaties to share her thoughts when that would only reveal that her dream was responsible for his grief as well as her own?

In desperation, the duke brought her here to Eunice. Instantly her haven, Eunice cuddled her for hours, never questioning her terror or insisting she be brave. For years a maid slept in her lighted room and the cost of extra candles was never mentioned.

Eunice enlisted Elizabeth's help with her precious gardening. She taught her the names of flowers and uses of herbs, insisting she dig in the rich soil with her hands to plant and weed. In quiet harmony, they shared the miracle of tiny seeds growing into living plants and flowers.

The entire household turned their efforts to help the newly orphaned girl. Cook needed her help in the kitchen, stirring and adding spices. Gingerbread men couldn't be made without her guidance and tasting ability. Maids were unable to change linen on beds without Elizabeth's tugging on the sheets to smooth them to perfection. Newly born puppies required her watchful eye and if she didn't stand on a stool and help brush old Molly, the poor horse would be ashamed to go out into the pasture with the other horses.

She recovered in body as well as in spirit. As she found the strength to tuck that horrible image away during the day, she was rewarded with the blessed peace to sleep soundly at night, seldom tormented by the dream.

Until the turning point of losing her parents, she'd had little reason to fear the flashes that came into her head, since the pictures were happy and it was fun having a peek ahead, like knowing what dishes Nanny would bring to the nursery or that Father's mare would birth two colts instead of one.

After the horrible dream, she didn't want to see the future anymore, didn't want to see that Cook would burn her finger, or that the gardener would accidentally scythe off the end of a lizard's tail. Even cheerful scenes were intrusions into a mind that wanted only peace, and the continual noise of others' thoughts irritated like mosquitoes buzzing at dusk.

She devised a strategy to fend off those encroaching images and sounds. When they intruded, she instantly began counting—twenty-two steps from her room to the stairs, one hundred fourteen to the breakfast table, six leaves on the wild poppy, twenty-eight on the yellow chrysanthemum. It gave her a small measure of relief and more important, some hope of formulating a better plan.

Two days ago, however, her system failed her. The vision of Mariane's impending death arrived without warning with a strength of its own, a picture complete with sounds, colors, and emotion that had stopped her cheerful descent of the stairs. She had clung to the railing, dizzily examining the scene before her for faults or some escape, but there was no mistake and the close of the scene left Mariane's hair caught in the underwater branches.

She had enlisted the aid of the gardener and stable boy to clear the blockage, but it was truly jammed, and with the constant addition of debris from the recent rain, it would take days to chop away enough branches to clear it.

Until she had seen Hawksley at table the previous night, she had been unable to see who the gentleman in the boat was, but Hawksley's unmistakable size fit the peripheral outline of the boat's occupants and gave her the first hope of vanquishing that awful vision of death. If only she could get there in time . . .

Eunice's sleepy voice broke Elizabeth's reverie. "Thank you, darling. I must have overset myself with the excitement of entertaining young Nathan. Is he all right, are you girls keeping him happy?"

Elizabeth raised her nose and replied with an adult air. "I believe at the moment he is driving three squealing young girls through the village, Auntie." She grinned. "I doubt London can offer such jolly entertainment."

A weak giggle escaped Eunice's white lips. "Oh, Elizabeth, how could you?"

"I do not think the damage to his lordship will be permanent, Auntie. I am sure there are hordes of people who will be happy to fill his bucket of consequence back to overflowing."

"He is still very young, darling. The edges will smooth off as he matures." She paused and added, "He was a very kind boy, you know, and that will govern his actions no matter his rough ways."

Her eyes drifted closed and she sighed as the drops began to soothe her toward sleep. "Would you mind reading to me while I fall asleep, dear? Something light and cheerful."

Elizabeth quickly lit a candle. Her glance flew to the clock ticking serenely on the mantel of the fireplace. Close to an hour had passed. She gulped back a bout of panic and reached for one of the books on the table.

Just then the sounds of a carriage rattled through the window of Eunice's bedroom. Hawksley's carriage? How could that be? In order for sounds to echo from that direction, he would have to be driving alongside the back woods on a road seldom used and almost completely overgrown with weeds.

She quickly slipped Eunice's latest novel under the bed and reached for something more likely to induce slumber. As she read *A Flower Garden of Embroidery Knots* in a soothing monotone, Eunice moved restlessly, but then her face relaxed and her breathing steadied. Elizabeth let her voice die away and waited. After a few endless minutes, she snuffed out the candle and tiptoed out of the room.

Feeling very much like a criminal for deceiving her aunt, she ran softly from the house, her heart thumping so loudly she could feel the throbbing clear up to her ears. Once outside, she sped down to the stream like a little hoodlum, hair streaming down her back, her clothes sticking to her in a manner no young lady ever allowed! She slid down the bank toward the stream, barely stopping herself by grabbing for the oak tree. She forced herself to look at the view before her, so terrified that it took all her concentration to really *see* what was happening. But she hadn't missed a thing.

The three girls were in the small boat, happily vying for every crumb of attention they could command from Hawksley, their young voices tripping over each other's so no conversation could be completely heard. Mariane raised her hand to pluck a blossom from an overhanging branch, then rose to her knees to reach still higher.

Just like her vision.

Like a cue from a play, Mariane promptly tumbled into the water, squawking and squealing her way down to the mass of debris stacked up against the low bridge. Lord Hawksley, looking equal parts stunned and disgusted, dug his oars into the water with magnificent strokes, almost overtaking her. It seemed a simple thing for Mariane to grab hold of the largest protruding branch, but at the last moment she saw some stiff, lifeless creature lodged in the spot she was reaching for. She screeched and threw herself backward. The current immediately pulled her down, and Mariane disappeared in an instant.

Elizabeth would never forget those next few moments. Now it was real, she thought, now it was truly happening. She watched the rest through a haze of tears, fearful that she had *caused* it to happen.

Lord Hawksley went into the water like an otter, diving swiftly under the blockade. Elizabeth grew light-headed and saw gray sparkles in front of her face. It wasn't until the water parted and

Hawksley grabbed the hanging rope that she realized she had forgotten to breathe.

He threw his head back, shaking it fiercely, gasped for air, and swiftly submerged again.

She felt calmer then, almost as if she could see through the tumbling water to the commotion below . . . Mariane clawing at her rescuer, grabbing and fighting at the same time, Hawksley tying the rope around her middle like a sack of grain, ripping her hair loose from the submerged branch with one brisk motion and towing her tightly behind him as he ascended with a single powerful lunge. In seconds he had her safely on the bank, grabbed her roughly around the middle, and shook her until she ejected the awful water she had swallowed.

Mariane moaned, clutching wildly at her head, wailing like a paid mourner as her fingers touched the snarls of wet hair clinging to her mouth and cheeks. Then she spotted the rope twisted around her ruined dress and tried frantically to pluck it loose, shrieking hysterically.

Elizabeth had never heard such a wonderful sound as her cousin's very safe and very alive fit of temper.

Hawksley brushed Mariane's fingers away and began pulling the knot free, growling impatiently for her to be quiet, in what Elizabeth suspected was supposed to be some soothing masculine nonsense. She chuckled and stepped forward to assist.

His head snapped up and his eyes met hers, halting her in midstep. His gaze seared her like a hot ember. She had never felt so powerful a connection with another human being. She felt his thoughts soar across the distance between them, curling around inside her—not words, but emotion of such clear intensity, forging together with hers until she couldn't feel the difference. Then he smiled, and she answered with a grin, thinking, *Now he knows it's true and he's not shocked or repulsed. It's going to be wonderful to have a friend who really understands.*

The precious moment evaporated as the screaming from Mariane's two friends finally penetrated. Hawksley turned to look back at the water. The forgotten boat bobbed against the offensive pile of rubble. Now he had to swim once more across the chilly stream to pull the boat and frightened girls to the shore. He motioned Elizabeth forward to tend to Mariane and swore fiercely. *"I hate cold water!"*

* * *

She smoothed the nonexistent wrinkles from the skirt of her dress, cleared her throat, and took a deep breath. Hours had passed since Hawksley had rescued Mariane and now, finally, she would have an opportunity to speak with him.

She had been summoned to the small library. Summoned by a maid, like an applicant for a position. She would have been more comfortable if he had stood in the middle of the house and roared her name. Or if he had teasingly enticed her to go for a stroll through the orchard. Or stormed into her bedchamber, demanding a moment of her time.

For once, she wished she could invoke a vision or listen to thoughts on demand. She would climb inside his head and save herself the embarrassment of such a formal meeting. Her fertile imagination produced one scenario after another consisting of his approval and admiration, only to be dispelled by the wide streak of practicality that ruled her.

Now that the specter of Mariane's danger no longer threatened, what could he want that demanded more than a casual word? Unlike Mariane, she had no hope that the tentative closeness that was developing between them meant anything more. She was only sixteen and no beauty like Mariane—more like a carrot compared to a lovely flower. Not that Hawksley was Mariane's picture of a charming swain. But dear heaven, she thought, as some emotion overtook her, he was *her* idea of perfection.

She paced to the bottom of the stairs as she contemplated the very tempting option of bolting up to her room. She didn't want to do this, she didn't want to have this hope of finally having someone to share her thoughts with and then be disappointed.

She knew what she did want, though. She wanted his friendship. She wanted to have someone who *knew* her, who knew of her terrible affliction and wasn't repelled. She wanted to feel safe, to feel his approval, to know that someone would care for her even after they knew her secret. She would always treasure that moment of closeness by the stream, and she wanted to be able to trust in it forever.

She wanted to be invited to London—not to be launched into society or be offered for sale in the marriage mart—but to be wanted, to be asked to stay with Nathan and Grandfather and be able to relax and be *herself*. Just for a visit once in a while, a treat she could look forward to. It gave her a warm feeling, like a sunny field of flowers.

The library door opened and Hawksley held out his hand. "I thought I heard you out here, Elizabeth. Come on in and quit nesting. Next thing we know you'll be dusting the banister or scrubbing the floor!"

So much for flowery words and charming declarations. "You're so gracious, Nathan, how could a girl refuse an invitation like that?" She marched in and stood waiting for him to follow her. Manners dictated that he either leave the door open or that a chaperone be present, but she knew the futility of either.

She knew something was not right when he carefully closed the door—instead of slamming it—and motioned her to a pair of chairs before the cheerful fire. The day had turned cold after all, with dark clouds preventing the summer sun from doing its job.

He sprawled in the other chair and stared at the fire. "This is serious business, Elizabeth, these visions of yours. You have lived a rather secluded life here in Paxton and cannot imagine how dangerous someone knowing about this could be."

"Really?" she murmured in a sweet tone.

"Of a certain." He leaned forward, thrusting long fingers into dark hair now drying to a curling thatch that must be the curse of Dunbar men and the delight of the Dunbar ladies. His elbows rested on his thighs and he spoke to the floor. "If it became known, there would be those who would want to control your power for gain or destroy it for fear of discovery. The ruling matrons in the *ton* might send invitations out of curiosity, but should one of their sons show an interest or their daughters offer friendship, they would soon show their claws. You might think they have no power to hurt you, but to see people you have grown to think of as friends turn their back on you would cause you more pain than I wish you to experience."

"Not to mention the shame to the Standbridge name," she offered in a soft, tortured voice.

"What?" He straightened up to look suspiciously at her, but her expression was all that was agreeable. He frowned and growled a sound that could have meant anything.

"Nathan, I do not have to be presented to these people nor do I care about finding a husband from among them. May I not just spend some time with you and Grandfather and go to plays and museums and bookstores?"

"You're missing the point, Elizabeth. It is not about avoiding people, but avoiding the problem of people knowing about your abilities."

"Would you have known, Nathan, had I not been forced to tell you? Do you think Grandfather would have guessed had he not known what to look for and had he not known someone else with the same abilities?"

She turned in the chair and looked directly at him. "I have lived with this for sixteen years, Nathan. Entirely alone, telling no one, and short of the danger to Mariane, have kept this to myself. If I need to interfere because someone needs help, I alone will make that decision. The point you are missing is that this is not your problem at all."

He threw back his head and laughed aloud. His long arm shot out and he mussed her carefully ordered coiffure as if she was a favorite pet. "Little Tiger has claws of her own, I see."

She turned to the fire, hating not having the last word. "Oh, give over, Hawksley, I probably will never marry in any case. I wouldn't bet on the likelihood of finding someone who would want such a liability." She couldn't resist one more dig. "Although, perhaps a gambler. With a little ingenuity I could keep him in money and mistresses all his life and he could give me my dozen babies."

"Elizabeth!" he protested, "ladies never talk about such things in company. In fact, they don't even think them." He paused. "I can see that I must arrange lessons for you before next spring to teach you all the ridiculous intricacies of proper behavior in London. Otherwise, the social lionesses of London will make a meal of you in very short time."

Well, she thought, that interview was over. First, though, she had her own questions. Admittedly, revenge should be left in the hands of the Almighty, but Hawksley's ego needed a little trimming.

"Tell me, Nathan, how did someone like you who knows all the intricacies of a complicated place like London find himself in a boat with three fifteen-year-old girls when he had been forewarned?"

He sighed deeply at her question, and his fingers drummed on the arm of the chair. Finally he answered. "Did you know that I am considered something of a phenomenon in the War Office, Elizabeth?"

"Really?"

"Oh, yes indeed. When Grandfather's spy friends need their codes deciphered, or complicated strategy plotted out, when they need traitors unearthed and identified . . . I am their man. I have a brain that sifts through information and finds answers." He looked at her with both eyebrows raised and a crooked smile. "Respected, that's me. Revered, you might say."

Giggles started boiling upward, but she wanted him to finish. She bit them back, took a deep breath, and nodded.

He looked pleased at her reaction, then assumed a pompous expression. "Mariane doesn't know how brilliant I am. Perhaps I should have explained it to her." He brushed an imaginary bit of lint from his sleeve. "I was outgunned from the beginning, but being a newcomer to the nursery crowd, I hadn't discovered how cunning they could be.

"The girls wanted me to row them in a boat, quoting something about a sketch in a fashion magazine showing proper bonnets for water nymphs. I almost choked on my tongue getting my refusal said. I think that was the beginning of their disillusionment with London gentlemen. They began making little faces, like goldfish talking to each other.

"I refused to race through the village, but finally gave in when they agreed to find a road without a lot of people or livestock on it. We drove around in circles until the horses were dizzy, looking for a suitable road. The clouds were rolling in by then and I lost track of east and west, which was, of course, part of the goldfish plan.

"Next, Mariane began pushing to go to London with you next year, giving me one last chance to redeem myself, I suppose. I didn't want to encourage her with a lot of maybe words, so I told her in plain language the answer was no."

He took a deep breath. "Imagine it was a bit hard on the girl in front of her friends. Didn't think of that when I told her what's what. She took it fairly well, I thought, and began buzzing to her friends again. Then she asked if I would stop and let them pick some flowers."

He leaned forward and stirred the fire, chuckling softly. "I hadn't a clue we'd come in on the other side of the house and didn't know how the road curved around so the stream was on the far side of the hill where I stopped. Good thing I'm not a foot soldier, I'd be delivering myself to the French at the first opportunity."

He looked up and smiled in satisfaction to see Elizabeth squeezing her crossed arms hard against her abdomen as she tried not to laugh.

"I was securing the cattle when the next thing I knew, I heard the sound of oars knocking against the wood of a boat and the girls were squealing, not that they hadn't been most of the morning anyway. I had to run like a fool to catch them before they got away. Had to wade to get into the boat. Ruined my boots."

He watched with enjoyment as she burst into long overdue laughter. Then he joined in. Her heart swelled with happiness and she thought, this was exactly what she wanted from Nathan.

Smiling, almost embarrassed now, she said, "Thank you for saving Mariane, Nathan." He cleared his throat and nodded briskly, clearly not wishing to elaborate upon his valor. Rather than prolong it, she stood and teased, "I must go. If you can maneuver your way safely to the dining room without mishap, I will see you at dinner."

Before she could move away, his hand shot out again and forced her back to her seat. She would have bruises in the morning.

She didn't like the feeling that was emanating from him, either. Usually when someone touched her, she had full access to their thoughts, but his were tightly under control and she heard nothing.

"We have one more thing to discuss, tiger mine. This is very serious, Elizabeth, and I expect your full cooperation."

She knew she wasn't going to like it, but she nodded.

"I want to hear the rest of the dream. The one you had this morning. Tell me the part where you claim I was cowering behind you and you were yelling for me to help you."

Oh, heavens, was he never going to let go of that? He was like a bout of measles, an itch that wouldn't go away. Reluctantly, she complied. "To be perfectly honest, you were bellowing my name in the dream before I was yelling for your help. Perhaps I was asleep and you were truly calling me. What difference does it make?"

He ignored her sarcasm and persisted. "What were you trying to do that you needed my help?"

She smiled, knowing that he was not going to like her answer.

"I was attacking the monster. I had forgotten you were there behind me and when I heard your voice, I knew you would be a
good match for him and so I called for your help."

"What were you attacking him with, Elizabeth?"

She grimaced. In the light of day, her efforts did seem rather
puny, but in the dream she had such energy and power, she was
sure she could push the monster over the side into the water.
Hawksley's voice brought her back to reality. "Tell me the dream,
again, Elizabeth. Every detail. Don't leave anything out."

He would never cease until she complied, so she gave in. She
recounted the entire dream, and he didn't speak until she was
through. She found that after all her resistance, telling him left her
with a solid, warm feeling, almost like having her wish, for
wasn't he listening like a friend? Now if he would only drop it.

Of course he didn't. "So, until this morning, the vision disappeared with both of us safely out of sight. But in this morning's
dream, you came out where he could see you and you attacked
him. He raised his knife to strike you and yet you persisted?"

"You would had to have been there, Hawksley. For once, I felt
I could defeat him, and I didn't care what he did to me. I only
needed to push him over the side to stop him and he would be
gone."

"And this was the first time he saw you?" He looked her full in
the face and asked, "Is this a vision that will come true, Elizabeth,
like the one you had of Mariane?"

The fire crackled and burned merrily as the clouds outside
rolled closer, dimming the light from the windows. Neither of
them spoke while she concentrated on his question. She had given
the dream-vision no more attention than she ever did, especially
after waking with Nathan in her room and the real danger of the
day facing her. She tried to analyze it now, and found she
couldn't give him an intelligible answer.

"I don't really know. I try not to let that particular dream
linger, and with you waking me up in the middle of it, I have no
idea what it means. I suppose I might have it again, but it could
be months or years before I do. It doesn't matter, Nathan, he's not
a real man, and I'm not foolish enough to fight a man with a
knife. It was not a real knife, anyway, it was like a large toy with
a golden dragon dancing on the blade."

"Dear God," he murmured, "did you say a golden dragon?" He

stood suddenly, frightening her with his abrupt action and the intensity of his expression.

She tried to swallow, but her mouth was too dry. What had she said to make him so angry? If she could just erase his fierce expression and lighten his mood . . . "Why should I be frightened with you standing behind me yelling ferociously at him?"

She wished he would retaliate with a clever answer—or grin and acknowledge hers. She wished the pounding thoughts that were growing louder and louder were not his. She began counting silently to keep his terrible thoughts a blurred jumble. Please do not speak the words.

He turned from her and walked to the window overlooking the front driveway. He pulled at his neckcloth and she heard a ripping sound and a curse of impatience. The gong of the clock in the hallway penetrated the thickness of the library door, its somber tones counting out the minutes of happiness she had left.

He returned and crouched down before her, placing her cold hands in his with a courtliness reminiscent of the duke. He captured her gaze and released a heavy sigh.

"I'm sending you away, Elizabeth. Just for a while, until I'm sure I can control the situation." She had known the words were coming, but still they drew a painful cry from her. She closed her eyes against the sight of his betraying face. *So there it is, the way of my past continues into my future, I must accept the fact that I will be forever alone in this. Why did I torture myself with the hope he would accept me the way I am?* She tugged at her hands, but he tightened his grip.

"I can't explain now, Elizabeth, and in any case this is far too serious a matter for a young girl to be concerned with."

He continued explaining, but blessedly, his spoken words were absorbed into the pulsating resonance of his thoughts. Later she might take the words out and examine them, but she thought she would rather not. She heard broken sentences, " . . . danger to you . . . you must be patient."

In the end, he was no longer there, but instead she heard Nanny's voice clearly over all the other noises in the room. "There, there, my sweet baby, you'll be all right as long as you remember to never tell . . . never tell."

Nanny was right, she thought, no simple friendship could survive the difficulties of her curse. She had lost sight of that in the

few hours Hawksley had been here, and opened herself to expect
too much. It steadied her to put that truth back into perspective.

However, it would not always be so.

She had an entire life ahead of her to find someone who truly
loved her. Her grandmother had found a way to be happy, and according to her diaries, so had other ladies in the family. Life did
not begin and end with Nathan, no matter how much that thought
hurt.

She stood, frantically craving solitude, needing time alone to
shore up all the breaches in the wall that so precariously enclosed
her heart.

He rose with her, opening his mouth to continue, but she uttered the words for him. "I will be ready when you are, Hawksley.
What do I need to take for living in . . . ?"

His face flushed but he answered. "Scotland. I will provide
enough money for you to have whatever you need. The family I
am sending you to will welcome you. He's the son of our doctor
in London. He has a lovely Scottish wife and they have children—"

He started to speak several times before he finally pounded the
last nail in the coffin of their friendship. His words were clipped
now and heavy with guilt. She knew he hurried to lessen her pain.
"Please don't write to us. Or to Eunice or Mariane. When it is
necessary, we will send messages back and forth through Dr.
Cameron's father in London."

The icy barrier she had gathered around herself cracked at that,
and unwelcome tears filled her eyes. He reached for her, but she
quickly moved back out of his grasp.

She turned to leave, and his voice followed her retreat, rough
and hoarse with something she didn't want to hear. "Someday
you will forgive me, Elizabeth."

Chapter Four

London, April 1813

THE liveried footman carried the ornate silver tray before him with the air of perfect confidence, his aristocratic mien equal to any peer of the realm. White-gloved hands steady, back straight, uniform clean, without a speck of dust or lint to mar the rich, dark green, he upheld the unequaled reputation of the Duke of Standbridge's London servants.

A white linen cloth rested squarely in the middle of the tray with its corners draping over the sides in precise, equal triangles. Gold-trimmed plates held sandwiches, crusts removed, stacked in a decorative heap, filled with meat and cheese, hearty enough for the old man and attractive enough to tempt the waning appetite of his distracted grandson. The last of the oranges from the conservatory at Standbridge filled a bowl, peeled and sectioned. Young Hawksley never could resist oranges.

A second footman marched cheerfully behind, his wide shoulders straining the seams of his livery. One work-roughened hand balanced a tray holding century-old silver urns filled with well-steeped tea for the duke and strong black coffee for the marquess. As if irreverently challenging the elegant silence of the house shoes worn by the footman he followed, the heels of his own sturdy boots echoed loudly in the hall.

The second footman's glance wandered to the gleaming parquet floor where, he observed with a roguish expression, the reflection of his polished tray danced ahead like a renegade spotlight. His strong square jaw relaxed with a quizzical twist and he one-handed the tray a few inches to the left, then to the right. The rhythm of his steps adjusted to the cavorting glint of silver on the floor. He looked almost disappointed when the trek ended before the double doors of the library where Marsh, the butler, waited with clenched teeth to grant them entry.

Unsmiling, Marsh conducted a swift inspection and nodded. His face betrayed neither his approval of the impeccable trays nor his disapproval of serving food at the incorrect time. The old duke kept country hours here in London, a source of near-disgrace for Marsh, though he would have chosen death before uttering such a criticism aloud.

The duchess had been able to coax His Grace out of such stubbornness when she was alive, teasingly insisting on keeping proper London hours. Upon her death the duke retreated to Standbridge where the disgracefully lax *country* servants allowed him to revert to his old ways. The trouble in Europe had gradually drawn the duke out of retirement these last few years, but now he had no intention of changing to please the servants or, God forbid, London's ruling society, the *ton*.

Marsh halted the troop just outside the closed door of the study, making no move to enter. The second footman gave Marsh a questioning look but Marsh ignored him. Finally, the door opened from the inside. Marsh's nostrils flared briefly as a miasma of wet wool and fish poured into the hall, immediately followed by a whistling cricket of a man who nodded cheerfully at Marsh and swaggered past, taking his wharfside manners to the kitchen where a hot meal and a cold bottle would send the little messenger on his way in comfort.

The kitchen staff maintained round-the-clock duty, as they had for several weeks as messengers of all sorts began arriving without appointment, each requiring refreshment befitting their station. It was a matter of extreme pride to Marsh that the household operated as smoothly as a well-oiled wheel, and that his masters were never privy to the strain such goings-on put upon proper London servants.

Marsh knocked on the open door and entered the study.

Hawksley sat at a long mahogany table, his chin leaning on the knuckles of his fisted hand, deeply engrossed in the oil-yellowed papers spread before him. His grandfather, the Duke of Standbridge, stood by the fireplace, absently poking at the glowing embers.

The footmen silently placed the trays on the side table. Marsh signaled the servants to depart and the first footman exited like an obedient shadow. Marsh held his temper in check as the second footman stalked to the window and raised well-muscled arms to grasp the edges of the drapes and pull them closed with a sound closely resembling a disapproving snort. The footman turned to eye the inhabitants of the room, dipped a respectful nod at the duke, and followed his counterpart from the room.

Marsh's eyes met those of the duke and they glanced in unison at the haggard young Hawksley seated at the table. An unspoken message passed between them and they performed their allotted roles with precision. Marsh took the poker from the duke's hand, replaced it in the holder, and began adding coal to the fire.

The duke crossed to the food and said heartily, "Well done, Marsh, a wonderful feast!" He reached for a clean plate from the stack, eliciting a barely concealed wince from Marsh at his casual rattling of the precious gold-crested dishes.

"Hungry as a wolf," the duke boomed, and piled several sandwiches on the plate. He added the fragrant orange slices to the assortment and placed it before his grandson, nudging his elbow sharply.

"What?" Hawksley started, coming out of his trance.

"Eat." Standbridge shoved a sandwich in Nathan's hand and nodded in satisfaction as his ploy worked and Nathan mechanically obeyed. Satisfied, he filled his own plate and joined his grandson. Marsh poured steaming liquid into cups and delivered them with quiet efficiency.

Nathan sighed as the fragrance of the rich brew drifted toward him. He reached for his cup. "You're a prince, Marsh," he declared, "you'll make a great king."

Marsh winced once more and bowed slightly. "Will that be all, my lord?" The duke waved him away and they were alone once more.

They finished eating in silence and the duke leaned back in his chair, giving Nathan an assessing look. "You look like a dustman, m'boy, with your hair all worried to a snarled mess and your clothes looking like you've slept in them. You'd make a marvelous study for Cruikshank's clever drawings. *Pugilist Dines with Duke* or *A Valet's Last Lament.*"

Nathan smiled in appreciation and tried to run his hand through the thick mass of black curls. "By the end of the day, I look like Harriette Wilson's lap dog. Why couldn't I have inherited your straight hair so I could just tie it back and forget it?"

"Raising you pulled out the kinks in mine, you rascal." The

duke waved at the paper-littered table. "You have a satisfied gleam in your eyes, sunken and bloodshot though they may be. What have you discovered?"

Nathan pointed to several stacks of paper. "I've piled these reports of deaths into individual groups. Three groups are significant and bear our Traitor's touch—torture, ending with a slashed throat and evidence that no matter where they were captured, their bodies were dropped on some remote spot of the English coast."

The duke quickly straightened up. "He carted them even from France just to drop them on our doorstep?"

Nathan nodded. "Not unlike a cat proudly bringing home his catch." He gestured to the paper-strewn table. "This plan of yours was brilliant, sir, running a compilation back for several years, because it reveals a definite pattern. The damning fact is that whether the victims were *émigrés* returning to France to work for Napoleon's overthrow or my people carrying messages, he took them only after they had been made privy to worthwhile information. Except those captured taking information from us—their torture was perfunctory, not enough to really extract information, but enough to entertain the torturer and thereby send us a message. Our Traitor didn't need to find out what his victims knew—because he already knew himself."

Nathan's voice took on a grim note as he picked up the latest message. "Our man in France, Pierre, was killed and an imposter took his place. Pierre was working closely with the French military and political leaders who were unhappy over the loss of their people and, more importantly, their wealth."

"It's a weakness always exploited in war, Nathan. When a population used to luxury is reduced to cabbage tobacco and acorn coffee, there is always time for negotiation."

Nathan continued in a lighter vein. "We've received some wonderful news from our last messenger. We've captured the imposter who took Pierre's place, but with typical French arrogance, he's brought us to our knees over the amount of gold he requires for revealing the identify of the Traitor. Unfortunately, he won't talk until Tangmere and Burnham deliver him safely to us.

"The Traitors' activities are far more encompassing than we had suspected. Had we not reviewed all these incidents together, we might have continued believing them random occurrences perpetrated by several different men. Then too, we would have still believed the rogue who killed my parents was simply a vicious traitor who retaliated against our family and never realized they were the same man."

The duke nodded. "For years after he killed your parents, I believed he was a simple smuggler incensed at losing his boat and crew and I was frightened because his note promised that he would be back to kill our entire family."

He chuckled. "Why else would I have put Marsh through such torment by hiring a crew of ex-soldiers to guard us? Sometimes I think he'll have a fit of apoplexy trying to make decent servants of them."

Nathan smiled briefly. "Walk with me tonight?"

The duke nodded and they exited to the hallway. Their outer wear awaited them in the hands of well-trained footmen. Marsh assisted, finally draping the duke's muffler over his shoulders with a flourish.

A footman opened the door and cold, damp air gusted into the hallway. Hawksley wound his own muffler around his head and neck, saying, "I hate this cold dripping weather."

Marsh cleared his throat and asked Hawksley. "Do you wish one of your men to accompany you this evening, my lord?"

"No, thank you, Marsh. My grandfather will guard my back tonight." Laughing, they began their stroll around the square.

After a few feet, Hawksley resumed their conversation. "While the Traitor has certainly outwitted us for years, it seems so *unwise* to me that he should have wasted his time killing innocent people like my parents when *you* were his enemy. He would have been far smarter to have eliminated you."

"I wondered the same thing and thought it just a fluke. However, looking back always makes geniuses of us, my boy." The duke's voice lowered. "I first became suspicious of his motive for not disposing of me when Lord Brownley's son was set upon by thieves and he retired and moved his family to Yorkshire."

"Yes . . . ?"

"D'you remember the scandal when Forster's mistress and son were found in bed together, murdered with their throats slashed, and everyone suspected Forster of the deed? He retired to his bottle."

Nathan's eyes narrowed as he picked up the thread. "And Johnstone and Wiggel before that."

He paused then nodded in conclusion. "All of them actively pursuing subversive enemies as we are, and our Traitor simply put them out of commission, preventing the instigation of a hue and cry for his own blood that would happen if he had killed such prominent men."

"And he gained the pleasure of torturing them by eliminating their loved ones. Torture distilled down to the most exquisite pain possible." A wagon passed, and they fell silent until the square once more grew quiet. Finally Nathan spoke, directing his compelling scrutiny toward the duke. "But you didn't quit."

"Don't give me a hero's mantle, Nathan, for I've questioned m'self time after time. After I put it all together, I made myself a very unpopular fellow by hounding his surviving victims until they admitted the truth. He left them all notes, each one a little more arrogant than the last.

"And then when he attacked you that winter before I sent you to Paxton . . . I thought of quitting, my boy, I'm not ashamed to admit that. You and Elizabeth are more important to me than the war or smugglers who ferry spies back and forth. But I couldn't do it. Never trust a man who leaves a task half done. I knew in my bones he would come for you eventually. I didn't believe he knew about Elizabeth, but I was worried when she came out of Paxton for her season."

The duke rubbed his gloved hands together and cleared his throat. "If your informer doesn't provide good information or even make it safely here, I've an idea that could give you an advantage."

"Yes?"

"Bring Elizabeth home from Scotland."

Hawksley stopped abruptly and stared at the duke. Finally he answered in a hoarse voice. "You can't be serious."

"I'm perfectly serious," the duke rejoined, starting forward again. "Our Traitor is watching us bloodhound around looking for him, no doubt. Not only might she be able to identify him, she might be able to anticipate any action against the family personally. And we have enough men to protect her at all times, of course."

Nathan stood silently for some time, his fingers drumming a rapid beat on one of the oak posts lining the footway. "The plan has its advantages, I'd be a fool not to admit that. But, after all our precautions to keep her safe from the Traitor all this time, why bring her back now?"

"Dr. Cameron came by today and brought some news from his

son in Scotland. Elizabeth is not exactly staying home safely tending to a little ladylike needlework as you instructed her."

Hawksley's lips twitched. "What has the little devil been up to?"

"She's been assisting the younger Dr. Cameron."

"So? A little lavender water on the temples of a malingering housewife never hurt anyone." He waited, then his gaze sharpened at the expression on his grandfather's face. "Oh, no, I should have known. She never could stay out of trouble. What has she been doing?"

"Well, what do you think she would be doing in the home of a physician? She's been assisting at the ladies' lying-in and—"

"Delivering babies?" He resumed walking. "Why, that's barbaric, she is only a child herself! And what do you mean by *'and'* . . . ?"

"And . . . a little stitching on a cut or two. He held up a hand to halt Nathan's remarks. "And before you go on, she's not a child any longer. I would have given her carte blanche on this doctoring business. Something m'wife would have done."

Nathan's gaze sharpened. "And if word leaks out about a member of our family mucking about in midwifery, it is bound to reach here eventually and she would be ruined."

"Yes. Then she would have to be moved in any case. She may not wish to come at all, after being shipped off like an unwanted parcel. I still believe you should have explained the real danger she was in, that her dream described our villain so clearly. She was young, but a right 'un, and didn't need to be treated like a delicate flower. All this business about it being better that she hate you than know her parents were murdered just shows how much you don't know about women, m'boy, especially a woman with Elizabeth's particular talents. Now she probably wishes us to Hades."

He met Nathan's scowl undaunted and plowed forward.

"Been thinking, she's twenty already, past time she finds a husband." He gave Nathan a side glance. "Should have brought her out before this, but with this muddle here, the timing wasn't right." Thinking out loud, he murmured, "When you have the Traitor safely under chains, I'll bring her to London. Suspect she'd like the museums and the theater, but the men will probably bore her to flinders. Still, you never know."

He paused in his monologue and looked askance at Nathan as if waiting for some response. Nathan's face had hardened to a deeply grooved mask.

A smile flickered quickly over the duke's face. Returning to the more pressing business at hand, he inquired, "When will your men be here with the informer?"

Hawksley's pace accelerated. "I'm not waiting for them to get here. I'm going to go meet them at the beach."

"Good, but take a guard with you."

A footman strode quickly to the front door as the knocker reverberated loudly in the hush of early morning. As he opened the door he heard Marsh's irritated whisper behind him. "Who on earth is making such a noise? They'll disturb the duke."

They heard a door slam above them followed by the duke's roar. "What's amiss, Marsh?" He descended the stairs, pulling the belt of his dressing gown tightly around his waist.

Marsh scowled at the messenger at the door and took the missive from his outstretched hand. He examined it quickly and offered the letter to the duke. "The message is for you, my lord."

"Not for Nathan?"

"No, Your Grace, it has your direction on it. It's from Paxton. Lord Hawksley left several hours past."

The duke's hands shook as he ripped the wax seal and quickly scanned the contents of the paper. "Oh, God, she's gone home to Paxton."

Chapter Five

THE door to the church opened once more. Heads turned. The swish and rustle of Sunday dresses moved through the room like a sweet wave, echoing up to the vaulted ceiling and back again. Ladies sighed as they watched the Wydner ladies enter. Gentlemen cleared their throats and looked back toward the vicar's frowning countenance, adopting sober, unconcerned expressions.

Two spinster sisters moved close to each other and whispered behind gloved hands.

Three lovely ladies moved toward their pew . . . *three*. Eunice Wydner, a little more softly rounded than her elegant daughter, still turned a gentleman's eye with her deep violet eyes and flushed cheeks. Mariane, all delicate shades of pink and blue and ivory, a bit high in the instep since her seasons in London and engagement to Lord Hawksley's friend. But all eyes were on the third lady. After four long years, Elizabeth had come home.

She was radiant, just as they had heard. Her animated, sunny expression invited friendship. Her eyes . . . such green, mischievous eyes! And tall. She towered over her aunt and cousin, yet glided forward straight as a willow. But the color, bless us all, the color . . . she was glorious autumn, come to life. Hair, like a child's, sunstreaked all russet, wheat, and daffodil. And that lovely skin, glowing apricot with a sprinkle of freckles across her nose; naughty girl, she still walked in the sun without a parasol.

Elizabeth inspected them all, one by one, as she followed behind her aunt and cousin, smiling and nodding and wiggling her fingers hello at the children, and grinning when they wiggled back.

Now they could find out the truth of all the rumors gone round the village three times at least. She'd been midwiving in Scotland? Well, one could believe anything of that heathen place. Molly, Elizabeth's maid, basking in her popularity since returning with her mistress, reported that Elizabeth has read at least a hundred books not even written in the good King's English, and she spoke French and some other gibberish Molly'd never heard of.

Molly's bragging her mistress has had a dozen offers of marriage or more. With her taking looks, she would have no trouble finding a decent *English* husband, now she was home. And about time; she'd almost passed her prime and must be twenty by now. It would be nice to have her home now that they were beginning to have a little society in their own village.

What would she think of them, of Paxton? While she'd been gone, they'd done a little changing of their own, they were proud to say. The Talbot and Dove, the mail coaching inn for so many years, had built an assembly hall with a musicians' balcony and a porch with a rose garden. Sold subscriptions and provided a place for the locals to do the pretty in their own town. The Tisburys' uncle stuck his spoon in the wall and left the family a little allotment. They'd promptly bought the place next door, had the front faced, and opened a store with bolts of cloth and ribbons for the ladies and a room full of sensible items for the men.

Wonder what young Elizabeth will think of her cousin, Mariane, carrying on just as if she wasn't wearing a betrothal ring, and her intended off fighting the damned Frogs? A great one for a dust-up, was Elizabeth, bet sparks will fly when she catches Mariane at that prank!

Looked like the pot would get a good stirring, and a dash of pepper, with Miss Elizabeth back.

Elizabeth ran her fingers over the rough bark of the oak tree, savoring the contentment that soothed her soul after receiving such a warm welcome at church and hugging to herself a full measure of happiness that her homecoming had brought.

I wonder how long I would have remained tamely in Scotland waiting for permission to come home, had I not been pestered beyond all reasoning with this feeling of danger. Poor Dr. Cameron, only threats of using her own medical wages and taking the mail coach had made him relent and send his own coach and servants to bring her home.

And what have I found? The village of Paxton has not burned down. Eunice and Mariane continue in good health. No villains lurk in the vicinity, preying on the inhabitants.

So why do I still feel so scattered, like a whirlwind of leaves, unsettled, disturbed—and, since my family is safe, do I want to pursue this *feeling?* After such an extended and zealous effort to subdue the affliction of my childhood, it is surely insane to deliberately invite it back.

While her banishment to Scotland had delivered an unequaled serving of pain, she had reaped benefits for which she would always be grateful. She had learned how to control her curse.

At Dr. Cameron's suggestion, she had agreed to study his medical books, and that had opened the door to solving her problem. Almost giddy with excitement when she discovered that intense concentration—difficult books and learning new things—was even more successful in keeping the visions at bay than her counting routine, she became obsessed with finding the resultant *silence*. Over the years she tussled with those intruders, fighting with her scholarly weapons—languages, mathematics, medicine, and literature—and usually the cowardly rascals faded away.

Yet, now that she was home, this feeling had grown more intense, greeting her each morning and churning up her sleep at night. Flickers of sight and sound beat persistently against her shuttered barricade, leaving her exhausted with the effort to keep them hushed. To regain the peace she had worked so hard for, should she let the image in and end the anxiety? But, she thought, shuddering at the possibility, if the veil was torn, just briefly, could it ever be mended again, or would it all come tumbling in, destroying her hard-earned control?

It was so overwhelming, and she was so tired.

She leaned back against the oak tree and closed her eyes, focusing on the spiraling, effervescent feeling that quivered inside her and took her breath away. Such a sure, strong feeling of danger, like an approaching wind violently bending the tops of distant trees as it came her way. She had felt this helpless terror before, the day when she held Mariane's life so tenuously in her hands, but she had no picture to guide her.

A flicker of light and motion vibrated on the periphery of her vision. Trembling, she softened the bulwark she had erected in her mind and tentatively permitted the flow to begin.

Harsh shades of red swirled. A man stood in concealing shad-

ows of an enormous building beside a waiting coach. Maroon liquid flowed over the shiny smooth flintstones of the footway and
down into the cobbled carriageway. Someone walked toward him,
all bundled up from the cold. Then moonlight drifted away from
the scene and it was gone.

The man in the shadows was the monster from her childhood
dream.

Shuddering, she searched her mind. Had she ever seen that
street, or those houses? The architecture in Scotland had a different flavor, and Paxton could never boast of such elegant struc-
tures. What had such a malevolent picture to do with the
monster . . . with her?

Furious with herself for weakening and believing something of
value could be gained by giving that vision space in her mind, see
what she had done to herself? Dreamed up a new version of her
nightmare.

No doubt if she remained *open* for very long, she would see
more pictures and begin to hear voices. And, to what end? As in
her childhood, they would most likely be random, seldom having any vital meaning for her. She sighed. This feeling probably
erupted from her longing to be home and a scene from one of
the gothic tomes she and Margaret Cameron had shivered over.
She had worried herself to a quivering mouse, and all for nothing.

Wanting to escape her uneasiness, she walked to the bridge and
stopped to enjoy the glimmer of sunlight dancing on the flowing
water. Then, before she could tighten her resistance, another sight
overwhelmed her, one with warmth and a honey-slow sweetness.
A soft smoke of light filled her, like floating bits of sun filtering
through a filmy curtain on a winter day. Then it came, approaching slowly, expanding until it filled her . . . she looked through a
tall, elegant window where endless candles flickered. She heard
laughter and the scatter of voices. She was outside, breathing the
fragrance of roses, held fast by the enchantment of water tumbling on rocks nearby. Her feet were dew-wet, but her shoulders
were warm. Someone was behind her. One large arm encircled
her waist, and the other crossed round her shoulders from behind.
His mouth was warm on the nape of her neck and his teeth nipped
a soft command of surrender. There was no need to turn around.
It was Hawksley.

Violently, she snapped the view closed. Where had that sensuous vision sprung from, so highly seasoned with a hunger she had never felt toward anyone? She trembled, hot and cold, flushed and shamed.

No, she silently wailed, no, she would *not.* She had no intention of admitting Hawksley into any of her thoughts, and if this scene forecast her future linked with him, it could just toddle along without her! Hadn't she once sent the future careening along in another direction by convincing Hawksley to rescue Mariane? Well then, she could certainly avoid spending any time in a garden with Lord Hawksley.

No doubt, she assured herself, that little episode was a result of coming home and sensing Hawksley everywhere she turned, knowing that she was no longer isolated from his powerful presence. She would not be surprised to see him come charging to Paxton someday in person with his bullying ways and arrogant demands.

Impatience tore through her. After four years of successfully banishing every memory of him, must she now be forced to cudgel every specter of Lord Hawksley that rose, past and future?

She was an adult now, fully capable of handling her own affairs. She had sent the duke a duty note, informing him of her arrival home. She was home to stay, unless she decided to see more of the world. She might find a respectable traveling family needing a governess or companion. She would like to journey to other countries, to speak French and Greek with authentic natives of those countries, and see the wonders she read about.

Eventually, when the hunger for children drove her to it, she would marry, a less attractive choice, given her unladylike independence and unusual situation. Perhaps she might find a husband during her travels. She grinned. Perhaps she might meet a sinister count with a haunted castle and recognize the dark picture she had just frightened herself with.

As for Lord Hawksley, he had played a heavy hand in her life, but there was absolutely no reason for her to ever spend another second of thought on the wretched man.

When she returned to the house, Chilton, the butler who functioned as doorman when his curiosity superseded his dignity, advised her that a courier and two coachmen from London waited for her in the kitchen. Disgusted with how her heart thrashed around inside her chest, she hurried to meet them.

The weary messenger stood at her entrance and handed her the missive. "I'm to stay here and watch over you." Elizabeth broke the seal and quickly scanned the ink-blotted writing. *"Remain in Paxton and wait for Hawksley's further instructions. Standbridge."*

Chapter Six

ELIZABETH strode into the parlor, her eyes glaring at the crumpled paper in her hand. "Hawksley, that . . . that *fiend*, that arrogant, insensitive, pea-brained fiend!"

From behind her a sweet voice responded, "Pea-brained?"

"Yes!" she hissed. "As in 'small as,' or—" She stopped and grimaced.

Flushing, she turned to the voice and apologized. "Oh, Aunt Eunice, I do beg your pardon, but I am mad as hops at this message from the duke telling me I am to await instructions from that . . . pea-brained Hawksley." She sank into the nearest chair and said, "You'll think I left all my manners in Scotland."

Eunice responded, obviously amused. "As well you should, Elizabeth, a house guest should always leave a useful gift. Now I can see that you are agitated over your letter. Whatever did he say?" The laugh lines around her eyes deepened. "Is Lord Hawksley sending you to India this time, my dear?"

Elizabeth's laugh broke loose, a full-throated blend that brought an echoing chuckle from her aunt. "Oh, Auntie, I'd forgotten what a treasure you are. And no, not to India this time, I am to wait in my room until I hear further from Hawksley. The duke has sent a guard and two coachmen to make sure I don't disobey."

She smoothed out the letter and began folding it. "I'll not be ordered about like one of his lackeys." She straightened up and shifted to the edge of her chair. "I'll give the messenger a suitable answer and send him back to London."

Eunice rose quickly and waved Elizabeth back. "Let's not kill the messenger, my dear, let's just feed him and give him a room for the night. Tomorrow is soon enough to take your answer back." She pattered out of the room, leaving Elizabeth alone with her steaming thoughts.

"I knew he was going to ruin everything," she fumed. "Just when I get my thoughts sorted out and I'm on the brink of deciding what I'm going to do with my life, I'm to wait for him to trespass where he's not wanted."

Eunice returned, her dove-gray gown covered with a white smock. She adjusted a wide-brimmed straw hat over her ash-brown hair. "I'm going to be outside with my flowers," she said cheerfully. "Why don't you take a brisk little walk to compose yourself. When you return I need a private conversation with you."

Elizabeth waited patiently for her aunt to disclose her reason for arranging a secluded conference. Eunice sat on her low drawing stool, sketching a tiny wild daisy growing alongside the garden path. *"Bellis perennis,"* she offered in her soft voice. "We only get them when they leave the field fallow and the wind blows them in. This little fellow is early this year. He goes to sleep each night, just like a baby."

How wonderful it seemed to hear her aunt's soothing talk of flowers once more. Eunice was a gifted artist and could lose hours wandering happily across fields and through the woods, much more at ease with blossoms than people.

Eunice stood and tucked the stub of charcoal and small sketching pad into the pocket in her smock. "Shall we walk?" she asked. They strolled toward the woods, with Eunice breaking the silence to point out early flowers. "This hairy little blue flower is a strawberry. Barren, though, poor thing. There, see how the tiny daffodil likes the spot of sunlight in the woods? Not much to see this early in the season. Wait until we reach the next turn, you'll love this patch of primrose." As promised, they found an exquisite cluster of fresh young plants, vibrant with a bright show of color.

They stood quietly before Eunice continued. "You are so like your mother. I was shocked when you returned from Scotland, it was like seeing a ghost. She was my dearest friend, and I was so pleased when she married my brother." She glanced at her niece and flushed in embarrassment. Elizabeth was furiously blinking back tears in an attempt to maintain her composure. She took Elizabeth's arm and they continued strolling through the stand of tall conifers.

"Tell me about Scotland. Not the scenery—I'll quiz you later in agonizing detail—tell me about you. What did you love and what did you hate, and are you sad or happy to be back? Or, should I not be asking such nosy questions?"

Elizabeth smiled and replied in a soothing voice, "I don't mind, of course. As to what I hated, being torn from you and Mariane was very painful. I thought I would never get past the homesickness. At first I hated the food and the strange accents and wished they would all go away and take their kindness with them."

Laughing in fond remembrance, she continued. "Dr. Cameron's wife, Margaret, was a dear and I could not stay distanced from her for very long. She bribes with sweet tidbits and convinces you that she needs your help desperately, while the truth is she can work like a demon without tiring. She soon wheedled me out of the sullens and beguiled me with her wonderful warmth and charm. And, of course, Dr. Cameron soon found out my besetting sin . . . curiosity. He, too, assured me that he was overworked and needed an extra hand."

Elizabeth's voice deepened with enthusiasm. "Medicine is such a complex subject to study. Scholars have been writing about it forever, with marvelous new discoveries each year. Yet some doctors' practices are still very primitive. Basically, a good physician will do what he can to fix whatever is offending the body and then stand back to let it heal itself."

She nudged the older woman playfully. "Like you, Auntie. You pull out the weeds, feed your flowers something nourishing, and let nature do the rest."

Eunice frowned. "But, letting an unmarried woman assist in childbirth. Why were you allowed to do such a shocking thing?"

"Who needs the knowledge more?" she teased, laughing at her aunt's gasp. "Seriously, Auntie, some people were shocked, as they would be here. But whereas *you*, that is *we*, the English believe we are the hub of information, the truth is that in many ways the Scots are far more educated and advanced in science and practical living. Ladies are expected to use their minds and girl-children study the same books as the lads." She flashed a bright smile. "And that's what I loved. Ladies are not expected to be little stuffed dolls."

She paused and laughed. "And, they *like* redheads! Margaret's hair is the color of one of your poppies and you couldn't put your little finger on her face without touching a freckle. You should see how her husband adores her."

The path led down to a wide spot by the stream and they

stopped to admire the sparkling water. Eunice crossed her arms and hunched her shoulders, staring intently at the grassy foliage. "Hemlock and gipsywort, they like the muddy banks. Nothing here blooms until summer, but the leaves are nice—"

Elizabeth interrupted, anxious to get past this dainty preamble and into the real reason for their secluded walk. "Auntie, what's on your mind? What's bothering you?" Eunice hesitated, and Elizabeth introduced her own concern. "It's Mariane, isn't it? I'm worried too, and wondered if I was the only one who noticed how that slug, Stanley, centers his attention on her."

Eunice brightened considerably. "That's it exactly, dear! You always understood what I needed before I even thought of it. She is betrothed to a wonderful man who is fighting for his country, trusting her to be all that she should be. How shocked Matthew would be to see her flirting with that worthless Lord Stanley. Whatever is she thinking of, dancing with him twice and welcoming him to visit whenever he wishes?"

Still practiced at jumping to Mariane's defense, Elizabeth offered. "She's lonely and flattered by his attention, Auntie, and probably not thinking at all. After her seasons in London, she must find this a very tame place."

"Will you talk to her, Elizabeth? I've tried, but she just gets sullen and refuses to discuss it."

"Oh, Auntie, I can't come back after all this time and begin telling her how to behave. She will feel I'm interfering, and with very good reason."

"I know it won't be a pleasant task, she's like a wet cat when she's crossed. But I can never find the right words to make her take me seriously. Stanley is so persuasive and clever with her. I don't trust him one bit."

Knowing that she could never refuse her aunt anything, Elizabeth sighed. "Very well, I will speak with her in the parlor after tea."

Elizabeth inserted the tip of her needle into the tightly stretched linen and wove it in and out, securing it safely in a resting position. She placed the hoop on the delicate satinwood dropside table, as if to free her hands for the coming battle. She had seldom risen the victor in a conflict of this kind with Mariane. The girl was softhearted about any creature hurt or in trouble, but stubborn to a fault about her friends, no matter how unsuitable they might be. She and Eunice had spoiled the girl and made a pet of her, foolishly protecting her from life's realities.

Since coming home Elizabeth had discovered that one might *converse* with Mariane, if the discussion included admiration of her exquisite face, her fashionable attire, or her charming manners, but divert the flow in any other direction and Mariane's attention disappeared like an underground stream.

She looked fondly at her lovely cousin. Framed in the morning sunlight, her golden blond hair shimmering like a halo, Mariane seemed the epitome of English maidenhood—conformable and sweet-tempered. Even as she fidgeted in her chair, she was so *perfect* to look upon that distressing her seemed almost cruel. But distress her she must, before the little ninny stepped through a door that opened and closed only once. Well then, she thought with a shiver of apprehension, *en garde!*

"Mariane. You have been betrothed to Matthew for two years. Are you planning to toss him away for a man milliner like Lord Stanley?"

Elizabeth bit back a smile as Mariane's head raised quickly, like a vixen spotting a pack of hounds. She had the instincts of a trapped animal when her judgment was under attack—having spent so little attention arriving at a conclusion, she resisted any efforts to expose the trail.

"He's not a man milliner, Elizabeth," she snapped. "He dresses in the first stare of fashion, something you would understand if you had ever ventured into society yourself."

"My poor unsophisticated brain is perfectly capable of understanding more than you wish, Mariane. As to Lord Stanley's fashion sense, never tell me that buttons the size of saucers and bilious, puce-colored waistcoats make him the more worthy man. He can't even turn his head for fear of blinding himself on his own collar—not that I would mind, it would add years to the life of your parlor looking glass."

Mariane's patrician nose quivered with indignation. "He's a sensitive, charming gentleman, Elizabeth, and he understands me the way Matthew never could."

"What you mean is that he writes poetry to every visible part of your person and brings you gifts every time he calls. You're like a little magpie, collecting compliments and shiny trinkets."

Mariane's face darkened. "You're just jealous that men are always attracted to me. Just like your precious Lord Hawksley.

Admit that you admired him first, but for whom did he risk his life? The minute he saw me . . . well, it's such an old story." She examined her perfectly manicured hand, watching through thick lashes to assess the damage of the hit.

Elizabeth swallowed hard, forcing herself to remain calm. Remember what's at stake here, she commanded herself, not your feelings, but Mariane's future.

"Mariane, what do you suppose Lord Stanley is doing in this tiny backwater village when the season is about to begin? Could it be that he's evading his creditors?"

Mariane snapped back. "He came on a duty visit to see his mother. He stays because he finds congenial company here. Why must you spoil it with criticisms of a few courtesies and attentions?"

"Ah, but what does Lord Stanley offer you besides courtesies and attention, Mariane? When you unwisely let him take you outside at the assembly, did he speak of his home or his family? When he entices you to stroll through the garden here, does he discuss his intentions, his expectations?"

Mariane raised her head and thrust her stubborn little chin forward. Oops, Elizabeth thought, here comes the evasive counterattack!

"Who made you my keeper, Elizabeth? Not my mother, and most certainly not the old duke. If you ask the duke for anything, he only instructs you to petition his so-wonderful grandson. If Nathan was so wonderful, he would be in the army fighting like my Matthew." Mariane's delicate ivory skin glowed as a pink flush invaded her cheeks.

Elizabeth couldn't resist. "He's still *your* Matthew, then?"

"I didn't precisely say I was ending the betrothal, Elizabeth. I only said that Rodn—Lord Stanley entertains me. I've missed hearing the latest *on dits* and witty conversation. I'm in danger of growing staid and provincial here, while *he* knows how to go on in society. Furthermore, how can you feel qualified to criticize a bosom beau of the Prince Regent!"

"I wouldn't value that as a character reference, Mariane. Prinny's chums are a pretty rackety bunch."

Mariane smiled with a touch of triumphant malice. "You're the odd one to talk about rackety people, Elizabeth. You were whisked off to Scotland, no doubt in disgrace yourself, and then you come slinking back home, with tales of practicing midwifery there."

Run through and run over, Elizabeth thought. Our little vixen has grown teeth since I went away.

"Is that what you wish for yourself, to be ruined and disgraced? Has Lord Stanley offered marriage? Is that why he persists in trying to arrange meetings without your maid, to discuss matrimony? Or does he only want to discuss poetry and steal a kiss?"

"Well, at least *he* is interested in something else besides crop rotation and draining fields. What fun is it going to be as the wife of a farmer?"

"Matthew is not a farmer, Mariane, he's a responsible landowner from a respected family and bosom chums with Lord Hawksley. Where do you think landed people obtain their funds—from the land—and if he didn't care for it, he would soon have nothing to offer you. Aunt Eunice tells me how Matthew captured your heart at first glance. Didn't he favor you with every attention when he was courting you? Oh, Mariane," she said tenderly, "I know you miss London society after your triumphant seasons, and I'm sure you've missed Matthew these past two years, but have you stopped loving him?"

Mariane's chin wobbled, and her lovely blue eyes filled with tears. She glared at Elizabeth and reached for her lace-trimmed handkerchief. "I'm not answering any more questions, you meddler."

She rose to leave the room, graceful and elegant even as she dropped the ferocious words behind her. "I shall see whom I wish, when I wish, and my feelings for Matthew are none of your concern. If I wish to spend a few moments with my friends, without a watchdog spoiling everything, I shall certainly do so. I have no intention of putting myself beyond the pale, *as you have,* but I am already nineteen, and I do not intend to grow old and boring while Matthew chooses to play soldier!"

Elizabeth sat frozen in the empty room. Adjusting her shawl closely around her shoulders, she slowly rose from her chair, feeling close to tears. Going nose-to-nose with Mariane had always left her feeling inferior, which is why she seldom had the inclination to do so.

She moved toward the front door, suddenly craving the feeling of sun on her face. She walked slowly past the stable and stopped at the edge of the fenced pasture. Leaning her arms on the wooden rail, she let the sun warm her while she strove to regain her usual serenity.

Had she only worsened the situation by provoking this argument with Mariane? If she let Eunice down and Mariane made such a seriously wrong choice, could she forgive herself? She took a deep breath and steadied herself. What should she do now? More important, what would Mariane do now?

Mariane would usually call *finale* to a confrontation like this by plotting and exacting some revenge and then giving in gracefully and doing the proper thing as if it had been her intention all along. But what gave Elizabeth chills was the inevitability of Mariane's foolishly weaving Lord Stanley into the fabric of her reprisal.

Maybe she could cajole Lord Hawksley into sending Mariane to India . . . or Scotland . . . *or, better yet, London* . . .

She knew then what she had to do. She must remove her troublesome cousin from Lord Stanley's influence, and London was a lure Mariane would not be able to resist. She would take her cousin and Eunice to Hawksley and he could provide another season for Mariane in London.

Stay in Paxton and wait for further instructions from Hawksley? She thought not. None of them was going to stay in Paxton. She inhaled the clear air, her good spirits renewed. A goal was a wonderful thing.

It was a delicious picture, Lord Hawksley's reaction when they all arrived together . . . like a present . . . one he couldn't ignore.

Chapter Seven

Paxton to London, April 1813

SHE marched back to the house, determined to do battle with Mariane once more. How dare her cousin grow so stiff and full of London pomposity? In days past, Mariane would have secretly closeted the two of them in a bedchamber and interrogated her, demanding all the grisly details of producing babies. She would have pored through Elizabeth's medical books and journals, eager for sketches over which she could shock herself badly enough to actually faint.

Mariane lived for drama, able to produce a scene filled with hysterics or confrontation if present company grew too boring—so, what on earth had changed her cousin? Obviously, hysterics and confrontation were still her forte, but for what purpose? To flirt with Lord Stanley, a popinjay she would have laughed at before? He wasn't her blond, blue-eyed hero, but a shoulder-padded, wasp-waisted bore who wore high heels and painted his face.

Though flighty and scatterbrained, Mariane had ever extended to Elizabeth a sweet friendship. What had changed all Mariane's plans and dreams? She certainly intended to find out.

She walked through the front door and slammed it closed with a force that would have matched Lord Hawksley's boorish manners. *No wonder he does that, it feels wonderful.*

Chilton came out into the front entry looking, no doubt, for the invading army that dared to make such a racket. "Miss Elizabeth?"

"Yes, Chilton, would you please arrange for trunks to be brought down to Aunt Eunice and Mariane's rooms? And summon their maids to begin packing their clothing for an extended stay in London."

Chilton masked his surprise, but recovered quickly enough to counter with a question. "I don't believe Miss Wydner's abigail has been informed yet, Miss Elizabeth. Shall I advise her of these plans, or shall we wait for Miss Wydner to do so?"

"No," she answered absently, trying to remember a servant who would answer to that description, at the same time alert to the humor in Chilton's mobile face. Like an old game, he was waiting for her to explore his seemingly casual question.

Elizabeth studied the man before her. He had aged during the time she resided in Scotland. Gray hair now claimed a place alongside the resident brown, and smiling crinkles had grown in number around his eyes. Still erect and full of energy, though, he was an old friend, one who had been a surprising comfort to her all those years ago when she came to Paxton, joining in the conspiracy to distract her back into life by punctuating her days with unexpected pleasures.

His firm hand had held her as she slid squealing down the banister and his serious voice had directed her in the proper manner to direct the servants. How many times had he delivered trays to her with grandiose bows, pulling back the covering to reveal sweet biscuits or hot cross buns? Once he had delivered a baby kitten on a tray, but had to reluctantly retrieve it when Elizabeth's eyes had turned red and itchy and she began sneezing.

They had perfected a system whereby their words were very properly mistress and servant yet their expressions and unspoken words told an entirely different tale. Judging by the look on his face, he had something very interesting to say . . . or rather, not say. In any case, the game was on and it was her turn.

"I doubt Mariane's abigail is aware of the plans since I haven't told Mariane herself yet, as you certainly have guessed, judging from the devilish look in your eye." She frowned and asked, "Who is my cousin's abigail? I wasn't aware of such a person in the house."

"Oakes is the abigail Lady Lowden sent to care for Miss Wydner's needs, Miss Elizabeth. She took to her bed about the time you arrived and hasn't recovered completely as yet."

"Aunt Eunice's sister sent an abigail home from London to stay here with Mariane?"

"Lady Lowden has some concern that Miss Wydner might wish to continue with the London niceties, I believe."

Elizabeth stopped to ponder this new information. What London niceties?—the latest fashions could be gleaned from Mariane's copies of *La Belle Assemblée* and no London manners could exceed the gentle kindnesses Eunice had drilled into both girls. Just what was going on? She had been home three days and had heard nothing of a seriously ill servant.

And why was Chilton smiling? A probe in that direction was definitely the correct path through the maze. "Then Oakes enjoys poor health?"

"No, indeed, she is a vigorous lady, Miss Elizabeth. Perhaps when you arrived it was a cold day and she contracted something."

"No, I believe it was a sunny day. But, perhaps I brought something from Scotland that affected her. I don't recall bringing home much more than a small trunk and a lot of interesting stories."

"A great one for stories is our Oakes, miss. And accents, she fairly dotes on picking out where a person comes from."

"Accents? Whose accent?"

"Begging your pardon, miss, but when you speak, you have just a touch of an accent. A few days home and I'm sure it will be gone."

Elizabeth was stunned. She had an accent? The idea pleased her enormously. How that would annoy Hawksley, to send her away an obedient little English cousin and find an outlandish Scottish lass dropping back into his life. A wild barbarian miss, as Mariane's abigail had obviously concluded. Elizabeth laughed softly, and sat down on the stairs. She knew better than to ask Chilton to sit with her to continue their delightful sparring.

"I see, Chilton. How foolish we are to think parlor conversation does not float somehow in the air to all corners of a house." She thought for a minute, then it all became clear. "Perhaps she was once frightened by a midwife?"

"I doubt that she has ever been frightened by anything, Miss Elizabeth."

"Perhaps frightened is too harsh a word."

"It's difficult to say."

Satisfied that she now had a clear picture of the way of things, she looked up at Chilton with a mischievous gleam in her eye. "Then the poor dear must be simply concerned, or perhaps repelled, by contamination from strange new sources. Perhaps I should attend her. I have learned so many wonderful treatments for almost every lady's ailment. What do you think, Chilton? I'd hate to see her suffer when one visit from me would certainly send her straight back to her duties."

"Would you like me to relay your message?"

"Would you like to do that?"

"Very much, Miss Elizabeth." He walked toward the back hall that would take him to the servants' stairway. He paused and turned, a twinkle in his eye. "Welcome home, Miss Elizabeth."

"So, you see, the only answer for my dilemma is for you to go with me to London. I daren't arrive at the duke's home with only a maid for propriety, not to mention remain there with two gentlemen who are only truly distantly related, no matter how kindly the duke bids me call him Grandfather." Elizabeth delivered these words with a serious expression, wondering what on earth she would reply should anyone challenge her with the recollection that she had traveled from Scotland with only the two coachmen and Sally for chaperone.

She adopted a guileless expression and waited.

Eunice's hands stilled, the tea pitcher she held halted, dripping a few golden spots into Mariane's cup, then continued with a shaky stream of liquid.

She felt guilty over the necessity of presenting her plea without warning, but if Eunice knew what was coming, her lovely face would display her thoughts for all to see, and Mariane would immediately know that this was a plot. The great difficulty for Eunice would be that she not only shied away from prolonged contact with her overpowering sister, but the thought of an entire city full of Lady Lowdens would be the ultimate terror.

As for Mariane, Elizabeth's mission was to present an avenue whereby her cousin could leave Lord Stanley behind and trip willingly off to London with her dignity intact. She turned her attention to Mariane as Eunice handed her daughter the fragrant cup of tea. A kaleidoscope of expressions danced quickly across Mariane's face and Elizabeth was tempted to dip into her thoughts. The impulse tantalized, nibbling around the edges of her hard-earned resolution. How she would love to know what schemes bubbled up in that young lady's mind. She hadn't long to wait.

"It's very kind of Lord Standbridge to invite us to London.

Elizabeth, but we couldn't insult Aunt Sylvia by residing with the duke instead of her." Mariane's eyes sparkled with excitement, giving lie to her demurral. Obviously, the thought of launching herself back into society from a duke's town house was responsible for erasing the sullen expression she had brought into the parlor.

The little minx wanted Elizabeth to ease her way out of Lady Lowden's clutches, so she obliged. "I suppose I could hire a respectable companion, Mariane, but if you and Auntie are not there to tell me how to go on, I'm sure I shall shame us all."

Mariane clearly agreed with that statement, inspiring Elizabeth to a little detour of revenge. "On the other hand, perhaps my years in Scotland have given me the skills I need, and we needn't upset Lady Lowden by forcing you to stay with me," she sighed, hoping her wretched sense of humor wasn't going to ruin this conversation—but how was she to keep a straight face with Mariane's dismay so obvious and Eunice choking on her tea? Better end this quickly and cease tormenting her cousin.

"If you would allow me, though, I shall ask the duke to send a note round to Lady Lowden, pleading for her sympathy and explaining how comforting it will be to have you both with me."

Mariane nodded graciously. "Very well, then, if you feel you need our assistance—"

"But, Elizabeth"—Eunice broke in, apparently unable to make such drastic decisions without protesting—"surely, it won't be necessary for me to go to London."

Both girls scowled and looked at each other, in tune for the first time today. Elizabeth gritted her teeth and spoke pleasantly, "Auntie, surely you do not wish Mariane and I to journey to London without a proper chaperone." A peep of the old Mariane smiled back at her as Eunice surrendered without another word.

Convincing Tarr, the poor messenger-guard, was not so easy. His orders, he kept insisting, were to keep Elizabeth safe, and short of tying her to a heavy piece of furniture, he was at a loss as to how that was to be accomplished. The three determined females rushing up and down the main staircase and double that amount of servants vibrating the back stairs gave him only moving targets, none of whom wished to listen to his demands.

Elizabeth took pity on the harried man and sent for Chilton.

"Chilton, Mr. Tarr is in need of your assistance. The duke has given him the unhappy task of seeing to my safety. In his mind, this does not include my traveling to London, but since I am quite determined to do so, can you help make his duties easier?"

The butler thought for a moment, then compiled his list of suggestions. "We'll send along the gamekeeper on the other coach to aid you, and he'll bring his Brown Bess to keep order. The man can down a deer with one shot, so you'll be in good hands."

Tarr nodded and Chilton continued, "There's a blunderbuss in the attic if you want to arm another man, perhaps the gardener or a footman."

At Tarr's horrified expression, Chilton shrugged. "The gun can be carried for effect and needn't be fired at all." Tarr turned to look at Elizabeth and his frustration evoked her sympathy.

"I promise to let you do your job. I'm just going to go to London and the duke can keep an eye on me himself. If you wish, you can go back now and tell him I'm coming soon."

When that didn't calm him, she gave up, wondering what kind of place was London when simply traveling through the streets seemed such a dangerous undertaking.

At last they were on their way, several days delayed while the problem of traveling vehicles was solved. The coach Tarr had arrived in could not transport them all plus their luggage, so the family's old town chariot had been refurbished.

Once Tarr had given the family chariot a thorough inspection for safety and pronounced it fit, Mariane had ordered a dusting and preening before she would deign taking it to London. A smaller conveyance than the duke's coach, it carried Sally and Oakes inside with mounds of luggage. The family coachman sat upon his hammercloth dressed in livery he had unearthed from somewhere and proudly handled the two horses from his high perch. In place of the lackey who normally stood between the hind wheels rode the equally proud game warden with his faithful Brown Bess fastened nearby and the blunderbuss resting in the boot below the coachman's feet.

Elizabeth entered the ducal coach in a mood of elevated spirits, thinking whimsically that the luggage decorating the outside of the coach resembled an aging matron trying to wear all her hats at once. She took the vacant seat beside Tarr, the guard, and faced her aunt and Mariane. Miffed that she was deprived of her chance to examine the still-illusive Oakes in close quarters, she cheered up immensely when she realized that Tarr was an equally worthy target for her curiosity.

"Chilton tells me you are a soldier on leave, assigned to the duke's employ. Are you happy in your position?"

His face took on a pained expression. An employee never revealed information about the family he served. Clearing his throat, he peered out the window over her shoulder and pointed to a man garbed in a tattered green jacket and trousers, limping away from a tethered horse. "I'm in better luck than that fellow and his companion, miss."

Elizabeth swiveled on the seat to look back at the lone traveler in question. "His companion?"

"We passed him back a mile or so, both of them was in the rifle regiment of the 95th foot. Out scouring the countryside for work no doubt, or a meal for chopping wood."

"But why did he leave the other man behind?"

"Didn't, miss, just doing a little Ride and Tie. The other fellow will catch up to the horse they share and ride past the first man and tie it down the road. Come dark, they'll stay together and billet in a barn or under a hedge and stand guard for each other. Not that they have anything worth stealing, save the horse and their lives."

Tarr then noticed Eunice's distress over the plight of the ex-soldiers and let the conversation die. He continued to look out the window, then the other, as Elizabeth plotted her next comment. She wanted to know if Hawksley resided in the London house, and if so, how much time he spent there.

"I'm looking forward to seeing the duke. It should be interesting to see him and Hawksley together. It seemed to me when I last saw the marquess, he had taken on much of the duke's looks as he matured." It wasn't precisely a question, but he would be compelled to respond.

"Yes," he responded, "His Grace has the vigor of a young man, much like my own grandfather." She nodded politely, thwarted as he slipped away from her real question.

"My grandfather was gamekeeper here in Townley Park. It seems the seventh earl celebrated his twenty-first birthday with a bonfire which promptly burned down my grandfather's cottage. In order to turn the earl's father's wrath away, Grandfather took the blame upon himself. When the earl came into his own, my father became gamekeeper and Grandfather opened a butcher shop in the village. A properly grateful man was the earl."

Tarr turned to Elizabeth with a serious slant to his mouth and a gleam of laughter in his eyes. She silently shared the humor of his ploy as he remarked, "He's a wonderful story teller, my grandfather."

She replied with a crisp voice, "As are you, Mr. Tarr."

She began again, "Does Hawksley—"

Mariane broke into the conversation, exclaiming, "This bouncing around is giving me the headache. Cook should take the cream for a ride on this road, she would have butter in a trice."

Eunice turned to Tarr and said, "Do you think we should stop for a while, sir?"

"No, missus," Tarr quickly disagreed, "this is a bad stretch of road. It's the ruts. Our coach's wheels don't match the grooves in the road. No doubt the local wagon builder likes a smaller size, like your own town chariot coming behind us, but the duke's carriage is too big. We're coming on to Leicester where Macadam had a go at the ground and we'll do just fine. Smart man, Macadam, built the roads up high where they'd drain, piled the ground with a ditch full of pounded rocks and gravel. Like driving through a park."

Elizabeth pulled free the cushions between her and the side of the coach and leaned over to tuck them around Mariane, saying, "When I traveled down through Yorkshire a few days ago, we came upon some wonderful roads built by John Metcalf. He's somewhat of a legend in the area, since he was born blind."

She glanced back at Tarr. "And the roads in London, are they—"

The coach lurched, throwing her against the window. She thought for a second that she had bumped her head since her eyesight seemed cloudy, but then she realized a picture was forming in her mind. She shook her head to clear it, but it was too late. She leaned back and closed her eyes, determined to make short work of this unwelcome interloper. Sickened by the sight of her dream monster, she nonetheless gave in and let it come, fearful that it bore some message for her family.

The same dark red water poured across the cobblestones and

the villain still waited in the shadows, but this picture was different. The person all bundled up was not walking toward the villain this time, but had passed him and was walking away. As she watched, the villain in the shadows moved forward into the moonlight, pulled a dark scarf over the bottom of his face, and followed his prey.

She opened her eyes and looked around. Eunice and Mariane were looking through the food basket, discussing the best way to serve the portions. Tarr had noticed her tightly closed eyes and said in a concerned voice, "Are you feeling badly, miss? Shall we stop?"

She shook her head but he ignored her and lowered the window and stuck his head out to instruct his coachmen to pull over as soon as possible. Mariane was delighted and they were presently parked on a wide curve near a meadow. Eunice and Mariane soon had the maids from the other coach engaged in arranging an impromptu picnic.

Still shaken by her experience, Elizabeth clung tightly to Tarr's hand as he assisted her from the coach. Frowning, he ignored propriety and placed her hand on his arm in a fatherly gesture, instructing her to walk a way with him.

"Best thing for the megrim, miss, a little walk in the fresh air."

"Thank you, sir, this does feel wonderful." They strolled a ways then Elizabeth's curiosity elicited another question. "Will I find London pleasant in weather as well as scenery, Tarr?"

He chuckled. "Miss, I'm sure you'll enjoy yourself just fine in London. The weather is fickle, ranging from not seeing through the fog and soot to bright clear winter days with snow on the ground. You'll find parks to your liking, Hyde, Green, and St. James, all pretty as you like in the spring. In your part of town it's all clean and sweet smelling."

"My part of town?"

"It's a big city, miss, with every kind of neighborhood there is. Just let their lordships show you how to go on, and you'll be fine."

Mariane called them to return to join in the picnic. They turned back and Elizabeth said, "What will the duke say when our little entourage arrives, do you suppose?"

The question was outrageous and she had no business asking, but he looked her squarely in the eye and answered. "He'll be relieved to see you safe and sound, miss. Beyond that, I can't say."

She fished a little deeper. "And Lord Hawksley?"

He shrugged his shoulders and said, "He's a deep one, his lordship, can't admit to ever knowing what he's thinking."

Then his face broke into a huge grin. His next remark made no sense at all. "I can't wait to see Marsh's face."

Chapter Eight

*B**RAVADO** always falters in the face of reality.* Elizabeth wondered briefly what fellow coward had uttered those words. One did not arrive on a duke's doorstep, luggage in tow, without an invitation.

She glanced quickly at Eunice, the only person who might be likely to see her true state of mind. Eunice gazed back, pointedly directing her attention to Elizabeth's nervously wringing hands. They both smiled, one with concern and the other with a rueful shrug.

Mariane, nose pressed to the window, excitedly pointed out familiar landmarks leading the way to the Standbridge town house. The horses slowed and stopped. The sun hung low in the dull sky as if sinking slowly into a gray mire. Breathing was now threefold, the inward breath conveying not only air for the lungs, but the flavor of smoke for the nostrils and soot for the tongue. Still, Elizabeth thought, if one had a choice between the aroma wafting through earlier neighborhoods through which they had passed and the air of Mayfair's Grosvenor Square, one would smack one's lips over the preferable flavor of Mayfair soot.

"We're here, ladies." Tarr sighed with undisguised relief. "I'll be getting out first, if you please." They no longer wondered at his cautious ways, his constantly looking out windows and keeping them inside the coach or an inn until he had scouted out the area for villains. Why he felt keeping them close in sight required this exaggerated care, she would never fathom, but without his courtesy and concern, the four-day journey would have been exceedingly less comfortable. As for her curiosity, it had long since suffered a travel-weary demise.

The coach leaned and rocked as he exited and the sound of

horses' shuffling hooves echoed on the cobblestones and bounced off the shoulder-to-shoulder houses lining the enormous square. Elizabeth's butterfly stomach discouraged any visual exploration of her surroundings; she wanted only to get past the next few minutes with dignity and composure. Tarr placed the steps beneath the coach door and reached for Eunice's hand to assist her—then withdrew it quickly at the sound of approaching horses.

"Hold, missus," he said and turned, withdrawing two pistols from beneath his coat. Mariane gasped and snuggled closer to her mother. Elizabeth slid over to look out the window facing the avenue, but her view revealed nothing. After a moment Tarr grunted, no longer alarmed at the oncoming vehicle, and stuffed the guns back in their hiding places. He resumed the business of emptying the coach, reaching for Elizabeth last and ignoring her questioning look.

Everyone's attention turned to the snorting of horses and the rattle of the oncoming carriage. The conveyance pulled over a distance in front of them, the duke's crest proclaiming its ownership. Determined not to cower behind the others, she stepped forward.

Her heart pounded and she drew in a shaky breath. Hawksley. Was it him? A *frisson* of dread surfaced, then subsided as a liveried coachman scampered down and opened the door of the diligence. He pulled a stool out and placed it on the hard ground with a flourish. A surprising feeling of peace flowed over her as she realized that this was His Grace, the Duke of Standbridge. He stepped down, ignoring the coachman's proffered hand.

She had forgotten how huge he was, wide and burly and a full preview of what Hawksley would look like at this stage of maturity. His laugh bellowed across the cold evening air and he opened his arms and exclaimed with surprise, "Elizabeth, come give an old man a hug!"

She walked into his arms and let him squeeze her in a enveloping embrace. It was not the welcome she had imagined. She was prepared for an angry confrontal, for bitter words, even the ignominy of the tears she might shed. But this welcome, this encircling warmth, this scene she had hoped for four years ago—were too much and were very possibly too late.

She clamped her teeth down on her lower lip, pressing hard enough to prevent the threatening flood of emotion. She lifted her chin and looked squarely at him. He turned them both so she was hidden from the others' view. "I was afraid of this," he said gruffly. He gave her a little shake and said, "Let's get the others settled and we'll talk later . . . all right?"

Without waiting for her response, he released her, turned, and bowed over Eunice's hand. "My dear lady, nothing could give me more pleasure than to welcome you to my home." He turned to Mariane and favored her outstretched hand with a kiss and said, "Back to torment all the young bucks, are you?" He laughed and ushered Mariane and Eunice into the house saying, "With all this beauty blowing in from the country, we'll be having a fine day of sunshine tomorrow."

Elizabeth turned and looked back at the bustling scene. Servants seemed to be multiplying as she watched, stripping boxes and trunks from the coaches, ignoring Oakes's strident instructions with an air of condescension. Tarr took over and herded the two maids toward the door with assurances that someone would see to their comfort and they mustn't worry about such lowly matters as luggage. Sally's eyes lit up and Elizabeth could imagine her maid's lively mind adjusting with ease to the thought of such an elevated status.

She surveyed the square, admiring the tall homes lining the streets and the lovely park in the middle. Something bothered her, but she couldn't put her finger on the culprit. True, it was unusual to see men standing at guard as Tarr and the coachman now were, but her feeling of danger was back and the beastly dream picture loitered near her eyelids, like a servant anxious to be noticed. How she wished she had never allowed it admittance in the first place. If only, like a servant, it could be given a glowing reference for effort and sent back to the agency.

She now lagged far behind the others, and by the time she entered, they had been shown to their various destinations. She stopped and stood still in amazement. How was she to remain aloof in this mansion?

It was so empty, yet spoke wealth from every corner. Footmen stood at guard like sturdy wooden dolls on a clock, all dressed in green livery—*was this guarding attitude a trait of all dukes' servants?* The inlaid parquet floor glowed as if it was alive, and already maids were erasing the signs of traffic from its pristine surface. Exquisite needlework adorned the few chairs against the walls and fresh flowers, from where she couldn't imagine, stood cheerily in vases on ivory inset tables.

She sighed. She wanted to go home.

The door behind her closed and Tarr's comforting, familiar voice uttered her very thoughts. "Intimidating, isn't it, miss. Not like your cozy house, which is a very fine place to make a body comfortable."

The duke's deep voice joined in. "Thought so many times m'self." He was descending the stairs, smiling like a man who had all he wanted before him. "No one makes a home like Mrs. Wydner, we'll all agree to that."

He looked at Tarr's red face and chuckled. "This place is more Marsh's territory than anyone's, but a warm house and a full table is not to be despised, so we'll just leave him to it." He thought for a minute, then a wicked look appeared. "I should take Marsh to Standbridge and see what he'd think of dogs in the house and livery kept in the attic unless Royalty comes calling." He turned to Elizabeth and said, "Go on up, m'dear, a whole flock of servants are waiting, anxious to fuss over you. We'll meet at dinner and afterwards we'll have our little talk."

As she reached a spot near the top of the staircase, she heard Tarr ask the question she most wanted the answer to. "Has the marquess returned home yet?"

The duke replied, "No, he hasn't and I don't know his direction or I'd go after the boy myself."

"Damned meal was like a march though one of Prinny's banquets. How the chef thinks a dozen removes gives a person a sense of importance, when all it does is give a bellyache, I'll never understand." The duke ushered her into the library. "Took me ten years to convince him not to cover everything with globs of Frenchy sauce."

She hesitated on the threshold, prompting him to reassure her. "Come in, come in, let's be comfortable by the fire." He guided her to a pair of chairs facing a glowing coal fire, taking her back to a similar scene between her and his grandson. He strode to a mahogany side table, rattled around in the tray of decanters, and emerged with two crystal goblets in hand.

It was a wonderful room, she thought, as he handed her a goblet half filled with a dark liquid. Her glance drifted over the book-filled shelves. She would like to be left alone to read every book, and that would take . . . perhaps the rest of her life, just the right time she needed before she was ready to begin this interview.

She gulped the liquid and coughed and choked. Tears rolled down her cheeks.

"Sip," he instructed.

"What is this? I'll go away quietly, you don't need to poison me." Oh, mercy, why did she say that? Typical of her to let her thoughts slide merrily down her tongue. Her face flamed and a streak of matching warmth followed the trail of the drink.

"I should have warned you. My Victoria and I used to share a tot of brandy when weighty matters were before us."

He sipped his own and placed both their glasses on the table between them. "And, though I don't expect you to believe me, m'dear, letting you go away is the last thing I want." He studied her with the usual twinkle in his eyes, then smiled. "You have the look of your mother, a stunning woman, had all the lads trotting along behind her like a pack of . . . ahem, lovesick fools."

He turned to the fire and a wicked grin engulfed his face. "Should be an interesting season with you here, Elizabeth. Looking forward to it."

This was her entry to the conversation, just the opening she needed. "I am not here for a season, sir. I am a little old for a debutante's introduction to the *ton*."

His smile dimmed a fraction. She hesitated, then continued firmly.

"I have another purpose entirely. My cousin, Mariane, is altogether too spirited to be left in Paxton without her fiancé to keep her occupied. A very unsuitable gentleman is rusticating with his mother nearby and has turned her head with the glamour—and if he is a pattern card of society—the overrated glamour of London."

His head snapped around. "What's his name, the rogue?"

She smiled at the typical masculine response. "Lord Stanley. I haven't a clue where his holdings are, nor anything about his family."

"A fop?"

She frowned in confusion.

"Minces, writes poetry, paints his face?"

She nodded, smiling again despite her vow to keep this a serious interview.

"Given name's Rodney?" At her affirmative nod, he barked, "Thought so. Only child of a foolish mother. Always under the hatches and dresses like a damned parrot. Sounds like one, too.

Got caught by him one afternoon at Lady Jersey's musicale and had to listen to him ruin the thing with an ode to someone's ear."

He sighed, sincerely suffering. "Love music, hate poetry. Never been back, though I'll say hello at an evening do."

"You snub Lord Stanley?"

"Not him. Lady Jersey. Don't snub her exactly, just don't go to her house."

She couldn't help it. She laughed. He smiled, pleased to have entertained.

So like Hawksley, she thought.

She sighed and continued in a serious tone, "I would appreciate it if you would send a note to Lady Lowden saying we will be staying with you. She'll be incensed not to have Mariane with her, but the woman tyrannizes Eunice."

"Nothing I'd rather do, m'dear, than prevent the woman from bothering our sweet lady. Lady Lowden has a voice like a fish peddler and ways of a Bow Street Runner. Parsimonious, squeezes every farthing, though she has more blunt than she could ever spend. Should have sent her to fight the French, would have settled the thing long since and saved us money besides." He rose abruptly and stalked across the thick Axminster rug. He opened the door and roared, "Marsh!"

She couldn't help it, she was being disarmed. She listened as he gave directions for the note to be delivered immediately. She had always felt a special affinity for him, especially knowing that he had accepted her grandmother, but that wasn't too unusual, considering—

The door slammed, interrupting her thoughts. The door opened a second time and he roared out into the hall. "Thank you, Marsh." Another crash of the door and he returned to his chair.

Yes, very much like Hawksley.

"You'll need some dresses to go about in, some ribbons and such. I'll arrange for an allowance. If that is not sufficient, just tell any tradesman who you are and—"

"That is very kind of you, but I have my own funds."

His looked perplexed. It gave her no little satisfaction to explain. "I have been employed, as Dr. Cameron has no doubt reported to you, and he trusted me to see to my own finances. A very enlightened people, the Scots."

She expected him to protest, but he surprised her by studying her with a bemused expression and extending a hand to gently caress her cheek. His voice was amused, but totally serious. "If you spend one of your hard-earned coins on the foolishness of London fashions, I shall lock you in your room and make you read improving books on the duty of young people to obey their elders."

Before she could respond, though what she could answer to that teasing nonsense she had no idea, he explained, "In order to watch over your foolish little cousin, you will need a wardrobe that can take you wherever she might wish to dart off to. Consider it a uniform, like a soldier in battle. The cost will stagger you, believe me, but my coffers will scarcely feel more than a feather's touch. In any case, you are one of my heirs and in addition to your dowry, which is considerable, I have settled enough money on you to make you independent, whether you marry or no."

Her head was spinning. None of this made sense. She felt she had wandered into another world. She rose, without realizing she had done so, clutching the back of the chair for balance.

He pulled himself out of his chair. "You're tired, m'dear. Had a few questions for you myself, as you can imagine, about your coming home. We'll talk again when you've rested."

Just what she had no wish for, she thought, and it must have registered on her face, for he added. "In a few days, when you're ready."

Then he blurted, "You're just like her, you know. Not your mother, though you've certainly got her beauty. No, I mean my Victoria."

She was surprised and murmured, "Your wife?"

"Yes, you have her quirky sense of the ridiculous, the merriment she found in everyday happenings. She said she loved me too well to let life's mishaps make me sad, so her task in life was to make me happy."

She was shocked; she had never thought of herself as light-hearted.

"It's in your eyes. You think you should be serious, and so you bustle around doing serious things. Inside, though, you're bubbling up, wanting to come out and play." He cleared his throat. "So, do it, hmmm? Vicky would have loved you and wanted you to be happy." He pulled her hair in a teasing caress. "So, you learn to have fun and don't look back until you've figured out how."

She was touched deeply. Imagine being compared to his dear wife. Imagine how much he loved her despite—

He broke into her thoughts, veering briskly off on another subject. "I've embroiled Nathan in giving a bit of grief to that mongrel emperor, Napoleon. The boy's brilliant, gives the old war horses a breath of fresh air."

She tried to mask her distaste of the subject; after all Hawksley was his cherished grandson.

He tugged at his neckcloth and cleared his throat. "We've run into a bit of a mess the last few years, but Nathan should have it cleared up by now."

He hesitated, but his voice was firm. "I've charged him with seeing to your future. God willing, we'll see this through to a fitting end." She opened her mouth to protest, but he threw a heavy arm around her shoulders and squeezed her close. "I know the boy's been a blockhead in dealing with you and hasn't a clue what a little sprite like you needs. I puffed him up in his duties when he was young, and now he's so earnest I want to box his ears. But his heart's good, and when he returns, we'll talk and shake the kinks out of this mess we've made of your life."

She pulled the drapery back further from the side of the window and began falling in love. The sunshine the duke predicted had indeed followed them into the city and filled her senses with its warm air as she watched the late-morning antics of London. She sipped hot chocolate from a delicate hand-painted cup and listened to the orchestra of enticements emanating from the early-morning peddlers. Flowers and fresh milk, hot buns and—

"Elizabeth!"

For a moment she thought it was Hawksley, he sounded so very like him. What on earth was the duke doing up so early? She thought Londoners slept until well after noon.

She opened the door just as his hand raised to pound on her door. "Yes, Your Grace?"

"For heaven's sake, Elizabeth, don't start 'gracing' me, I've told you to call me Grandfather." He looked like a boy ready for a tantrum. "Come and do something about that woman in my parlor. She's routed Marsh, a thing I hoped never to live long enough to see."

Eunice's door opened partway and she looked out at them. He hurried over to her. "No need for you to worry about this, dear lady, we'll deal with it."

Eunice and Elizabeth looked at each other, trying to make sense of his confusing words.

"Lady Lowden," he whispered.

Eunice tried to scuttle back into her room, but the duke reached for her hands, now the gallant, his voice gathering strength. He leaned over and looked into her face, coaxing a smile. "Just need a little advice from your niece, you know, on the care and feeding of a man-eating lioness."

Eunice's soft laugh escaped and he straightened, smiling paternally. Just then Mariane slipped out of her room and joined the group.

"What is it, Mother?"

"Aunt Sylvia," Eunice confided. "She's in the parlor."

"Wonderful, I cannot wait to see her." She fairly flew down the hall toward the stairs. Elizabeth followed with far less enthusiasm.

"Well, that tears it." the duke said with a heartiness none of them felt. He tucked Eunice's hand securely onto his arm. "We'll face it together. We'll just slink in behind your idiot child and my intrepid Elizabeth and see if we can remain unscathed."

Elizabeth entered the parlor, still smiling from the antics of the duke. Sylvia and Mariane were seated closely together on the upholstered settee, chattering with feverish intensity. They looked up when she entered, greeting her with almost identical expressions. Not exactly scorn or disgust, but more a polite distaste. As they exchanged pleasantries and she took a chair near them, she mentally reviewed her morning toilette and decided she had left nothing undone to offend them. She couldn't help her streaky red hair or the sprinkle of freckles that would only get worse come summer no matter what precautions she took, but that surely was old news to both of them.

The duke and Eunice entered the room and Sylvia's eyes narrowed to see her sister's arm resting on that of the duke. She blinked the sight away and rose to greet them. The air near her sister's cheeks received polite kisses and in the interchange, Sylvia arranged the group to her satisfaction with her back to the duke and Eunice neatly separated from the others.

"Well, sister, what is this nonsense about not coming to me?"

Eunice's hands gripped tightly before her. "Elizabeth cannot stay here without a chaperone, Sylvia, and we—"

Sylvia's glance swerved to Elizabeth and her nostrils flared,

this time in undisguised contempt, but when she spoke, her voice
was sweet enough to satisfy any arbiter of manners. "How very
like you, dear, to put your own wishes aside to help your little
niece."

She seized Eunice's hands and pulled her down to join herself
and Mariane on the settee. When she had her settled, much like
coddling an invalid, she continued her thought. "But, I believe
that you are still thinking of her as the child she was when she left
home to live in Scotland."

Her voice rose to match the very real emotion that drove her. "I
believe you should put the needs of your own sweet daughter before this nostalgic fondness you have for your brother's child.
Mariane is such an innocent and needs the guidance of someone
familiar with the pitfalls of London, while dear Elizabeth has experienced more of life." Her voice rose another notch. "Much
more, from what I have heard. Why, to see them together is to assume that Mariane has the same—" At Eunice's horrified expression, she stopped, teetering on the brink of insulting the duke's
relative and guest in his own home.

Elizabeth wondered at the duke's silence and looked back to
discover why a stream of oaths had not filled the room and why
the duke had not come to Eunice's rescue. He stood quietly, entirely engrossed in the scene, with an almost disappointed look at
the woman's aborted monologue. Where had she seen that expression?

Of course. It was identical to Hawksley's when he was dissect-
ing her dream.

The duke was analyzing, reserving action until he had the answer he was seeking. And Lady Lowden had quit before he had
all his answers. God help the woman when he struck, Elizabeth
thought; she might find herself chained in the dungeon or ab-
ducted onto a ship bound for foreign places.

Lady Lowden recovered with a speed that impressed even Elizabeth. "We have time to discuss this later, dear Eunice. For now,
we have a full day ahead of us. Mariane's clothes are sadly out of
fashion, despite Oakes's efforts to keep her *au courant*."

Elizabeth mentally nodded, realizing what missing information
had eluded the duke. Oakes had very likely sent her own note to
Lady Lowden, describing Elizabeth's unsavory activities in Scotland, and that lady had decided that once that information became

known, it would taint Mariane's reputation, not to mention her own, the duke's relationship to Elizabeth notwithstanding.

Lady Lowden stood, turning to the duke. "Your Grace, might we have the pleasure of your ward's company today, or might she find shopping a bore?"

Elizabeth cast a pleading look toward him, but he smiled as if Lady Lowden had just given him the greatest boon. "Just the thing, dear lady, you can see that Scotland is slow in receiving the latest fashion news and she could do nothing than benefit from your gracious advice."

That rogue, how could he do such a wicked thing? Look at him beaming beatifically at them both like the village moonling. He'll pay for this dastardly trick, she thought, just as soon as I can concoct a little revenge of my own.

Her opportunity came in the middle of one of the most confusing days she had ever spent.

If she never saw another Bond Street establishment, she would be happy. No one could possibly need all the clothes she was forced to consider. She liked the stringency of the Scottish household and the high-necked, practical gowns she wore. Evidently one changed clothing here every time one changed direction. Morning dresses, afternoon dresses, riding habits, ball gowns—every occasion must needs have a particular dress and footwear designated especially for it. On and on it went, and the only saving grace was Lady Lowden's defection from her in a feverish dedication to shaping Mariane's wardrobe.

Elizabeth was listening in open-mouthed awe as a clerk displayed the wonders of the shocking new silk drawers—and had agreed to ordering several in pink—when she heard a familiar voice.

"Elizabeth Wydner, is it really you? The last time I saw you, you were happily settled with Douglas and Margaret."

She looked up to see one of her favorite people. "Eleanore Cameron, or should I say Lady Barton, now you are a married lady?"

She quickly made introductions, noting the mixed emotions crossing Lady Lowden's face as she placed the newcomer. Although Eleanore's mother was daughter to a viscount, she had married a younger son of a baron who had put himself into the even more distant reaches of society by pursuing medicine. Since

Eleanore's brother not only followed in his father's footsteps, but had defected to Scotland, the family was definitely *suspect*. The dilemma for Lady Lowden was Eleanore's recent marriage to an earl which, like a cork, bounced her back into the mainstream of the *ton*.

Dear Lady Lowden, with her feverish dedication to pure bloodlines, would have made a wonderful horse breeder.

As soon as the other ladies became once more entrenched in fashion, Eleanore said urgently, "Elizabeth, I know this is such short notice, but we are hosting a small masquerade ball tonight at our home. Do you think you might be spared from your other commitments to join us?"

Elizabeth's imagination took hold. A masquerade, she had never been to one and would love to join her friend. Mariane and Eunice had neither plans for the evening nor gowns ready as yet, so she would not be reneging from any previous plans with them. Furthermore, hadn't the duke bid her to "come out and play?"

As Eleanore's excitement grew with plans to find Elizabeth a suitable costume among her own things, Elizabeth remembered her decision to pay the duke back for his mischief. Arrangements were quickly made, and Elizabeth excused herself from the others. "Pray tell the duke I shall return after Lady Barton's ball tonight."

Three weary men slipped into the Standbridge town house through the door leading from the back garden. The guard headed for the back stairway. Hawksley led his friend into the library and bid him remove of his wet coat and sit by the fire. The duke, asleep in a voluminous high-back chair, woke at their entry.

"Good evening, sir."

"Good grief, m'boy, I'm glad to see you. You both look fagged to death and wet besides. Is it raining out now?" He turned to the other man, "Woolfe, I'm glad to see you back in one piece." He turned an inquiring glance to Hawksley.

"No, sir, it's not raining, just cold and misty."

"Well, tell me all. I can smell disaster in the air."

Hawksley shed his greatcoat and woolen scarf and draped them over a Windsor chair alongside the fireplace. He sunk into a chair near Woolfe with a tired sigh. "As you can see, we have neither Tangmere nor the imposter. I'll let Woolfe tell you what happened."

Woolfe leaned forward, his coal-black hair falling forward across the side of his narrow face. "We anchored offshore and rowed in. Etienne Bedard, the damned Frenchman, had driven us to near insanity and we were more than ready to dump him in someone else's lap. Had he not held the key to the Traitor's identity, we would have dragged him across the channel on a long rope."

He pushed his straggling hair off his face and leaned back in the chair. "He had insisted we bring his possessions with him, knowing he would not be welcome back in France once he squawked. One of the smugglers and Tangmere rowed him and some of his things in the first boat and I followed with the rest in a little dinghy with a sailor from the ship to take it back."

His voice faltered, "Tangmere beached a considerable way ahead of me and they were waiting for him. Two men with torches. Tangmere hailed them as if he knew them, so I didn't worry. The damned dinghy was slow, going back one wave for every two forward, and we were both soaking wet and rowing hard.

"All at once the tall man dropped his torch and went crazy, attacking them while his fellow held his torch high and watched. I could see this knife flashing yellow against the light, and in the next instant, he had killed them all."

He paused and said with a tired irony, "My brave smuggler companion promptly dove over the side as the two men started out to meet us. I was so angry I wanted to kill them with my bare hands, but considering that was my only weapon, with my pistol soaking wet, I followed the smuggler."

Woolfe leaned against the arm of the chair and said in a slow voice. "You're not going to like the information I have. I regret I couldn't make out the assailant's features, but his voice was pure aristocratic English and he called me by name."

They sat in silence as the implications of Woolfe's story sank in. The duke spoke first. "An aristocrat who knew your name?"

"Yes, Your Grace."

"You know what that means. He has never been a smuggler or a hoodlum grown bigger with power as we thought. That scoundrel, he's one of us! He eats at our tables and gambles in our clubs. Dances with our ladies and we probably think he's a fine fellow."

Hawksley added, "And works in the War Office?"

"No doubt, m'boy." He paused and said heavily, "We have no more time to waste, then. We'll use Elizabeth."

"Absolutely not," Hawksley snapped back, "leave her where she is safe. It would take too long in any case."

The duke chuckled, surprising the two young men. "It should take you about thirty minutes, if you're in a hurry. She's out dancing at Lord and Lady Barton's ball."

Chapter Nine

THE red brick mansions in St. James's Square lent a rosy warmth to the spectacle of polished carriages and perfectly matched horses conveying their occupants toward the brightly lit house of Lord and Lady Barton. The long line of conveyances pulled forward a few feet, then halted to wait for the first coach in line to liberate its passengers and depart.

Far back in line, Hawksley swore and nearly ripped the door from its hinges as he exited his coach. He strode past the cavalcade, ignoring the dismayed whispers his unthinkable action generated in the passengers waiting dutifully to reach the proper place to vacate one's coach.

He would not be here long, he calculated, just time enough to grab his little cousin by the nape of her neck and carry her back home. Unfortunately, it would also be long enough for the gossips to speculate over what had brought the Marquess of Hawksley out of his lair.

Damn her, why couldn't she have stayed in Scotland? It would have been over soon and he could have gone for her as he had planned.

He passed through the doorway and stared in dismay at the crowd before him filling the hall and stairway up to the ballroom, more boisterous than usual with the anonymity of costume and mask.

A damned costume ball! Trust Elizabeth to complicate his life and turn the simple task of plucking her out of the evening's festivities into a game of hide-and-go-seek. He hated masked balls.

Eleanore, Lady Barton, would be pleased at her success, for the evening was a *shocking squeeze*, which only demonstrated the absurdity of a society that measured a hostess's triumph by how tightly a house could be packed with guests.

Not too many years ago he had joined enthusiastically into the daily round of activities, enjoying the camaraderie of races and boxing as well as the feminine delights available. It all paled now, fading into the background as he drove himself to find his parents' killer and rid the country of a vicious traitor.

Already people were hailing him, wishing to tell their friends they had participated in a private conversation with the elusive Marquess of Hawksley during one of his rare outings. He wondered, his searching glance stopping at each gentleman who might fit the description of the Traitor.

She was having a wonderful time.

She had expected to find the people highly affected and decidedly unfriendly, but on the contrary, not only had the ladies been pleasant, but she had found gathered around her a bevy of swains, each vowing undying devotion. It was all a hum, of course, but she was enjoying the laughter and frivolity.

The evening had evolved into a series of surprises, just one more example of how her life never behaved itself or followed her careful plans.

She had never wanted a season, yet here she was, in the midst of the crème de la crème of London society, self-propelled if she wished to be precise, since she had accepted Eleanore's impromptu invitation with the alacrity of a child released from her lessons.

She had never wished to display the generous bosom maturity had bestowed upon her in anything other than the matronly gowns favored by Margaret Cameron, yet here she stood in a dress borrowed from Eleanore, covered modestly everywhere—except for her décolletage. Her fingers itched to grab the neckline of the gown and pull it up to her chin. Or better yet, pull off the gauzy veil covering her hair and stuff it into the bodice. When she explained her dilemma to Eleanore, that dauntless lady pronounced the ensemble perfect for her figure and her coloring, and to cease fretting. A natural reaction, since Eleanore had proudly created Elizabeth's pasha's harem look herself. Delicate golden gauze veiled her features and bright hair, and cunningly enhanced the simplicity of her gown.

Elizabeth seldom left events to chance. Indeed, she always prepared ahead, planning meticulously for every event. Yet, here she stood at the edge of a dance floor, holding a fan with each blade displaying the name of a gentleman—and she barely knew how to dance.

When Eleanore, always a tease, presented her only as "Elizabeth Wydner, a friend of mine from Scotland, formerly from Paxton in Leicestershire," Elizabeth, having explained that she knew only a few country dances, had expected to be left sitting alone. Once again she was mistaken. Sitting out dances, it seemed, did not mean one necessarily sat, but if a persistent admirer still wished the company of a lady, the pair could stroll around the floor greeting friends or partake of champagne punch to pass the time.

She had always kept a sensible attitude toward her suitors, never daydreaming or sighing over their nonsense. But tonight she found herself actually flirting—and blushing at the most outrageous compliments one could ever hope to hear. No wonder Mariane's head full of windmills had turned a little at such breezy nonsense, even if only from the lips of Lord Stanley.

Yet, despite her life tilting once more at an unexpected angle, she was having a wonderful time.

She wondered if Hawksley hovered near his own lovely lady and uttered such nonsensical remarks as these young men who paid her such amusingly extravagant court. Should he return in time, she wondered, might she find him in attendance?

And then she felt it. In the midst of the noisiest room she had ever occupied, with the largest audience vying for her attention, she could feel Hawksley's presence.

She raised her fan and discreetly surveyed the crowd. No matter that he was four years older, she would be able to find him anywhere for his sheer size alone and would recognize those charcoal eyes in any crowd. She turned slowly and surveyed the entire room. He was not in sight.

Good. Excellent. Splendid. She certainly did not want him here to spoil her fun. She leaned forward to hear the question directed to her by Mr. Woodhouse, her favorite gallant.

"I believe my name is inscribed on your fan for the next dance, Miss Wydner, pray do not disappoint me."

She laughed at his exaggeration as he led her onto the floor for the reel. As they went through the movements, she watched him. Of medium height and soft brown hair, he reminded her of an owl with his neck buried in the popular high collar and neckcloth. He wore a university professor's robe and pair of spectacles as costume. His eyes blinked rapidly as he concentrated on the steps, but his smile when he caught her glance was sweet. She had men-

tally applauded his actions before as he led out several less favored debutantes, helping them forget their nervousness with his
droll comments.

The dance ended and her partner led her from the floor, contin-
uing his clever banter.

"Here is Lord Stafford waiting for you, trusting you are suscep-
tible to his famous good looks. Pray promise me that you admire
my steadiness of character above all."

She laughed again. "And Lord Stafford has a shaky character,
Mr. Woodhouse?"

"The words *blanc mange* come to mind," he said with mock
seriousness.

"But you are defaming your own good friend, so I must find
your own character less than steady as well."

He raised a hand to his forehead in a dramatic gesture. "I am
undone!"

He bowed and left her with Lord Stafford, the oldest of her admirers. Blond, gray-eyed, with a Corinthian's physique, he was
indeed a handsome gentleman, a viscount who had fifty thousand
a year. This supplied by Eleanore who kept her apprised of the
pertinent details of the most eligible gentlemen. The only catch,
her friend had warned her, was that after so many years of resistance to all the hopeful ingenues and persistent mamas, it had become perfectly obvious to all that Lord Stafford was not looking
for a wife.

Dressed as a Royal Mail coachman, Lord Stafford offered his
arm to lead her into the dance, but she hesitated. "It is the La
Boulanger, my lord, a dance I am not familiar with."

"Come, Miss Wydner, this is the easiest of dances to learn, the
first one we tackle after escaping the nursery."

Her first impulse was to resist further, but the duke's decree to
"come out and play" still buoyed her spirits and gave her courage.
She was not here to comfort an ailing patient, she was here to
enjoy herself.

"Very well, Lord Stafford, but if you are sporting a cane tomorrow, be a gentleman and do not reveal how you came by two
bruised and broken feet."

He looked startled, an expression she had noticed more than
once on the faces of her swains. He recovered quickly and proceeded to teach her the steps as the music began. It was great fun
and soon all their neighbors were good-naturedly giving her ad-

vice.

If only she did not continue to have shivers of dread that Hawksley would soon be here. If only she not sense his anger.

Blast, this was worse than he had imagined. His gaze quickly skimmed across the chairs lining the walls, stopping only to inspect the diminutive girls. Not there. Was she hiding behind a pillar or potted plant? Poor girl, she must be frightened to death.

"Hawksley, reduced to coming uninvited to balls now, are you?"

Hawksley turned to his host, laughing. "Stubble it, Barton. I am here to rescue my little cousin from the clutches of all your lecherous friends."

"Your cousin?"

"Elizabeth Wydner. Little redhead, freckles, shy. Just returned from Scotland."

"Ah." Barton's face creased with laughter.

"No, you dunce, I am not in the petticoat line. Just need to take her home."

"She's shy, you say? Poor girl, what a shame. Allow me to offer my assistance." Lord Barton motioned Hawksley to join him as he moved toward the couples on the dance floor.

Hawksley moved alongside his host, irritated by the enigmatic smile still quivering on the lips of his old friend. Annoyed as well by the onlookers who fell silent as they approached, then buzzed louder as they moved away. They circled the room slowly. He didn't see her anywhere.

He wished again, as he had done countless times before, that he could shake the dust of the metropolis from his boots and retire with Grandfather to Standbridge. And Elizabeth. He would make up for all the years of friendship they had missed. He would fill her life with luxuries and treats. Perhaps bring her to London occasionally, as Grandfather suggested, and show her the sights. She would laugh at the circus and—

He halted abruptly, every thought fleeing, as the arresting sight before him struck with the strength of one of Gentleman Jackson's blows—dead center in his solar plexus—and spread out to the rest of him with a heat of lust no gentleman should feel in the middle of a public ball. A vision so enchantingly beautiful he had to fight for air.

He stood still to watch her dance. No, not exactly dance. She was misstepping and laughing at her own untutored attempts, a sound so imbued with sunlight and music that he felt transported to a magical place. And everyone around was laughing with her. Not censuring with their aristocratic noses in the air, but smiling indulgently. Of course, Eleanore was bound to invite the more pleasant of society's inhabitants, and this was a masquerade . . .

Who on earth was she?

And what about her did he find so damnably arousing?

She was tall, but would fit in his arms perfectly. A dip of his head and her mouth would be his. Long legged and slim hipped with a curve of shoulder and bosom that fueled his insane fantasy. Eyes that danced with pleasure. A body that moved naturally with the music while she fumbled with the correct steps.

He wanted to rip that flimsy scarf from her face and see her laughing mouth, wanted to drag her into the garden and pull every inch of her close to him . . .

"Do you see her, Hawksley?"

"What? Who?" He tore his eyes away from the woman and looked at his host. "Oh, Elizabeth. No, her looks are very distinctive, so I could not have overlooked her. Where is your wife, Barton? She's her guest, they might be together." Good grief, how could he have forgotten his mission here? He was not a green lad who became smitten with every girl whose enticing shape and laughing eyes attracted him.

Barton motioned to a servant. He gave the man a low-voiced command and turned back to Hawksley. "I'll have her join us. You can find your little cousin and be on your way in no time." With the same enigmatic smile, his host turned back to watch the dancers. "You have the room humming, Hawksley, with your unexpected appearance. Perhaps you should get out more, it wouldn't be such a shock to the chaperones."

At Hawksley's ungracious "humph," Lord Barton extended his hand to encompass the room and said, "Look for yourself. While you stand here, fair game with no spouse or betrothed on your arm, they are scheming how to bring their little darlings to your attention."

Hawksley bit back an oath and looked around. Barton was right; dozens of bright eyes looked upon him like beggars at a feast.

Lord Barton's shoulders heaved with silent laughter. "Never mind, Hawksley, I'll deliver you out of their clutches. Here's

Lord Stafford, every mama's dream son-in-law, probably the only man rich enough to draw the scent away from you. Shall we let him beat off the avaricious mob while you dance with his lovely partner?"

Lord Stafford hesitated as the music ended, searching the edge of the dance floor. "Our hostess has moved, Miss Wydner, pray give me a second to find her." Finally spotting Lady Barton, he held Elizabeth's elbow and guided her through the milling guests.

Elizabeth was grateful for his assistance since her knees had lost the ability to work correctly. Hawksley was nearby. She had felt him again, this time watching her. And his thoughts, surely she had misunderstood his thoughts, surely what she had heard was some distorted combination of other masculine musings. Not that she was a stranger to lascivious thoughts, for some rather shocking fragments had slipped past her barriers over the years, but surely what she heard was not Hawksley thinking of her.

Lord Stafford broke her train of thought. "Who is your next partner, Miss Wydner?"

Grateful for a distraction, Elizabeth opened her fan to examine it, but the crowd surged too close and with her hands shaking so badly, she couldn't read the name. She raised it up to take advantage of the light shining down from the chandeliers . . . and looked directly into a pair of simmering charcoal eyes . . . Hawksley!

Her heart lurched and her throat spasmed. Dear God, he looked so . . . so powerful. She halted, her thoughts suspended out of reach while she tried to remember her rehearsed strategy for this anticipated moment.

She had planned to be indifferent, cold, and condescending. Instead she was almost overpowered by the impulse to walk into his arms, as she had the duke's, and have him welcome her, to feel his arms around her. What was wrong with her? Had she not already fought this battle against her feelings for Hawksley—and won?

Of course she had. This small fissure in her resolve was simply the result of the *presence* of the man which had always awed her, and four years had possibly made him more attractive.

His thick hair rested on the collar of his black velvet coat. He was leaner than she remembered, yet his broad shoulders seemed wider while his muscled thighs strained the fabric of his black knee breeches. With maturity had come shadows and mystery, barriers beyond which she suspected no one ever intruded. Dark shadows beneath his eyes betrayed a fatigue not born of boredom, but of someone having reached past his limits to drain his very soul.

Once again she fought against her feelings, this time ones of compassionate concern. Idiot, she scolded herself, how can you feel sympathy for a man who even now is probably hatching schemes to dispatch you elsewhere?

She looked away from him, determined to salvage what she could of her composure and perhaps regain the pleasure of the evening. She smiled when she saw Eleanore walking toward her. Dear Eleanore, she was a wonderful ally, and had already promised to help her keep Mariane occupied in the days to come.

Eleanore's husband, Lord Barton, reached for Elizabeth's hand and said, "Might I ask a boon of you?" Before she could agree, he continued, "You must rescue this poor man from the avalanche of approaching females."

Before she realized what he was about, she found herself delivered into Hawksley's arms. Truly into his arms, with his hand actually on her waist. Shocked at such advances, she pulled away, only to have him draw her firmly closer.

She was furious. She looked around for someone to come to her aid and realized that all the couples were similarly arranged. *Oh, no, it was the waltz.* People whispered behind their fans about the waltz. At least they did in Scotland, and she had no intention of contributing to her own social disgrace.

"My lord, I do not dan—"

"I know. I have been watching you."

He swung her to the side, turning with her. "Slide, step step. Just lean on my arm and listen to the music." In a low voice, he murmured directions in time with the melody, and in desperation, she followed his lead. She had never been so embarrassed in her life. Or so exhilarated.

She risked a peep at the other dancers—and fell in love with the waltz. She relaxed in his embrace and smiled. This was not a frolic like the country dances, it was poetry. The couples looked so beautiful gliding to the wonderful music, the ladies' dresses flowing like water as they turned. It was heaven. For a moment, she forgot with whom she danced and smiled with sheer joy.

He returned her smile. "Lord Barton quite forgot his manners when he pushed us out on the dance floor without benefit of an introduction. I am Hawksley, grandson of the Duke of Stand-bridge."

She thought he was attempting a little humor and she searched in her mind for an appropriate rejoinder. He spoke again.

"You wish to remain a mystery until the unmasking?"

He didn't know who she was.

Her smile froze in place and she looked away, furious that she had let his words distress her and frustrated that of all the fiendish plots for revenge she had devised, she had no plan for his not recognizing her.

Her thoughts bounced back and forth like a shuttlecock. She knew now that his earlier thoughts had been of her. He wasn't interested in her as the Elizabeth he knew, but he *was* interested in the woman she had become, thinking she was a stranger. It was a heady feeling, this admiration as a woman from Hawksley. She was tempted to savor it for a while, for when he discovered the truth, she had no idea how he might react, and prudently, she had no wish to find out in a ballroom full of people.

Should she withdraw with him someplace quiet and reveal who she was, or should she leave it to chance? Honor jousted with the prospect of an unexpected opportunity for reprisal, like a game where she was the only one without a blindfold. How delicious. She couldn't resist.

"Tell me about your family, Lord Hawksley."

He looked surprised at her direct question, but he answered. "Just a couple of bachelors, my grandfather and I."

That hurt a little, but it firmed her resolve. "No other family?"

His eyes darkened and a shutter fell over his face. He whirled her around until her unrestrained delight at the dance returned his good humor. His smile had returned, and with it his next probe. "Now my turn to ask a question. What about you, are you the season's incomparable?"

"Since this is my first social, it is difficult to predict. But now my turn. Tell me, are you the target of every matchmaker in town?"

He looked startled by such frankness, then amused. "Of course. And you no doubt are the target of every gentleman in the room. Could it be that are you an heiress?"

Her mouth lifted at his rudeness. "Yes, actually, I am." After Grandfather's pronouncement of last evening she could answer that question without blushing. Since this was a duel in bad manners, she added, "Are you hanging out for a rich wife?"

He threw back his head and laughed aloud. Heads turned, and mouths fell open. Her prim little conscience nudged her with the charge to behave herself—but how could she when Hawksley seemed to bring out this mischief in her? Once more she realized that she was having a wonderful time.

Until a moment later when he danced her through the doors opening onto the balcony and into a darkened corner. Light flickered across his strong features as dancers briefly blocked the illumination from within, then swirled gracefully on around the room. His gaze held her captive while they stood still poised as dancers of the waltz, so innocent in a ballroom, so provocative on a darkened balcony.

His thoughts were audible now—clearer, too, as some strong emotion propelled them toward her. *Who are you, I wonder . . . a cheerful little innocent or a magic sorceress?*

And, who are you, Hawksley? The boy I loved or the man I hate? As she listened to her own revealing thoughts, she made an amazing discovery—*she had loved Hawksley.* A fledgling, hero-worshipping love, true, but powerful enough for its remnants to affect her even now. It was, of course, the reason for her terrible despair when he sent her away, and the reason her admirers had inspired no more than lukewarm interest. She felt relieved, for now she would see to it that this spark of love did not survive, for there was no happy ending for them.

She had no wish for a husband who could treat her so callously and who was so uncomfortable with her "affliction." Hawksley, of course, had proclaimed years ago that nothing could be worse than a wife who could invade his privacy and over whom he had no control.

She was relieved when she heard Eleanore's voice.

"Elizabeth."

She turned then. "Yes, Eleanore?"

"This will never do, my dear."

Lady Barton turned to Hawksley. "Would you shame your own cousin, my lord?"

"My own—?" His hands fell away and he stepped backward. His incredulity was worth the hours of apprehension she had suffered. She stood defiantly as his appraising inspection slid over every inch of her. She had nothing to be apologetic for and everything to be proud of. She had been told she was attractive and now she saw the truth of it in Hawksley's eyes and knew that she had not misunderstood his thoughts as he watched her dancing.

Returning stare for stare, Elizabeth was confident that she would not be found lacking. After all, she was more than just a woman he lusted after. She could bring a child safely into the world and ease a mother's suffering. She could stitch a cut and diagnose an ailment. She could read a medical book written in Greek, and if she felt so moved, she could fluently curse him in French.

She watched his face as he finally grasped the situation. He nodded as if putting a long-lost puzzle piece in place. She looked into his eyes and felt a deep satisfaction when she found a glow of approval blaze before he shuttered it behind an expressionless mask.

Eleanore held her hand out to Elizabeth and instructed, "Smile as we return to the ballroom, just as if we had been out here sharing a pleasant conversation while we sought the cool air."

Eleanore paused and said to Hawksley. "Walk with us, my lord. There is nothing wrong with dancing with your own relative and wishing a few private words after such a long time apart."

When Eleanore left them a few minutes later, Hawksley said in a terse undertone, "I have come to bring you home, Elizabeth."

She lifted her fan and spread it to display the names inscribed thereon, and replied in a calm voice, "Certainly, my lord, just as soon as I have honored my commitments."

Hawksley slammed the front door of the Standbridge town house. "I'm sending you back to Scotland, Elizabeth. You should have waited until we arranged for your return."

"I did not want to wait to return in a coffin, my lord."

"You needn't be sarcastic, Elizabeth, you know better than that."

"The point is moot, Lord Hawksley. I am not going anywhere until I am ready to go. And certainly not in any direction you point."

"Cease calling me Lord Hawksley, Elizabeth."

"It is the least offensive of my choices."

Hawksley ran his hand through his tangled hair once more. Elizabeth stood poised, ready for the next onslaught when the door from the library opened. The duke stood in the doorway, obviously just awakened from a nap.

"Children, children, lower your voices, the servants need their sleep even if you plan to stay awake all night and argue." He ushered them ahead of him into the library and closed the door. Like an amused referee, he waited for them to continue.

Elizabeth and Hawksley looked at each other, both contemplating the next move. She spoke first.

"Your grandson is up to his old tricks and, as is his custom, thinks he is going to shuffle me back off to Scotland. You know my plans and have agreed to them. Tell him to give over."

"Your foolish ward has no idea what she is getting into and must return immediately."

She shouted, "I am not sacrificing Mariane's happiness to your overweening belief that you can order everyone around. Tell him, Your Grace."

"You are my responsibility, Elizabeth, and will do exactly what I say. Tell her, Grandfather."

The duke yawned and stretched. He sat down on the edge of his chair and pulled on the boots that lay on the floor. He stood and retrieved Hawksley's coat and muffler from the Windsor chair beside the warm fire and slipped into them.

"Anyone want to take the air with me? We're not sleeping anyway."

Their voices chimed together. "No!"

Elizabeth couldn't believe he was deserting her once more. First cheerfully relinquishing her into Sylvia Lowden's clutches and now abandoning her to Hawksley's biting remarks. Very well then, she didn't need any help.

She yelled after the duke. "Abandonment clearly runs in this family. The family crest should proclaim 'Abandon all those who enter these doors'" At the sound of the duke's fading chuckle, she turned back to Hawksley and glared.

He changed the subject. "If you do not wish to be my responsibility, Elizabeth, you should certainly be someone's. What were you thinking about attending a ball dressed as you were? It was far too provocative for a young girl. You should be wearing a modest white dress like the other debutantes."

"Honestly, Lord Hawksley, at a masquerade?" Then, deserting all her previous misgivings about the low neckline, she attacked. "Besides, my lord, Lady Barton, whom you seem to respect, prepared my costume herself. And if you bothered to notice, other ladies' necklines were lower than mine. Perhaps you would like to go back and issue some orders to them?"

Hawksley turned abruptly and stalked out into the hall. Elizabeth followed him out into the hallway. He grabbed a cloak from the coat rack and threw at the nearest footman. "Go walk with the duke. Don't let him out of your sight."

He turned and marched past her back into the library and she followed once more, still not satisfied. Their voices rang out again and the two remaining footmen smiled at each other, happy to be so well entertained.

Endlessly patient, the Traitor stepped back silently into the shadows near his waiting coach as Lord Hawksley began his nightly stroll. He shivered involuntarily as the damp cold penetrated, but he was neither tempted to stamp his feet nor rub his hands. His comfort came from within, conveyed on the twin pleasures of remembrance and anticipation. *Anticipation,* he thought, running his tongue slowly over his dry lips. What a wonderful appetizer for the feast to come. The moon glowed briefly then winked out as heavy clouds moved once more into place.

How very beneficial . . . a dark night. He thrust his long fingers into the deep pockets of his dark woolen coat. Easing the knife out of the soft leather sheath sewn into his pocket, he ran his fingers down past the smooth handle and caressed the golden dragon on the blade. One slash across the throat of the young pup and his message would ring clear to his favorite enemy, the Duke of Standbridge. Saliva filled his mouth and he swallowed the warm, revenge-filled liquid. One foot began soundlessly tapping the rough stones of the wet street, and he hummed softly, almost light-headed with pleasure.

Tonight is only Act One in my plans for Lords Standbridge and Hawksley. And the girl.

His eyes closed as he indulged in his favorite pastime, seeing in his mind's eye the live dramas, satires, melodramas . . . the tragedies that he produced from afar. He was a brilliant, powerful director standing in the darkened wings, controlling his own chosen actors. The comedies and farces were a bonus. People were such sheep, such a maneuverable, predictable lot. The more power they held, the greater pleasure it was to pull their strings. Start their mouths watering for what you offered, be it the forbidden sensualities such as the old Hellfire Club or the prestige and admiration so craved by politicians, and they rose to the bait *en masse*. To add tartness to the glut of his pleasure, came occasionally a worthy opponent such as the Marquess of Hawksley.

He only regretted not being able to witness firsthand the duke's devastation when his grandson's lifeless body was carried home.

He pictured the scene, Lord Standbridge sitting by the fire, sipping a smooth, rich Scotch whisky, savoring the pleasure of the moment, gloating over the nearness of trapping Napoleon's master spy at last. After following the spy's bloody trail through the labyrinth of carefully placed false clues, his precious grandson, Hawksley, had finally narrowed the trail. The knocker would pound against the brass plate . . .

A cart rumbled by, closely packed barrels grating against each other as the heavy evening dew loosened the enclosing ropes. His own henchman grumbled in French as the coach horses moved restlessly, rocking the vehicle and making unwelcome noises in the dark street.

He swore viciously as his lovely scene disappeared. Damn the waiting! A red haze glowed hotly in his brain and he chanted the soothing dirge that would clear his sight, *"Someone will pay, someone will pay . . . "* A cold trickle of water dropped from the brim of his hat and ran down the back of his neck. He shuddered. Yes, Hawksley had escaped his knife once before, but now he would pay; it was past time.

It had amused him to watch the young fool's first fumbling attempts at espionage, the flush of excitement at his initial successes. He had watched with almost paternal indulgence as the young aristocrat drove himself from success to success, building a network of informants with a combination of persuasiveness and, of course, the necessary lubricant of all spy work, gold.

But he thought gloatingly, at the same time, *my* stroke of brilliance was in manipulating that masterpiece of idiocy, the secret trade agreement. The fools, France and England, fought their way to bankruptcy and then stopped and did a little horse trading— England's skillfully made boots and clothing for France's stolen European gold—and then continued fighting each other. What a marvelous protective shadow for increased business when the *legal* trade lent its protected umbrella over the smuggling I control.

But Hawksley, the bird of prey, was watching too closely and too many of my fat plums ripened and began dropping into someone else's basket. Hawksley would pay for the lost plums, the lost gold, the lost power . . . and the lost pleasure. *Hawksley would pay!*

"You went too far, my young friend," he murmured as his prey's footsteps grew nearer, "when you tampered with the flow of currency into my coffers. So I had to punish you a little and show how fragile a thread you had woven and how simple it was to sever it with the bodies of a few of your pawns. A pool of blood is such a visual warning to comrades in a network and it echoes like a shout in a mountain canyon." He smiled at his own cleverness. "A *yodeled* warning."

His smile faded and his eyes filmed over. An unblinking glaze concealed turbulent memories. Then, my dear Hawksley, he thought, you have grown to maturity a little too quickly for my tastes, trusting no one, forming no more traceable links, leaving no more currency trails. You never understood how fortunate you were to escape my golden dragon. Other agents pulled in their claws when I laid on a few lashes, but you just wrapped up your wounds and grew more determined. Stupid boy, too intelligent for your own good.

And finally you surpassed the limit of my indulgence when you began deciphering *my* codes, young Hawksley. No one is allowed to surpass my brilliance. A few have tried, but alas, they are no more. I salute you, dear boy, but now that Napoleon, my golden goose for all these years, is about to be cooked, your entertainment value is at an end.

He stretched and cleared away his reflections. Now, back to his delicious plan . . . yes, there sits my old enemy at his fire . . . the door will be answered and they'll bring in his beloved Hawksley. He'll read the warning note pinned to his chest and that will be the end. Ah yes, I see his anguish, his fury and . . .

His heart began to thunder as his quarry's footsteps grew louder. His eyes glittered with satisfaction as he reviewed his plan with lightning speed. He stepped farther back into the shadows of the side street as his target walked toward him.

He pulled his muffler over his mouth and nose in a smooth, practiced movement. His mouth was dry with the bitterness of not being able to spend more time with his victim and the loss of his usual pleasure, but with powerful control, he assured himself that he regretted nothing.

His prey's footsteps beat a vigorous pattern along the footway, oblivious to the dark personage waiting for him.

Chapter Ten

HAWKSLEY'S fingers dragged a new path through his disheveled hair as he glowered at Elizabeth across the expanse of the long mahogany table. Elizabeth glowered back, her hands gripping the chair behind which she stood—feeling breathless, rather like a pugilist given a moment's respite, invigorated yet drained. So this was why men fought, she marveled, for the exhilaration of pitting their finest skills against a worthy opponent, for the thrill of a telling hit and the tantalizing promise of victory. It was heady stuff.

Still, she was exhausted and longed for her bed.

Using her most conciliatory smile, she said, "Hawksley, let us not continue this endless quarrel. It is obvious neither of us wishes to relent."

She did not like the amused twist of his lips or the easy way he strolled around the perimeter of the table to stand near her. His arresting dark eyes held her motionless as he slid sideways onto the edge of the well-polished surface and settled himself with the ease of a stalking leopard, his leg swinging lazily to and fro.

The urge to step backward seized her, but she stubbornly resisted, vowing that his bullying strategy would not send her scurrying away. Never mind, she could be beautifully persuasive when necessary.

"Let us compromise. You wish me gone. I wish to rescue Mariane from the danger of a rogue who attached himself to her in Paxton. Let me dangle London in front of her for a short time and see if that will not give her a more balanced view of things. Or, perhaps her fiancé, Matthew, will return soon. Since Matthew is your good friend and you were responsible for introducing them, surely you wish to assist me. In either case, I shall fade into the woodwork like a good little chaperone, and no one will even notice me."

There, how could he resist such an articulate and commonsense answer to everything?

He lowered his head and closed his eyes, rubbing them with strong fingers. Oh, she chastised herself, as he began to massage his temples, he looks exhausted. Why am I prolonging this ridiculous conversation when he clearly needs to be in bed?

Automatically, her hand flew to his face, then she snatched it back. She stiffened in alarm as he seemed to tremble. A low rumble escaped his throat and his shoulders shook.

Then she realized that the wretch was laughing. Laughing!

She turned angrily away and walked to the window that overlooked Grosvenor Square. A wild tirade of verbal abuse danced behind her clenched teeth, threatening to break out and spoil her veneer of control. She stepped forward to put more distance between them.

Soothing herself with the beauty of the lamplit square beyond the window, she smiled, pleased to be distracted by the amusing view of Hawksley's conscripted footman hurrying to catch up to the duke. The oversized cloak fell off the servant's shoulders and he stopped, a pantomime of frustration as he fastened it at the neck, his breath puffing white exclamations into the air. She searched the square for Grandfather, intending to distract herself with a guessing game of how long it would take the footman to reach the older man.

From her vantage point on the ground floor of the duke's town house, she could see that Grandfather had traversed perhaps one fourth of the short side of the square, and strolled serenely along the footway.

She smiled, thinking how healthy he looked, then shivered as a dizziness flowed over her. Of all the times for the intrusion of a vision—why could it not come at some appointed hour when she was prepared, or have the decency to know when she was locked into an important moment in her life? She would love to deny it admittance, but each time it occurred it seemed to be changing and progressing, frightening her so that she daren't ignore whatever warning it might convey.

She closed her eyes to fix her attention on the sensation and waited to see what was coming. Strangely, although the foreboding persisted, no vision appeared, no swirling red, no monster. She leaned forward to rest her brow against the cold glass, and the sensation grew stronger. She opened her eyes—and gasped.

"Elizabeth?"

She shook her head at Hawksley's urgent tone while before her unrolled the reenactment of her most recent vision, not a view that would swirl in and out—but this time the participants were real.

The duke had wound the knitted scarf around his head and ears to combat the cold night air, bundled like the man in her vision. His erstwhile guard's legs were not as long as the duke's, and he trotted along a way behind him as a good servant should, discreetly, nonintrusively.

She could not see her monster, but she knew he was there. Yet, how could that be true, when her monster was only a representation of death and not a real person?

Oblivious to it all, Grandfather kept walking.

"Oh, no," she moaned, scrambling away from the window to run to the door. "No . . . noooo." She fumbled in her hurried attempt to open it, but by that time Hawksley was beside her. He quickly turned the knob to open the heavy door, but as she surged forward into the hall, his arm snaked around her waist, catching her in mid-flight.

He pulled her back tightly against his broad chest, "Elizabeth, what is it?"

"Grandfather—my monster is outside, waiting for him." She fought him to escape, but he whirled her back into the library. He pressed her against the wall with both hands and growled, "Stay here, Elizabeth."

He moved out into the hall and looked upward and roared, "Woolfe, Tarr!" He turned to one of the now anxious footmen and said, "Give me your weapon, then one of you run up and awaken my men and the other stay and guard the door." He grabbed the proffered pistol and ran out of the door.

Elizabeth ran to the fireplace, snatched up the poker, and followed him out into the shadowed street.

Hawksley carefully surveyed the square as he began running silently along the footway in front of the houses where he usually walked on his evening stroll. Grosvenor Square being a high-rate paying area, the oil lamps were still burning and placed close enough together to light the footway and lend a faint glow into the carriageway. Following the path they took on their evening strolls, he kept a steady pace lest he miss something along the way. Hawksley cursed, damning the shrubs and plants in the park blocking his view of the narrow end of the square.

Where was Grandfather? Was he lying hurt, or worse, somewhere along the way? Should he yell to warn Grandfather, or would that only increase the danger?

If the Traitor had not yet encountered Grandfather, where would the murderous villain be hiding in wait? Crouching on the steps of an airy between houses and watching through the iron railings? That would provide an easy escape route back through a garden to the mews, but his chances of observation by a servant would be greater. Did he wait quietly in a side street with his accomplice holding a carriage on alert, risking identification only by moving travelers? Even more menacing, might he live in the square and simply vanish back into his house?

A coachman atop the seat of a hackney at the first intersection saw him running toward him and waited for him to pass.

His heart pounded. Was this the Traitor's conveyance? He ran to the coach and flung open the door. It was empty. He searched the face of the coachman and found an older man, far too frail to be the Traitor or his henchman. He slammed the door closed and waved the hackney forward.

Then, with a thrill of relief, he saw two figures walking in the shadowed front of the far corner building. Was it Grandfather and the footman? Woolfe's footsteps joined the muffled cadence of Hawksley's and his low voice passed quietly between them. "Tarr's coming."

He started to run forward, then saw another sight in his peripheral vision that frightened him more than anything—Elizabeth flying across the carriageway, skirts lifted, brandishing a poker in her hand. A nightman's wagon rattled in the street behind her, its noxious odor heralding its approach. If the Traitor didn't get her, the wagon would. That girl was going to age him twenty years this night.

He veered off toward Elizabeth, but Woolfe streaked ahead of him, throwing back a terse directive. "Go after the duke, I'll get the girl."

Hawksley angled slightly toward the corner, keeping an eye on Woolfe's progress. Then with a thrill of relief, he saw that the gentleman ahead was indeed Grandfather.

Hawksley cursed as Elizabeth, seeing her pursuer coming, ran even faster. Woolfe's longer legs made easy work of it and just as the wagon neared, he stretched one arm around her middle and pulled her off her feet. The curving motion swung her arm around in an arc and the length of metal she carried slammed into the side of Woolfe's head. He staggered, stunned enough for Elizabeth to pull out of his grasp as the night wagon passed. She started running forward once more.

Hawksley winced in sympathy, grateful to see Tarr approach Woolfe. He allowed himself a brief glance over his shoulder and realized that she was not hysterical as was his first impression, but rather, furiously on the attack.

Would she wildly assault the villain with no care for her own safety? Of course she would—just as she did in her dreams—and she was heading straight for the street just ahead of where Grandfather walked. Hawksley moved out into the carriageway to get away from the lamps in order to allow his eyes to adjust to the darkness that matched the street Elizabeth had targeted. Strangely, no lamps lit that distant intersection, and the resultant darkness was an instant clue to where the Traitor waited. He sprinted forward at top speed, his hand tightly gripping the pistol.

Then several things happened at once.

As Grandfather crossed the street where the Traitor surely waited, a figure moved out of the dark, his head and lower face covered. As he quickly closed in behind the duke, the stalker's hand slipped out of his pocket and a knife glinted briefly. The footman saw the obvious danger and ran forward, exclaiming in a voice that echoed clearly, "Here now, m'lord, watch out."

The duke turned to see what was amiss. He raised his hands to grapple with his attacker, and at the same time, the footman flew at the villain. With a dancer's grace, the villain turned and with a smooth motion, felled the footman. By now the duke was on the offensive, and the villain reeled from the duke's blows but still managed to parry with his wicked weapon. As the duke fell forward, the villain chopped down on the duke's head with the other hand. He leaned over the duke, grabbed a handful of his hair, and lifted.

Elizabeth screamed—just as the sound of Hawksley's pistol echoed across the square. Hawksley's bullet found its mark and the villain jerked and twisted, leaving the crumpled duke at his feet.

The attacker grabbed his wounded arm, the knife quivering in his hand as he tightened his grip around its handle. He looked up and hesitated, obviously stunned by the scene before him. He looked down at the duke, then back at Hawksley. He recovered quickly, gave Woolfe another quick appraisal, then melted back toward the waiting carriage. By the time Hawksley reached the duke, the coach was escaping briskly down the street.

Woolfe passed the macabre tableau and ran after the coach, but the distance between them soon became too great to offer any hope for capture. He turned and ran back.

Hawksley knelt by his grandfather and pulled him into his arms, swearing and praying as his fingers felt the wet cloth. The duke was covered with blood.

"Hold him away from you." Elizabeth gasped as she fell to her knees beside him. As Hawksley complied, she examined the duke with swift moving fingers, pausing at the throat, and then skimmed over his scalp and face. She ran her hands over his chest and down his arms and stopped, quickly shoving his right sleeve back. Blood pulsed slowly out, beat after beat.

She took a shaky breath and commanded in a terse voice, "Give me your neckcloth," and began tearing at the ends of the white bands herself. As they ripped free, she quickly wound it around the duke's arm, knotting it firmly on the wound.

Tarr and Woolfe joined them just as doors began opening nearby. A few curious neighbors walked cautiously forward. Elizabeth ignored them all and said to Hawksley, "Carry him quickly home and take him to his bedchamber." She looked up at Woolfe. "You run ahead and tell the kitchen I want water boiled now and some strong lye soap. Wake my aunt and instruct her to bring my medical case to the duke's chambers and send someone for Dr. Cameron."

Elizabeth moved to the footman and examined him quickly. She bowed her head and covered her face with her shaking hands. "Tarr, could you . . ." Tarr, who had joined her on the footway, said, "I'll stay here with the lad. You send the boys at the door and we'll bring him home."

Hawksley lifted the duke in his arms and began carrying him. Several neighbors assisted him and the procession moved carefully back to the duke's home. Elizabeth ran silently ahead.

The footmen were just leaving to perform the dismal task of retrieving their comrade when the grim cavalcade reached the town house. Hawksley thanked his neighbors as he entered the house and assumed the full weight of the duke into his arms. Marsh accepted their good wishes and the errant poker—and closed the door firmly behind Hawksley before the anxious neighbors could follow. Marsh followed Hawksley upstairs, managing to tender his help before the two flights were fully reached.

Hawksley stopped as he entered the duke's bedchamber. A profusion of lamps transformed the room into daylight brightness. The bed had been stripped, save for a thick padding of spotless white sheets ready to receive the length of the injured duke.

Elizabeth, her dress covered with yet another white sheet, stood at a table, washing her hands. She instructed, "Before you put him on the bed, please remove his coat and outer clothes." Hawksley's first impulse demanded that he ignore her and immediately give his grandfather the greater comfort on the bed, but she forestalled him by saying, "His outer garments carry filth from the foot traffic in the square. If you dirty the bed where he will lie, his chances of recovery are greatly lessened. Untie the bandage from his arm and leave it with his clothes."

The duke moaned as he was moved in the undressing process, but fell quiet as Hawksley finally transferred him to the bed. Blood still seeped from the duke's arm wound. Hawksley's hands shook as he straightened up and his knees felt like mush. Elizabeth looked up at him and quickly said, "Sit down, Hawksley. Eunice will give you something to drink."

Eunice materialized beside him. He had not realized she was in the room. He had no intention of being treated like an invalid and scowled her away.

Elizabeth held her trembling hands out before him and said, "Look at how badly my hands are shaking. You have had the added strain of carrying a man as large as yourself across the square and up the stairs. No matter that you are as strong as an ox, in a moment your body might betray you and render you unconscious." Her voice softened. "Please, Nathan, I need your help. Sit down for a moment." He nodded and lowered himself to a chair beside the bed, suddenly grateful for the support beneath him.

He watched in amazement as she turned back to the duke and once again began her examination of his arm.

"Excellent," she breathed in relief, "he has only severed small blood vessels." She quickly washed the bleeding arm, placed a thick pad on the wound, and wrapped it firmly. After propping it upright on several pillows, she said, "Eunice, please press steadily on this bandage. It will stop bleeding by itself, God willing."

As her aunt complied, Elizabeth reached for a fresh bowl of

water and washed the duke's face and neck, issuing little sighs as she discovered the sources of the blood that covered him.

It sickened Hawksley to see what damage the Traitor had done in a few deadly seconds. He must have made some sound, for Elizabeth glanced up quickly and said, "It's not as bad as it looks. These cuts here"—she pointed to his hairline—"he probably sustained when he fell to the ground. They bleed profusely, but will heal quickly." She covered the wounds liberally with basilicum ointment, then placed a bandage around his head.

She turned the duke's chin to the side, which revealed a gash from the jaw down to the edge of the throat. Hawksley gasped and Elizabeth quickly assured him, "This is a wicked one, and will need sewing, but will not cause his death."

She nodded at the thick bandages on the duke's arm. "The duke saved his own life by guarding his neck with an upraised arm. Probably the neck and arm wounds were made with the same swing of the knife. We must keep applying pressure and keep this arm raised for the bleeding to stop. Any deeper and it would have been very serious. Our greatest enemy now is the fever that might follow."

Elizabeth's fingers stilled and she turned her attention to Hawksley.

"Remove your coat and let Eunice poor some water so you can wash your hands. She will cover your clothes as she has mine. I will need you to hold him steady as I repair this wound. If he awakens, I must still go on. Reassure him with your voice and tell him exactly what we are doing. He will respond to you with less confusion than anyone else."

Grateful that the duke remained unconscious, Hawksley followed her instructions silently, wondering all the while at how completely he trusted her with his grandfather's life. Minutes ago she had argued fiercely with unreasoning stubbornness, yet a moment's transformation had revealed a confident, courageous woman whose voice had barely flickered in her authoritative ministrations.

He watched her face as she turned her considerable skill toward the last ghastly wound. Her soft lips pursed as she carefully plied her needle—somehow an endearing touch, he thought, to see her thus.

Though still furious at her deception at the dance and irritated as always at her unreasonableness, at this moment he felt strangely drawn to her nurturing warmth, and from somewhere came snatches of a similar loving comfort he remembered from his childhood, memories which he had relegated to the painful past when he knew his mother would never return, and he had learned that a strong man could survive without the soft touch of a woman.

Was this reaction to Elizabeth simple gratefulness for her care of his grandfather?

Simple? He marveled at the myriad emotions she had evoked in him this night alone. In the span of one evening he had impatiently gone to drag his scrawny little cousin home, lusted after the lovely woman she had become with the most powerful feeling he had ever experienced, argued mightily that she must turn around and leave, then watched in terror as she ran fearlessly to slay her own dragon.

Whatever he felt for Elizabeth, it was not simple.

A gusty sigh escaped Elizabeth's lips and a smile broke out as she finished her work. She came across to Hawksley's side of the bed and sat down, replacing the pressure of her aunt's hand on the duke's arm with her own. "Eunice, it's time to bring the warmed blankets and get this dear man tucked up snugly. Leave the arm out so we can continue holding it until the blood stops flowing. We will leave the jaw uncovered so Dr. Cameron can inspect it when he arrives."

She glanced at Hawksley and her smile grew. "I know he looks terrible, Nathan, but I have seen worse. I once had to sew a man's finger back . . . oh, dear." A flicker of the impish Elizabeth he remembered crossed her face, then vanished beneath a countenance of solemn contrition. "I apologize. Sometimes my tongue goes on without any assistance from the rest of me."

Eunice finished her task and turned to lower the lamp wicks. The softer glow was welcome and comforting, as if signaling that the emergency was past and the harsh danger had receded.

Hawksley and Elizabeth turned to each other. Their glances met and held. He swallowed hard to ease the tightness of his throat. Words came out unbidden, propelled by the emotions of the evening.

"We almost lost him, Elizabeth. If not for you . . ."

Elizabeth's eyes overflowed and wet streaks adorned her cheeks. "Thank God he didn't awaken."

Hawksley said, "How did you ever become involved in medicine, Elizabeth? Was it your idea or Dr. Cameron's?"

She rubbed her eyes tiredly, then said, a smile on her face. "It was his idea. His is a country practice as you know, and he is an extremely forward-thinking physician. It was very difficult for husbands to accept the necessary examinations of their wives while they were in the family way. I would go along accompanied by a maid and it eased the anxiety in the husbands. Then, of course, Dr. Cameron couldn't resist teaching me everything and soon had me actually assisting in the births."

Eunice interposed. "But you were a young girl, Elizabeth, did you not find it offensive or frightening?"

"Oh, yes," she said with a laugh, "the first time it seemed so shocking, but the beauty of seeing a healthy child come into the world completely erased the seemingly repulsive part of it. I soon discovered I had a talent for bringing a child forth safely. I seemed to be in touch with the baby and able to sense its discomfort or danger." She wanted to say to Hawksley *So there, my abilities are good for something wonderful.* She watched his expression as she talked. Did she detect a softening as she told her story?

"The word spread among the ladies and soon they were asking for my help and Dr. Cameron and I became a team. After a time it wasn't unusual for the doctor to be busy in the surgery while I attended the lying in alone."

Hawksley raised his hand to interrupt, his tone curious and earnest. "Yet tonight you were not simply tending an expectant mother, and it was clear you were not a stranger to this other kind of work."

"Bless Dr. Cameron for that too, if you will. Knowing I was keen to occupy my mind, he enticed me into reading his medical books and pamphlets. I found them very engrossing and was eager to learn more. After a while, occasions arose where I could put the knowledge to work—it seemed a natural progression. Then I was even more pleased to find that I have a light touch with simple wounds that was appreciated in our little country town."

Eunice walked over to sit beside her niece and spoke to Nathan. "This is enough talking for now. Nathan, you go now and get some sleep. I shall obtain some instruction from Elizabeth and then I am sending her to bed as well."

For a moment they both looked uneasy, but Eunice was resolute. "I know you expected to stay up all night watching over him, but you will be of no use to His Grace if you become ill yourselves."

Grateful for the opportunity to confer with Woolfe and Tarr, Hawksley hurried from the room. There would be little sleep for him this night.

Chapter Eleven

T HROUGH a cloudy haze of exhaustion, she heard the whoosh of a door opening and the sound of many footsteps. She sat up and immediately thought, how fared Grandfather? She opened her eyes and blinked, trying to stop the room from whirling.

Before she could transform her thought into words, her maid, Sally, relayed her answer. "Mrs. Wydner said to tell you that the duke is fine and you are to"—here the girl hesitated—"to not put you head out of your door until you have soaked in this bath and awakened properly."

Before she could decide whether to obey her aunt, the servants had completed their task, and the steaming bath was waiting.

The room finally ceased its circular motion and her brain began to function more clearly. Clever Eunice, she thought, in guessing that I would collapse upon the bed fully dressed and knowing that I would rush to the duke's side without a thought to my appearance.

She stood slowly. Her joints were stiff and her back ached. She looked in disgust at the wrinkled dress she had slept in, trying not to imagine of what the rest of her must look like.

A few moments later she stepped out of the pile of clothing at her feet and lowered herself into the high-backed tub. A groan of pure pleasure escaped her smiling lips and she slid down farther yet to immerse her aching neck and tangled hair in the wonderful lavender-scented liquid. She could easily become accustomed to the pleasures she found in the duke's home, she mused, from the thick towels and scented soaps to the mahogany-paneled water closet at the end of the hall. She soaped herself vigorously, beginning to feel alive at last. Sally rinsed her hair with clean lemon-water waiting for that especial purpose, a recipe handed down from the duke's wife, Victoria. She recalled now that her own mother had used just such a mixture, coaxing her to cease complaining at the taste as it streamed into her mouth.

Pleasant memories, indeed, but no time to dwell upon them now. She must rush to see the duke and corner Hawksley with her multitude of questions.

As she dressed in her sober gray gown, she thought longingly of the frivolous creations she had seen other ladies wearing during yesterday's shopping trip, for while she did not wish to attach the impossible Hawksley, she did want him to find her attractive. It made no sense, but still it was her unreasoning heart's desire.

She pulled her boudoir chair before the fire, leaned forward, and began to brush her hair. As it slowly dried, sparks snapped through the golden-red tresses to mingle with the crackling of the wood fire. She was pleased to find that though the public rooms in the town house used the latest coal-burning fireplaces, the private rooms still offered the fragrant pleasure of burning wood. She stood and shook her hair back over her shoulders and looked in the mirror. Wild strands floated out to halo her face and fall heavily down her back. It felt wonderful, unconfined, and since she was housebound by virtue of her nursing duties, she decided to tie it back at the neckline and let it hang free.

When she stepped out of her room, she was surprised for a moment to find two footmen standing at the end of the hall, almost as if guarding the staircase from attack. They wore black arm bands, obviously in honor of the courageous footman who had fallen in defense of the duke the previous evening.

She hurried to her patient's room. The door was open and she heard Marsh's voice. "Dr. Cameron has still not returned home, my lord. Shall I send for another physician?"

Dr. Cameron was not coming? She clutched the door handle, her heart threatening to pound out of control. While tending the duke, she had managed to control her shaking fingers and assume a confident air that the younger Dr. Cameron had insisted was an integral part of treatment, but through it all she had counted on the affirmation and further direction of a competent doctor to take over. What would she do should Marsh or Hawksley bring in a bloodletting physician or one of the charming quacks who thrived in today's society, peddling their drops and pills?

Hawksley's voice answered smoothly. "Wait until I call you, Marsh. Miss Wydner will give us some direction when she returns."

She slowly let out her breath, grateful for the reprieve.

Marsh waited for a few seconds, ones filled with heavy disapproval. Mercifully, he gave in to duty and left the room, nodding distantly to her as he passed.

Hawksley stood at the window, his back to the room, freshly attired in a dark blue coat and gray pantaloons, and shod with gleaming black Hessians. Thank goodness she had not rushed to Grandfather at first awakening.

Her attention went swiftly to the duke. His arm lay on the mountain of pillows and the bandage, obviously changed by Eunice, was blessedly white. She hurried to his beside and felt his forehead for fever and ran her fingers down to his throat to monitor the speed of his heartbeat. By the time she finished, her hands were shaking, a reaction she often had when good news brought relief.

Eunice bustled in, bringing her cheerful peace with her. She, too, had changed into fresh clothing and looked fit and ready to meet the day.

Elizabeth spoke to her aunt. "Did he awaken while I slept?"

Hawksley quickly turned at the sound of her voice, but said nothing as Eunice answered her question.

"No. He seemed restless at times, but mostly lay very quiet."

Hawksley crossed the room to stand beside her. "Should he not have been yelling at us all by now?"

Worry creased her brow. She checked the time on the mantel clock. Several hours had passed since his attack and he should have awakened.

She ran her hand over his scalp and head, stopping at the base of his neck. "His attacker hit him fairly hard in this area and he has nasty lump back here. He might be suffering from that."

Hawksley extended his hand and she guided it to the raised area. They exchanged a concerned look. Elizabeth turned to the night table where the boiled water Eunice had brought last night sat waiting.

Perhaps she was proceeding too carefully concerning such monitoring of the water, but the word *antiseptic* had been a serious drill for young Dr. Cameron, who was a devotee of the writings of Sir John Pringle, who coined the word. Thus water was suspect until found innocent. London water was freely available but she had heard that no enlightened person actually drank it until it was determined whether its source was clean rainwater, a private well free of contaminants, or a water company that might draw from the Thames, which was a virtual sewer. She must investigate the matter at the first opportunity.

She poured a small amount of clean water into a tumbler and held it to the duke's lips, letting a few drops fall into his slightly opened mouth. "Grandfather, wake up now."

The duke's mouth closed upon the water and his lips moved, seeking the moisture. Again she let the water seep into his mouth. "Wake up now, Grandfather." She gave Hawksley a beseeching look.

He joined in. "Sir, it's time to get up now. The room is full of pretty girls wishing to speak to you." Eunice's cheeks flushed at his words.

The duke's eyelids fluttered and he began sipping the trickling water Elizabeth administered. Elizabeth said to Eunice, "Get the laudanum now, Auntie, please. In a few moments he will be roaring his discomfort."

The duke slowly came awake, sipping the water in rationed drops while a stormy expression began to gather upon his face. He opened his eyes and frowned at Elizabeth. A bubbling relief flooded through her, loosening a tight band of anxiety across her chest.

His first words made them all smile, so pleased were they to see him in his usual form. "Gads, woman, I want a drink, not a demmed infant's sprinkling! My head hurts and I feel like I've gone through the hedge face-first."

Elizabeth nodded at Eunice, who in turn poured an allotment of laudanum onto a spoon and spoke to the duke. "Here is something to make the pain go away. It is not enough to put you to sleep, but it will help." Eunice's soft voice caught the duke's attention and he turned his head slowly to look at her.

"Pretty lady, indeed," he murmured and swallowed the dose and the small portion of water to follow. Eunice shook her head in embarrassed silence and looked at Elizabeth. They smiled fondly at the charming rogue.

The duke turned back to look at Hawksley, wincing as he moved. "The Traitor?"

Elizabeth's head snapped back to the duke, then across to Hawksley. What were they saying? They *knew* who her monster was? Had Hawksley understood her, that the attacker of the night was the same villain from her dreams?

Hawksley's expression hardened and his eyes turned to black obsidian as he answered. "The Traitor escaped."

"And my footman?"

"I am sorry, sir. He tried to stop the Traitor from attacking you and was killed for his efforts."

A long moment passed before the duke responded. His eyes were bright with unshed tears. "Will you see to his people for me? Tarr will have the particulars."

"I have already taken care of it, sir."

"Good."

After a moment's reflection, the duke took a deep breath and said, "Now if you please, I wish to know what damage the demmed villain inflicted upon me."

"Elizabeth will explain, sir. It's her handiwork after all.

"Elizabeth? You mean to say you let the gel work on me?" He turned carefully to look at her.

Elizabeth could barely speak, she was so frustrated. Questions fought to be asked and she must hold them back rather than distress the injured duke. She briefly explained. "You have a bump on the back of your neck, small cuts on your forehead, a rather deep gash on your jaw, and a cut on your arm that bled freely for some time. Please do not move your arm or turn your head too quickly."

"Well, by Jove. Wouldn't Vicky have loved to see such a thing." He smiled contentedly for some time, then gingerly turned to face Hawksley.

"Did you see who our Traitor was? The coward had his face covered when I was tussling with him."

"No. I shot him in the arm but he got away in a carriage. His wound might identify him if he is fool enough to let us see it, which he certainly is not. One advantage is that we may now see who is not the Traitor and narrow our suspects down."

Elizabeth's temper rose with each snippet of information about her monster they so casually dropped into the conversation, just as if he was the neighborhood dustman. There would be no more hazy mysteries for her when they talked about him with such apparent ease—she wanted answers and she wanted them now.

First, though, she must get Hawksley out of the room. "Lord Hawksley, give me a moment to give Eunice and the duke's valet some instructions for Grandfather's care and then I would like just a wee word with you."

Hawksley's face was comical to watch as he realized that she was seriously giving him his marching orders. The duke started to laugh but very quickly his injuries changed his mind and he settled for a feeble chuckle. He said weakly, "This is no conversation for the ladies, anyway, m'boy. We'll talk later."

Hawksley studied Elizabeth for a moment, raised that hatefully superior eyebrow, bowed in her direction, and left. The door slammed behind him, then she heard a low oath as he obviously remembered that this was a sickroom.

Elizabeth's estimation of a moment to settle the duke was far off the mark. While the duke may have been amused and pleased with her medical care, the old curmudgeon had no intention of forfeiting any of his comforts or pleasures to her "wild Scottish nonsense." He particularly wanted his beefsteak and ale, not some "baby's pap."

The maids arrived, unusually solemn, to clear the room. She instructed the valet in caring for the duke's private comfort and by the time Elizabeth freed herself from his chamber, Hawksley was nowhere in sight. The coward.

She realized when she reached the hall that she had no idea of the layout of the house, other than the library and dining room, which were on the ground floor. One could not walk along knocking on bedroom doors, so below stairs she must go.

She ran nimbly downward. Halfway to the next level she slowed, surprised that, in the midst of such terrible events, she was so lighthearted. Her hand glided lightly over the polished banister as she studied the riddle of her good cheer, finally perceiving the answer as she reached the first-floor landing. Of course—the oppressive vision no longer sat upon her shoulders, flapping its dark wings at her. Despite the heartbreaking death of the young footman, her vision had come to pass and the intended victim had escaped from the monster.

But, oh, she thought, with a fierce thrill of fury, she would like to have hit him with her poker!

She nodded to the next pair of footmen. She was correct in her first impression of them—*guarded* was the right term for their militant stance. Today, of course, their added solemnity at the death of one of their own in defense of the duke gave the household a hushed, expectant aura. The footmen watched her with matching quizzical expressions as she opened doors, looked at each room, and continued on to the next. Finally, one spoke. "Are ye lost, miss?"

"No," she replied absently, "just curious." Where was that dratted Hawksley?

The next room she looked into netted her a worthy quarry and, while not Hawksley, he was certainly worth investigating. He leaned across the billiards table, carefully aiming his stick at a colored ball. She entered, leaving the door properly open behind her. "Good morning, sir. Are you not the fellow who chased me through the street last night?"

Chapter Twelve

HE whirled from the baize table where he had been playing and stared at her. His thoughts rode clearly upon his features as his appreciative glance ran over her face and figure. He brought his fingers to the side of his cheek where a red welt revealed where she had accidentally hit him. So he knew who she was, but for the moment he had the advantage.

He casually reached to his side and deposited his cue on the table, saying, "Miss Wydner?"

"Yes. And you are . . . ?"

He bowed with a lazy continental manner, never taking his gaze from her face. "I am Woolfe Burnham, Miss Wydner, and completely at your service should you desire to again race through the streets or wield your poker against unsuspecting men."

She laughed aloud. His grin widened in response. This was more like it, she thought, a charming, *accessible* man with nothing to hide. Here was the perfect person to answer some of her questions.

"I am delighted to meet you, Mr. Burnham. Please accept my very sincere apologies for decorating your poor face with the imprint of the duke's poker. My arm kept moving without my permission last night, I assure you. The poker was meant for . . . what is the name you all call our resident villain?"

"Hawksley and the duke refer to him as the Traitor."

"And you call him . . . ?"

"I am sure you would not recognize the expressions used, Miss Wydner, but rest assured they are not what any mother ever christened her child."

"You certainly appeared quickly last evening, Mr. Burnham, are you a resident in the duke's household?"

"Were that I could claim that honor, but I had a short piece of business to conduct with Hawksley and will only be able to accept their kind hospitality for a few days. And you, Miss Wydner, will you be in London long?"

"Yes, actually, I am accompanied by my aunt, Mrs. Wydner and my cousin Mariane. My cousin is blue deviled with missing her fiancé who is in the military. We have brought her to town to cheer her up with the social life of London."

A fleeting frown followed by another approving appraisal of her face preceded his drawled answer. "I usually leave the tiresome job of socializing to my cousin, Geoff. However, for the pleasure of dancing with you, I might be persuaded to attend a few functions myself."

Elizabeth shook her head, smiling at his embellished words. "I am at a loss here in London, Mr. Burnham. All gentlemen from eighteen to eighty find it impossible to carry on a normal conversation with a lady without mouthing these fulsome compliments, which can mean nothing since they flow out of their mouths within seconds of meeting." She paused, then with a shrug of her shoulders said, "All save my kinsman, Lord Hawksley, who speaks with almost painful honesty."

"Hawksley has insulted you?"

She laughed at his incredulous expression. "Oh, for goodness' sakes, Mr. Burnham, do not rush out and challenge him. I have irritated him from childhood, and we speak freely with each other. I was only commenting about London manners."

The frown slowly left Woolfe's face as he explained, "I have never heard a lady complain about flowery words or compliments before, Miss Wydner, but perhaps they should. The words are indeed an habitual politeness, since we are drilled from an early age in the ways to converse with a lady. One boon we find from it all is that, should we find ourselves smitten, we may speak the words of our hearts without fear of embarrassing either party."

He shrugged. "Who can say which way is best, that of total honesty with occasional bursts of heart-on-the-sleeve poetry or that of habitual flattering words which smooth the path and bring a smile to a lady's lovely face. Save yours, of course."

"Please do not exclude my smiles, Mr. Burnham, for I do not believe I was actually complaining, now that I think on it. I admit I found myself perfectly happy to hear such nonsense during last evening's ball, no matter that it was just good manners."

"And Hawksley? Would you welcome such nonsense from him?"

She laughed again at his impertinence. "One might wish for a pot of gold, Mr. Burnham, but would faint dead if it arrived."

"Hmmm." Woolfe mused with a faraway expression. "And I have always considered Hawksley to be the most brilliant man I have ever met. Perhaps he has been hermited away from society too long."

"Hermited?"

"I daresay his appearance last evening was the first for several years."

Having always pictured Hawksley blithely enjoying London society, she was amazed at this information. The question fairly asked itself. "Why?"

Woolfe hesitated, but answered slowly. "He works. Night and day, week after week. More than that, you must ask him yourself."

"And yet he attended the Barton's ball last night."

"To fetch you home, I believe."

She couldn't help it, once more she laughed aloud. Hawksley had told her that was his reason for coming, but she had discounted it.

Oh, my, the thought of Hawksley being forced to break a habit of years to come get her, to don evening clothes and wade through the packed rooms, and then not recognize her, but instead to find himself attracted to a stranger who in turn . . . oh, it was such a delicious picture. Better than all the retaliatory scenes she had conjured up over the last four years, and some of those were diabolical, indeed.

She sunk onto the cushioned settee near the window and Woolfe sat in a nearby chair, watching her diminishing laughter with a bemused expression. As she caught her breath, she studied him in return.

His demeanor seemed to soften as he relaxed with their easy banter. At first impression, he had appeared thin, almost gaunt, his tanned skin tightly drawn over wide cheekbones and a strong narrow nose. A second examination belied the first impression of frailty, when she realized that his shoulders were nearly as wide as the enormous Hawksley's and that he almost stood as tall.

He seemed to move slowly, almost with the awkwardness of a too-quickly growing youth, folding his long legs as he sat, as if no furniture could accommodate his long limbs. Then she remembered the ease with which he had scooped her up when they were both running, a difficult task for anyone, and one requiring strength and coordination beyond the average man, no matter now fit.

His smile was slow and lazy now, and furrowed laugh lines framed his deep blue eyes. His drawling speech boasted an excellent schooling, but some other blood joined the Celtic in this interesting man. His shiny, almost blue-black hair, tied back at the neck, was negligently long, and like the man, a little out of the mainstream of things.

Impulsively, she leaned closer to inspect the welt she had inflicted on him. Something flashed in his eyes as she did so, but quickly disappeared. He was a man who did not like a quick motion directed at him, she decided, and she was grateful she was not a mortal foe. His reaction evoked an almost maternal response from her. "I do apologize, Mr. Burnham, please know the blow was unintended."

He grinned. "It is a badge of honor, one I wear with pride."

A low voice from the open door interrupted, anger underlining every syllable. "You were anxious for a word with me, Elizabeth?"

She turned her attention toward Hawksley, but was drawn back to Woolfe when she felt his hand on hers. She watched in stunned silence as he then turned to Hawksley and gave him a rather bored expression. Why had he done such a thing?

She turned to look at Hawksley once again, wondering at the anger on his face. She had indeed been looking for him, searching the house room by room. True, she had been sidetracked by Woolfe, but since Hawksley had not requested the conference, nor had he waited for her, what reason could he have for his display of anger at a slightly tardy meeting?

Hawksley smoothly strolled across the parquet floor to stand before them and graced them with a charming smile that failed to reach his eyes, "Breakfast is waiting downstairs. Cook seems to think we must needs drown our worries in food, and I cannot face it alone."

Before he could answer, Hawksley lifted her suddenly popular hand from Woolfe's grasp, saluted her fingers with an unprecedented kiss as he expertly propelled her to her feet. Wrapping his free arm possessively around her waist, he steered her toward the door, throwing back in a friendly, satisfied voice, "Come along, Woolfe. Cook loves you more than all of us put together. He has been in a cooking frenzy ever since he learned you were in the house."

He looked down at Elizabeth and confided, "Woolfe recuperated here once for several months and Cook managed to put some meat on his bones—it was his finest hour."

Confused at Hawksley's cheerful change of mood, she glanced back at Woolfe to appraise his reaction. Woolfe's eyes shone, a glow she had seen often at the Scottish tournaments. Oh dear, so that was what all this was about. Two males in competition for a female. Sometimes she wondered if men even realized they carried on so. In fact, she wondered if either of these two men would notice if she left without them.

Breakfast was a frustrating experience for Elizabeth in her anxiety to speak with Nathan. The men gave unhurried attention to the wonderful array of food and yet consumed enormous quantities. Nathan was still an impressive trencherman, and the Scottish men she knew could clean a heavily laden table like a proverbial swarm of locusts, but Woolfe had them all beaten. Like a hungry schoolboy, he shoveled it all in and filled his plate with equal enthusiasm again. Cook made an appearance at the end of the meal, his mustache quivering with pleasure when he glanced from Woolfe to the empty sideboard.

Eunice and Mariane were agog. Dressed as was fitting in the magnificent room with its gracious Rembrandts and Turners overlooking the stately dining appointments, they looked like two blossoms in a lovely portrait themselves. Elizabeth, used to hearty Scotsmen, was equally torn between hiding her amusement at the women's amazed expressions and wondering how the men could accomplish such a feat without compromising their table manners.

Expecting Hawksley to be as anxious as she to discuss the life-and-death drama in which they were enmeshed, she was flabbergasted when the two men stood to leave at the end of the feast, dripping the pleasantries men are wont to do when they are relieved to be escaping back into a man's world and leave the ladies fluttering behind them.

Elizabeth had no intention of remaining in the dark about her monster for one minute more than necessary. She smiled sweetly and rose, following them into the library. Their consternation was a joy to observe. No lady would be so lacking in decorum as to follow the gentlemen when they had bid her adieu with a bevy of compliments, plenty to keep her happy until they were forced to do the pretty again. Among the multitude of unwritten rules for polite behavior, they obviously knew of none to dictate their behavior for the situation she created by following them.

She seated herself at the end of the long mahogany table and bid them join her. Dumbfounded, they sat, squirming awkwardly—floundering like fish out of water.

Hawksley regained his composure first. She assumed that he had finally remembered that she was not a pliable female who could be dismissed. He looked quickly at Woolfe and smiled that devilish grin, the one that meant he was ready to be entertained.

Was he daring her to discuss their situation in front of someone she had just met, in fact calling her bluff? Why then did he wait so gleefully to see Woolfe's reaction to whatever she intended to do next?

Men! They behaved so irrationally in these competitive situations. Perhaps Hawksley hoped she would shock Woolfe and discourage his attentions, not that Hawksley truly wanted her for himself. Moreover, at this point, she cared not a whit for Woolfe's flirtatious intentions; she simply wanted her answers now so she might return to her care of the duke.

"Who is this Traitor you speak so familiarly about? I do not mean his identity, for you obviously do not have that information, but what do you know about him? I assume by 'Traitor' you mean 'traitor to the realm.'"

Hawksley looked surprised, but quickly recovered. His grin expanded as if she had not disappointed him in the least and turned his overly polite attention to Woolfe. Woolfe looked shocked, obviously not so much at her question, for she had been present at the attack the previous evening, but at Hawksley's cavalier attitude toward what was very likely a highly secret subject.

When neither man answered her she stood and said, "Very well, I shall go to the War Office and start asking questions until I get my answer."

"No!" They both stood, answering in unison. Woolfe's tan had faded to a chalky white and Hawksley's grin was gone.

She turned to Hawksley, speaking directly to him as if no one else was in the room. "Did you understand last night that your Traitor is the same man as the monster of my dreams?"

"Yes."

Amazed at his unemotional answer she thought aloud. "You were not surprised at that . . . you already knew . . . in fact, you were not even surprised at the attack. You moved immediately without questioning me."

She was not surprised by his affirmative nod. Nor did she try to stem the anger that mushroomed inside her as understanding came. She leaned forward and looked him straight in the eye. "He was my monster before he was your Traitor, Hawksley. I dreamed about him until I was afraid to go to sleep at night. I came home from Scotland because the specter of his evil was once more pounding in my brain."

Hawksley would have responded had she given him the opportunity, but she pointed a finger and pushed it against his chest. "I saved your grandfather last night. Do not ignore my questions and do not play games with my feelings. If I have to advertise in the newspapers for information, I will have my answers."

They stood frozen, a tableau charged with emotion. Finally, Hawksley sighed resignedly, gently touched her shoulder, saying, "I can be such an ass, Elizabeth. Please forgive me."

She couldn't agree with him more, but was shocked to hear him admit it. Was he patronizing her? She searched his eyes and was relieved to read genuine contrition. She clamped her teeth down over her lower lip to keep her emotions in check, nodded once, and sank to her chair. Now, she thought, I shall finally have my answers.

Hawksley massaged the back of his neck, clearly under stress as he organized his thoughts. He turned to Woolfe and said, "You may stay or go, Woolfe, but if you stay I must have your word what you learn will never leave this room."

Woolfe replied in an affronted tone, "Have I ever given you any reason to doubt my loyalty to you or to our country, Hawksley?"

"This is more than friendship or patriotism, Woolfe, and I must have your word that no matter what you hear, whether you believe it or not, no one will ever know what was said here."

Woolfe stood very still, looked at Elizabeth for a long moment, then turned to Hawksley. "Very well, you have it."

The men sat down as Hawksley said, "Carry on, Elizabeth, ask whatever you need to know."

She was still shaking with emotion, but was determined to have no more uncertainties between them. "First of all, Hawksley, I want you to know that I am furious with you. How do you think I felt when you and Grandfather calmly discussed my monster in front of me when you knew how he had tormented my life? Did you think I was of so little importance that I did not even deserve an explanation, however belated? And then when you had your chance this morning, you trotted off without granting me the audience I asked for. I thought I had seen the height of your callousness before, but this is beyond belief."

Some unnamed emotion crossed Hawksley's face, but before he could respond, she continued. "Who is this man? Why did he attack Grandfather? Why is this house like a guarded castle with men on every floor, looking like they would like a good fight? How did he get to be your Traitor when he was my monster?" She took a deep breath and said, "I would like those answers first."

By this time Hawksley's face was flushed with color, but his voice delivered the answers without a trace of emotion. "To fill you in, Woolfe, Elizabeth's parents and mine were lost on a yachting trip when she was a young child." He turned to Elizabeth and placed his hand on her fists, holding them tight as to keep her anchored while he continued. "Our Traitor—your monster—was responsible for their demise."

She gasped, and tears gathered in her eyes. She blinked furiously to stem the flow. If she became a watering pot, Hawksley would relegate her back to the status of the helpless female who could not withstand unpleasantness, and that she couldn't endure.

Hawksley asked, "Shall I not go on?"

"Sorry," she responded in what she hoped was a confident voice, "It's simply that I hadn't realized they were murdered."

"I had hoped to spare you, Elizabeth, and I shall if you wish."

At her firm head shake, he gave her an approving nod and released her hands. "The Traitor was enacting a revenge on Grandfather for destroying his smuggling crew. He was adding to his coffers by transporting English secrets and French agents back and forth between our countries. He boasted about the killing in a note to the duke."

His grim face relaxed in a smile. "Grandfather began hiring ex-soldiers to guard us and placed Tarr over them. Marsh has threatened to quit a dozen times since the rough manners of the soldiers do not match his strict standard of Standbridge servants, but Grandfather is unrelenting in this. Even when we travel, the coachmen are trained and armed." Elizabeth nodded, remembering Tarr's strange actions and the footmen who had followed her on Sylvia's shopping trip.

He smiled grimly and said, "The only weakness in the plan is that he forgets to guard himself. He maintains that the Traitor has no intention of killing him."

"But," Elizabeth interjected, "he tried to kill him last night."

"I do not believe the duke was his target. He was wearing my coat and I am the one who usually walks at night. Grandfather occasionally joins me, but I usually go by myself, with guards, of course. The Traitor must have thought he had a windfall last night to see a lone figure with a trailing guard."

Hawksley hesitated briefly, then carried on. "This is not the first time he has attempted to put an end to my life." At Elizabeth's gasp, he shrugged. "It seems I have the proverbial nine lives."

Elizabeth's heart pounded painfully at the thought of Hawksley as a target of the madman. Still, the story made no sense. "I do not understand. Why does he not want the duke's death?"

"The Traitor uses the same vicious trick on all who stand in his way. He does not harm his enemies, but only part of their family. That way he holds them captive in fear of more reprisals and prevents them from ever mounting a search for him. In addition, he is a sadist who loves his work."

Woolfe frowned. "All these years . . ."

"We had no idea he was a member of the *ton* until last week when you gave us the last clue. Up until then we believed he was a smuggler or an underworld character." He turned to Elizabeth and said, "Woolfe barely escaped an ambush just last week and discovered that the Traitor not only must be operating directly from the War Office, but that he is almost certainly an English aristocrat, probably someone we number among our acquaintances."

During Hawksley's explanation to Elizabeth, Woolfe's fingers absently tapped the table, his brow furrowed as he stared into space. She was entirely surprised when he finally turned to her and asked, "What did you mean when you said you saved the duke? And what are these dreams you speak of?"

Drat the man. Why could he not accept Hawksley's story and let it rest? Could she lie and say she recognized her monster? But no, Woolfe knew he had waited in a darkened street across the square.

Elizabeth looked to Hawksley for direction, a mistake, for the
unexpectedly tender understanding she found emanating from
him drew her into a dangerous torpor. She wanted to throw herself into Hawksley's arms and beg him to make it all go away.

Then, like a beam of sunlight, she realized that not only did he
offer her the choice of remaining protected from baring her pecu-
liarities before someone else, but in not speaking for her, he was
granting her the respect and freedom to tell her own story if she
so chose. He had extracted Woolfe's promise that their words
would go no further, and now the decision was solely hers.

Her resolution was quickly made. She tore her glance away
from Hawksley and said briskly to Woolfe, "I began having a terrible feeling of danger and, fearing for my aunt and cousin, came
home from Scotland. They were unharmed and so I believed I had
overreacted. Then I began having a childhood dream again, a
dream about a monster who killed my parents and Nathan's on
the yacht."

Woolfe looked shocked and Hawksley emanated an almost pal-
pable alertness. He growled, "Elizabeth, you do not have to do
this."

That was almost her undoing, but she wanted to get the story
told while she still had the courage. She shook her head and continued.

"Now the scene I saw was different and came at odd times,
even when I was wide awake. And the picture was changing."

Woolfe's demeanor had changed completely, the casual slouch
now gone. "Amazing. What did you see that warned you about
the duke's danger?"

"In my vision, a man bundled up in a coat and scarf walked
past a street where my monster was waiting. When I looked out
the window last night I could see it happening in reality just as I
had seen it in my vision. I told Nathan, and you know the rest."

Woolfe turned to Hawksley, "And you believed her?"

Hawksley smiled. "It's a long story."

Woolfe's lazy grin was back as he turned to Elizabeth. "And
you were going to slay the dragon with your mighty poker?"

She quipped, "And got you instead."

Woolfe kept his attention on Elizabeth as he spoke. "If no one
wants this amazing lady, I'd like to keep her. She reminds me of
my childhood playmate, a perfect lady until her temper blew, and
then heaven help the enemy."

Hawksley snapped, "Perhaps you should hurry home and court your childhood sweetheart, rather than dangle after a substitute."

Woolfe's smile dimmed just a fraction. "Alas, we are not sweethearts since the lady loves another, who is also perfect, and who never loses his temper." His face lit up with an angelic smile. "And he has no idea she even has one."

He eyed Hawksley's stormy face, then Elizabeth's sympathetic frown and asked, "What say you, Miss Wydner? I must confess I have nothing to offer save a weak connection to my cousin, Geoff, the Earl of Kingsford, who although I consider him my closest friend, is busy gaming away his inheritance. Dare I hope you are flush in the pocket?"

Since Elizabeth knew Woolfe was tweaking Hawksley, she answered in kind. "Actually, the duke has informed me that I have some expectations, but since I shall be much too busy pursuing the Traitor, I am afraid I must decline." She paused and teased. "It is marriage you are offering, is it not?" Then she laughed and Woolfe joined in. They glanced in unison at Hawksley and the laughter died.

Hawksley looked at both of them in turn, reminding Elizabeth of a statue she had once seen in a museum of a Roman gladiator— hard, fearless, relentless. For some reason, this only incited more chuckles from Woolfe, but Elizabeth felt uneasy. The last time Hawksley turned to stone, her life had changed in an instant.

She waited while Hawksley made the transition back from wherever his brilliant mind had traveled. He seemed to have reached some favorable conclusion, for his face cleared and he granted them his full attention.

"We have much to do and must act quickly."

"Surely you are not suggesting Miss Wydner aid us in this."

"We cannot stop her from pursuing him, Woolfe. Therefore, we shall work as a team. Our strength lies in our sifting through the combined knowledge we bring to the whole. I thought to do all the sifting myself after talking to each of you, but her fresh outlook might be the very thing we need. Lord knows the Traitor has outsmarted us at every turn. You have seen him in even darker circumstances than last night, but you have heard his voice. His attack on me came at night here in town, and although his face was covered, I have some idea of his size and build."

Hawksley paused, his voice gruff now, sounding more like the duke than ever. "He, of course, knows now that Woolfe has re-

turned safely with damning information about him. To balance
that threat, however, we now have the added bonus of Elizabeth,
unless he already knows she is here, which brings me to the most
difficult part of our plan."

He turned in his chair and reached for Elizabeth's hand. "In all
honesty, the rest is not my idea but the duke's, one I have rejected
as too risky but now must accept. It presents a considerable peril
to you, since the Traitor may discover he has another possible
victim at hand to threaten us with. In any case, you are in grave
danger. He knows he is in jeopardy and would not hesitate to kid-
nap you to get back at the duke."

After pulling her captured hand into both of his, surrounding it
entirely with his warmth and strength, he spoke with a voice she
did not recognize. "He would never release you alive, Elizabeth,
and your incarceration would be hell on earth."

Woolfe protested, "Here now, Hawksley, don't frighten her
so."

"That is exactly what I must do, Woolfe. You saw her last
night and probably thought she was acting the hysterical female."
Woolfe grunted his agreement and Hawksley laughed softly.

"She always attacks him in her dreams—without any thought
to her own peril—and even after knowing how dangerous he is, I
doubt she can do any differently now."

With a catch in his voice, Woolfe replied, "Keep her in the
house, then. Set guards on her door, until we catch him."

Elizabeth sent him a scathing look and opened her mouth to
protest, but Hawksley interposed smoothly. "You don't understand, Woolfe, the fact is . . . her dreams always come true."

Woolfe looked at them both in turn, clearly not accepting the
inevitability of Hawksley's unorthodox pronouncement.

"It matters not if you believe me, Woolfe, what matters is that
we are going to use her visions, just as she did last night. Instead
of bowing to what seems to be fate, she schemes and plans and
circumvents the danger. I have experienced the phenomenon myself years ago. It works, Woolfe. We cannot ignore it."

Woolfe leaned back against the chair, his folded arms demon-
strating his opinion of Hawksley's plan.

"You see," Hawksley continued, "Elizabeth wields a weapon
far more deadly than a mere poker. Like a magnet, her dream will
bring the Traitor and Elizabeth together and I shall be there with

her when it happens."

Elizabeth pulled her hand away and retorted, "You were also in the dream when I attacked him, Nathan. Perhaps you, not I, will be the one to draw him forth."

"Ah, but according to you, my actions were somewhat less . . . courageous than yours."

Elizabeth laughed. "Shall you be sitting here in the house beside me, waiting for your Traitor to announce himself."

"No, my little firebrand, we shall not sit here doing our needlepoint, we shall go-a-hunting."

"No!" Woolfe stood abruptly and glared at Hawksley. "How dare you endanger her like that."

"Endanger," Hawksley said with a deadly calm, "now that is an interesting word to use, almost one would think you her champion and I her enemy."

"Explain yourself, then."

"We shall throw ourselves into the social arena and see if we can find our vicious prey with a broken wing."

"Famous," Elizabeth explained. "and I shall already be there with my cousin, Mariane. You two may stand on the sidelines while I dance with all the suspected men. I shall cling tightly to the appropriate arm while you watch to see if they wince."

She was sure Hawksley would object, but he surprised her by nodding absently at her outrageous suggestion. Then she understood his complacency when he made his next pronouncement. "I must ask your cooperation in one small matter, Elizabeth."

She cocked her head suspiciously at him while he continued. "Give us three days before we begin. We have already sent out men to watch our suspects. If we move quickly, we shall find him."

At the sight of her stubborn face, Hawksley restated his request, speaking in a humoring tone she distrusted. "Give us three days, Elizabeth. If in that time we have made no headway, you may join in the search."

He threw her another bone. "Besides, you will need clothes. Take Tarr to protect you and buy whatever you wish. Send the accounting to me and never mind the cost." He looked at her faded gown as if seeing it for the first time. "Take Lady Lowden and go to the best modiste."

At her insulted silence, a touch of desperation crept into his voice. "Take dancing lessons."

She opened her mouth to give him her scathing opinion of his arrogance when she was stopped by the sound of an ear-splitting scream.

Chapter Thirteen

WOOLFE rushed from the room before Elizabeth could rise from her chair. Pausing to grasp her arm, Hawksley followed, stopping at the door briefly before he allowed her to pass through.

Elizabeth rushed to Mariane's side when she realized whose scream had penetrated the heavy library door. Mariane stared, horror stricken, at a young man who stood hesitantly at the front door. Eunice, her face reflecting her concern, hurried down the stairs as Hawksley strode cheerfully toward the new arrival.

"Matthew, it's great to see you home, old boy. I see you have upset the delicate sensibilities of your betrothed with the shock of seeing you home safely after all her worry. You always did rush your fences and should have sent word you were on your way."

Eunice joined in as she reached the men. "Matthew, how wonderful to see you. Thank God for your safe delivery."

Elizabeth took in the situation at a glance, despite the covering dialogue of the other two. Matthew was not a pretty sight. He leaned heavily on a cane, barely able to stand. Sweat stood out across his forehead and the rosy blotches highlighting his cheeks clashed with a tired gray complexion.

The worn blue jacket of the Ninth Light Dragoons hung loosely on his thin shoulders and his once-white breeches showed a wear equal to his tired black boots. His blond hair—Mariane's requirement for a perfect suitor back in Paxton so long ago—fell in uneven lengths past his shoulders.

Mariane, the author of the unpleasantness of the scene, looked as if something spoiled had been served for breakfast.

"Mariane!" Elizabeth whispered, "I shall slap you silly if you do not welcome him this instant. Now, do it nicely so your terrible manners do not hurt the poor man any more. Can you not see that he has hurried to find you when he should be in bed?" She poked a finger into Mariane's back and prodded her forward.

Mariane's voice shook but she smiled prettily, just as she had been practicing in her mirror for years. "Welcome home, darling. Please forgive my manners, but my sensibilities are much too finely drawn of late."

Mariane lifted her hand to him, but floundered when she realized that he held the head of his cane tightly with both hands and daren't reach for hers. Elizabeth could see Mariane blanch, but was relieved to see her recover with a smooth aplomb and lean forward and kiss his cheek.

By the time Hawksley presented Elizabeth and Woolfe, she had decided that Matthew was perfect for her cousin. He looked at Mariane with love in his eyes, yet was obviously not deceived by her flustered excuses. He was clearly hurt, but not destroyed, exuding determination and confidence in his own worth.

It occurred to Elizabeth then that this untitled soldier was the reason Oakes had been assigned as abigail to Mariane. Not to keep Mariane's clothing up to date, but to insinuate herself as a second voice of Lady Lowden, to convince Mariane that she could do much better for herself than Matthew.

Yet, Mariane must have already run the gauntlet of their disapproval two years ago and made her choice out of love for Matthew. However, after two years of Matthew's absence and Oakes's constant prodding, Mariane had evidently lost her confidence in that love, thus her tentative acceptance of Lord Stanley. Reflecting on Mariane's actions of late, Elizabeth feared that Oakes had done her job too well.

Matthew had a difficult road ahead of him to help Mariane realize that she did, indeed, still love him. Elizabeth grew concerned as the young man seemed to lose his balance for a moment. In his condition, would he have the strength to battle his enemies, Lady Lowden and Oakes, who surely thought a mere soldier not worthy of their Mariane?

In that same moment, the young soldier's eyes rolled back and he fell heavily at their feet.

Mariane cried out and knelt down beside Matthew, uncertainly touching his shoulder as if afraid to disturb him. Elizabeth knelt on the other side and touched her skilled fingers to his face. Eunice wept softly and Hawksley bellowed for Marsh.

Fervently praying that Dr. Cameron would arrive soon, Elizabeth found her worst fear to be true—Matthew's skin was dangerously warm.

Marsh arrived immediately, took in the scene, and began giving orders. Elizabeth had to admire the stiff-rumped butler. Despite his wariness of her, he remembered everything she had done for the duke, and maids and footmen were hastily dispatched to obtain mounds of clean sheets and boiling water. Eunice offered to fetch her medical bag while Mariane continued to pat her betrothed as if to reassure him.

When Matthew's bedroom was ready and cleared of servants, Hawksley and Woolfe carried Matthew upstairs, and at Elizabeth's direction, removed his outer garments and settled him in bed.

Eunice gently removed Mariane from the doorway and Woolfe excused himself. Hawksley remained at Elizabeth's request. She immediately began sponging Matthew with cool water to bring down the fever, grateful for the Scottish doctors whose journals had revealed the benefits of icy baths. Fever was such a frightening part of sickness—on one hand it seemed necessary to bring a malady to an end, and on the other, it could destroy by itself if let run free.

Hawksley took over the sponging while she began her search for the cause of Matthew's troubles. Almost immediately, she found an area of heat and swelling in his leg. She recognized the danger to Matthew, but daren't risk his life with her limited experience in surgery. What was she to do with this young man if Dr. Cameron did not present himself soon?

Furthermore, she worried, how long had it been since she had last checked on the duke? It seemed hours since she had tripped so lightheartedly down those stairs, and she was beginning to panic. Then she felt Hawksley's arm encircle her shoulders and looked up, surprised that he was in the room and amazed that he seemed to know how she felt. The feeling that engulfed her was overwhelming. Relief, comfort, a sharing of fear, gratefulness that she was not, after all, alone. She let herself lean against him for just a moment, just long enough to garner her strength.

They worked together over the next few hours, doing their best to keep Matthew from danger before the doctor finally came trudging up the stairs.

Dr. Cameron's eyes lit up at the sight of Eunice sitting in the chair. As a widower, he obviously appreciated the sight of a comely woman. Introductions over, he turned his attention to his old comrade ensconced among the covers.

"Marsh tells me you met an enemy in the square last evening, my friend. From the looks of all those bandages, the fellow didn't much like the way you tied your cravat."

The duke smiled as he turned his head to face the doctor, but did not reply. Eunice said, "He was given a few drops of laudanum, but that was before dawn. Perhaps the pain has returned."

"Ah, yes, why don't you see to it, Mrs. Wydner, before I stir him up too much."

As Eunice administered the potion, Dr. Cameron sat on the edge of the bed and began examining the injury on the duke's jawline. "Perfectly natural to be more uncomfortable as the day wears on, Standbridge. The body has a way of playing dumb when it's first hurt and now it's beginning to feel again."

He frowned at the sight of the long strip of stitches and turned to Hawksley.

"If I didn't know better, I would swear m'son sewed this up. Who'd you get to do the job?"

Hawksley nodded toward Elizabeth and said, "You remember Elizabeth Wydner."

The doctor's eyes lit up. "Ah. Should have known. Fine young lady, met you in Scotland. Never saw anyone so keen to learn. Had your nose in a book from dawn to dark." He smiled at her as she returned his teasing with a shake of her head. She glanced at Hawksley, pleased to see his sudden frown.

Dr. Cameron unwrapped the bandaged arm and asked, "This bleed a lot?"

Elizabeth answered. "Yes, pretty steadily for some time."

"In beats one after the other?"

"Yes."

As he began wrapping a clean bandage on the arm, he said to Hawksley, "You'd better buy the girl a new hat, m'boy, although she'd probably rather have a subscription to the lending library. If you'd called a leech in, he would have done some serious damage and we might not be smiling this morning."

Dr. Cameron frowned at Elizabeth who stood anxiously at the foot of the duke's bed. "Don't be worrying, m'dear, he's doing fine, just fine. Tell me how you're liking London. M'daughter tells me you had the gentlemen in a tizzy over you at the ball the other night. Just like Scotland with the lads wearing out the door knocker and filling the house with flowers."

She blushed and changed the subject. "The duke has an impressive bump at the base of the neck, Dr. Cameron, and he slept rather heavily after we brought him home."

The doctor slipped his hand behind the duke's head and said to him, "Blessing they hit you where no damage could be done, eh, Standbridge? How's your sight, are you seeing things in twos ere you woke?"

The duke answered in kind, "Not unless I count your chins, Cameron."

The doctor bellowed in laughter. Hawksley looked at Elizabeth, pleased to see her relax and join in the fun.

What a marvelous woman she had become, Hawksley thought. Proud and strong, and damned if she would give an inch. He liked her immensely, and if he could keep resisting the overpowering desire to seduce her, perhaps they could regain the friendship they had begun so long ago in Paxton.

He watched her fidget as Dr. Cameron brought his examination of the duke to a close. He knew she was worried about Matthew's condition, yet hesitated to speak until she knew the duke had gained a full measure of care.

He found himself eager to bring a smile to her face, assuring himself that he would do the same for any young female in his charge. He addressed the doctor, "We have another patient requiring your services, Dr. Cameron. I'm rather anxious for you to look at him."

He watched Elizabeth's face beam with gratefulness as the doctor assured him he would be finished in a minute.

True to his word, the doctor followed them to Matthew's room in a very short time. He and Elizabeth remained just inside the door as the doctor bustled into the room.

Matthew slept heavily, not moving when they entered quietly. Hawksley spoke to the doctor. "Should we let him remain asleep?"

"Not at all, not at all." Dr. Cameron strode quickly to the window and pulled back the draperies. A groan emanated from under the bedcovers, but the doctor ignored it as he opened the window to let the spring air in with the sunlight.

He sat down on the edge of the bed. "Well, now, son, I'm Dr.

Cameron. Let's see this injury of yours." He pulled back the covers with a flip of his hand.

Matthew sat up and pulled his leg away from the doctor's hands, saying fiercely, "Hawksley, if you value our friendship, please take this man away."

The doctor leaned back and nodded his head. "Rightly so, rightly so. You have the ruling of your own limbs, my boy. But I'll tell you right now that I've never removed an arm or leg. Wouldn't know how, if truth be known. Just want to see what's giving you trouble, if that's all right with you."

Matthew looked quickly at Hawksley and when he saw the marquess's nod, he took a deep breath and said, "Very well, then."

Dr. Cameron proceeded to examine the leg, moving his fingers carefully over the entire surface as he watched the young soldier's expression. "Achh," he said as his hands stilled, "here we are."

He looked at Elizabeth and said, "Come look at this, m'girl and let's see what you think."

The look of alarm in Matthew's eyes when he realized Elizabeth was not only in the room, but intended to examine him, was too much for Hawksley to keep a straight face. He turned to Elizabeth to hide his laughter and murmured. "I suppose the sight of a grown man hiding under the covers at your arrival is a familiar sight?"

"Oh, yes," she murmured back, "and hiding in barns and even once up a ladder."

Hawksley's chuckles followed her as she approached the bed. Dr. Cameron said to Matthew, "You remember your sweetheart's cousin, Elizabeth Wydner, don't you, m'boy? She's been in Scotland helping my son with his patients and I want to ask her opinion on this leg of yours."

Elizabeth smiled sweetly at Matthew and added, "We met downstairs, Mr. Stephens. I am sorry you are not feeling well."

Hawksley watched, fascinated as Elizabeth became totally absorbed in the soldier's wound. Without hesitating, she pressed her hand to the area the doctor indicated, then sent her searching fingers on their own expedition of the exposed skin. Without embarrassment, she looked at Matthew and asked, "Does this hurt in a pounding rhythm when you first stand up?"

He frowned, "Why, yes, but—"

"And when it's up on the bed it's better?"

At his nod, she continued, "You're unusually weary—" She broke off as her hand stilled, then, "Does this hurt?"

She nodded as he gasped and she said to Dr. Cameron, "Hot and swollen, but not too deep or we couldn't feel it."

"What d'ye think we should do, lassie?"

"Something's lodged in his leg and its septic. Time's a problem—it should be gotten out immediately. We go through the skin and what little fat the poor boy has—"

"Good. And then . . . "

"Cauterizing as we go to stop the bleeding and pray we don't have to cut too much muscle to remove whatever it is and—"

At the mention of cutting, Matthew drew a startled breath and his leg jerked. Elizabeth broke off their friendly debate over packing the incision with sugar or basilicum, realizing their patient was definitely not enjoying their conversation.

Fascinated as Elizabeth soothed Matthew, Hawksley found himself imagining her as a mother, capable yet tender, fiercely defending her own time with her children against society's demands they be shuttled off to the nursery. He could feel himself being lured into a fantasy of keeping her with him. The woman was a witch. He smiled and scolded himself that he knew that back in Paxton and should have procured a spell to safeguard his heart against such errant nonsense.

He snapped out of his daydream as Dr. Cameron's voice said briskly, "No time like the present, m'girl, no time like the present. I shall be back in no time with a few things we'll need while you prepare the boy."

Elizabeth knocked, then opened Mariane's door, praying fervently that she would find the right words to say to her cousin. She could hear muffled voices in the anteroom.

"Mariane?"

"Yes?" Mariane hurried into the bedroom, a worried frown tightening her lovely features. "Is it Matthew? Is he worse?"

"He is very ill, Mariane. Dr. Cameron has been in to see Matthew and will be back soon to perform a vital surgery on his leg. I have something important to ask you." Mariane nodded eagerly, which might have encouraged Elizabeth if her request was not so unusual. "I want you to come and hold his hand to help him through his ordeal."

Mariane clutched her throat and caught her breath in shock.

Elizabeth knew her request was outrageous, but Matthew would benefit greatly from her presence and it was time Mariane began to grow up.

A choking sound came from the direction of the anteroom and Elizabeth turned to see the abigail storming into the room.

"Absolutely not," Oakes insisted, her thin voice nearing a screech. "I forbid it!"

"Forbid?" Elizabeth tilted her head and stared at the older woman.

Oakes stared back haughtily. "You think to force a young girl to not only enter this soldier's bedchamber, but to remain while the doctor—" Oakes halted as words failed her. She grabbed the turned post of Mariane's bed, her thin fingers curling tightly as she controlled the anger so apparent on her face. "And to continue to ally herself with such a man as this under any circumstances is past enough."

Elizabeth looked at Mariane to see her reaction to Oakes's words. Elizabeth's heart sank as her cousin responded. "I know I should be thinking of Matthew, Elizabeth, but . . . as it is, everyone says I have chosen badly and now to tie myself to . . . " She sent a helpless look toward Oakes.

Impatient to abridge Mariane's confused explanation and determine exactly what her approach should be, Elizabeth turned to the abigail and said, "What exactly is Mariane's dilemma, Oakes?"

Oakes had no difficulty expressing herself, indeed she clearly felt explaining to Elizabeth was an exercise in condescension. As she lifted her chin and drew herself up, she reminded Elizabeth of a bit of laundry being twisted and wrung dry. Her pursed lips spit out the words like pips from an apple.

"Miss Wydner she was very young when she became betrothed to Mr. Stephens, which she did against the advice of Lady Lowden. During the time he has been gone, she has reconsidered her decision and realized that a girl with her advantages and connections can aim higher than a mere landowner with no title."

When Elizabeth did not immediately agree, Oakes sighed and continued, speaking more precisely, as if to a foreigner. "Mr. Stephens has chosen to leave her alone these two years, expecting her to sacrifice her youth and beauty. Then he thoughtlessly comes home in that wretched condition, unkempt and unsightly, looking ready for his deathbed at any minute. Should she be expected to marry such a man with no manners or polish, who would inflict such a distasteful choice upon her?"

What a mull, Elizabeth groaned silently. It would take more than the few moments she had to surmount Oakes's influence. Clever Sylvia to plant her creature in Eunice's household.

Issuing a prayer for forgiveness for lying in her teeth, she said, "Very well, Mariane, let us arrange it thus. I shall help you find your titled husband. In the meantime, you must go through the motions of devotion toward Matthew lest you be condemned as cold and heartless by his family and friends. I imagine the thought of you here waiting for him has given him the will to live, else that wound of his might have left him dying in Portugal."

A little cry of pity escaped Mariane, stirring Oakes to another rousing attack, this time on Elizabeth. "Why the duke lets someone like you run tame in this house, I'll never know. Mrs. Wydner hasn't the courage to say boo to a goose, but she knows what's proper. I shall still put the matter before her this instant."

Mariane stopped the older woman. "Oakes?"

"Yes, Miss Wydner?"

"I know you are overset in my behalf, but we must set something aright at once." Oakes looked quizzically at her young charge, but Mariane continued in the same firm tone. "My mother is the finest woman you and I ever hope to know, and I will not tolerate any misspeaking of her. Because she is shy does not in any way indicate that is a fault. And," said Mariane pointedly, "neither will any criticism be allowed of my cousin."

Elizabeth could see storm clouds gathering on Oakes's face and decided she had no more time for arguments. "Mariane's mother has given her wholehearted approval, Oakes."

Oakes puffed up like a toad. "Very well, then, I shall petition the duke. His Grace will certainly know better. I shall send Marsh to enlighten Lord Standbridge of this wickedness immediately."

Oakes waited for Elizabeth's reaction and when she realized the younger woman was not going to answer, she sniffed and marched out of the bedroom. Elizabeth would liked to have seen Marsh's reaction to such a disturbance of the duke, but she had no time for such entertainment. She went right to the point. "The decision is yours, Mariane."

Mariane reacted just as she had always reacted once she had reached a decision. "What shall I wear?"

Elizabeth smiled, her heart lifting. "Something simple and cheerful."

Mariane moved with surprising efficiency and moments later she called from inside the dressing alcove. "Come and see, Elizabeth. Is this suitable?"

Elizabeth walked to arch of the alcove, pleased at the sweet smile on her cousin's face as she adjusted the high-waisted sash of a simple white dress.

Elizabeth nodded and took Mariane's hands in hers. "This is a serious business, Mariane. Matthew has some bits of shot in his leg. If they are not removed immediately, he may not live. It's a miracle he has made it this far. If I am not mistaken, he drove himself to come home to you and that has been his only thought."

Elizabeth found satisfaction in the tears that sprung to Mariane's eyes. It was past time she saw life from a different angle.

She heard the hall door creak behind her and sensed someone enter the room, but ignored it. It was important that Mariane comprehend why Elizabeth asked this of her.

"Sometimes a man may be close to death and his belief that he is needed or that he has some strong reason for living will overcome that weakness. That is what you must now give to Matthew, Mariane. Think only that he is hurt and he loves you. Forget what Oakes thinks or Lady Lowden or all the hostesses of Almack's. The people we care about are more important than what a room full of strangers think."

At Mariane's slight frown, she persisted, "If you knew no one in town would ever speak to you again, would you turn your back on him and take the chance that he might die?"

She heard the sound of movement behind her and hurried to finish as Mariane's face crumbled in horror at her words. "You may think the worst thing in the world would be to be tied to a man who is not only untitled but might be crippled for the rest of his life, Mariane. But open your mind and give him a chance. You may find that the worst thing in the world might be losing him."

"Elizabeth."

She whirled at the sound of Hawksley's low voice, amazed to find him there when she expected Oakes. His expression was one she had never seen before, serious and determined, as if he had made some great discovery and still pondered over it.

No doubt her words had made him more worried for his friend, and for that she was sorry. However, she knew she had a powerful experience at hand to mature Mariane and bind her to Matthew. If the moments Mariane gave to him did not bring them closer and give her the growth she needed, then they were better off apart.

Hawksley cleared his throat before speaking, "Dr. Cameron is ready for you," he said softly, opening the door fully for them to exit.

Elizabeth motioned to Tarr as they entered the hall and murmured, "Will you bar everyone from Matthew's room, please?"

They slipped into Matthew's room and stood quietly just inside the door.

Chapter Fourteen

H E'D once jumped out of a tree and fallen flat on his back. He hadn't been able to breathe for a long time, just long enough to scare the jumping fool out of him. That's how he felt right now, and all because of the words Elizabeth had just spoken.

"You may find the worst thing in the world may be losing him."

He might actually lose Matthew? The empty feeling that followed made him realize that he had always expected they would be friends into old age. As neighboring boys they had enjoyed wonderful adventures—bruising rides over adjoining fields, inventive pranks, and exhilarating rivalry. Unlike many friends who had grown apart, they still shared the same sense of humor and deep love of the land. The thought of going home to Standbridge and never seeing Matthew—

Then, a more pressing thought pushed forward, and he heard the words again, a little differently this time *". . . the worst thing in the world may be losing her."* Only this time he saw the world without Elizabeth. The despair that followed was surprisingly painful. Elizabeth had always been there as part of his life, even when they were separated.

He recalled scenes from their life together, surprised at the clarity of his memory.

Elizabeth at family gatherings, and his amusement at her childish antics. How she followed him even then and mimicked his every action.

Elizabeth after the death of their parents, and the comfort he felt, but would not admit, from her attempts to protect him "from the monster getting you."

Elizabeth at Paxton, the young girl, so frightened yet determined that he would save Mariane from the dangerous stream. The skinny, red-haired piece of impertinence who fascinated him even as she mocked his attempts to control her. Their camaraderie and shared laughter at how Mariane had outwitted him and foiled their preventive strategy.

Ultimately, Elizabeth's unwanted tears when he sent her away and the pride he felt at her courage and bravado shining through.

Then last night—upon discovering her real identity, he was immediately set at odds—the child he had sworn to protect was now a woman he desired, a beautiful woman who had endured and thrived despite her terrible banishment. Who upon returning, heated his blood as no woman ever had, with whom a simple waltz had aroused his body like the strike of a lightning bolt.

Today, being with her again, she had blasted his solid, purposeful control and turned his emotions into a whirligig spinning out of control. And he couldn't imagine life without her.

He was brought out of his reverie by the laughing voices of the joking pair before them. Matthew lay cheerfully girding himself for what was to come with generous portions of Scotch whisky donated by Dr. Cameron. The jovial doctor sat casually exchanging jests with his patient as if nothing untoward was about to happen. One would think they hadn't a worry between them.

Matthew looked back over his shoulder and said, "What, ho, Hawksley, I b'lieve I'm cured. B'lieve you should send this fellow packing." He grinned cheerfully and twisted his head back to slump comfortably on the pillow. "Send the fellow packing, Hawksley, but tell him to leave his malted quackery here. I b'lieve it's cured me."

Dr. Cameron topped off the soldier's glass and asked, "You were mentioned in the dispatches, lad. Is that where you got this injury?"

"Got shot in m'ankle whilst picking up messages from Old Wellington's French spies. You'll never find that story in the dispatches."

Dr. Cameron perked up at reference to the famous general. "Wellington's spies?"

"Ask Old Nathan there, he's the one who organizes all the . . . sorry, Nathan, forgot myself." He gave Hawksley a sheepish grin and shook his head.

Hawksley waved him on, unable to reprimand his friend.

Matthew cheered up and continued. "Well then, I was on patrol, and slipped away from my companions to pick up a message supposed to be in a hollow oak. Dismounted so I could climb down to a little stream. There I was, off my horse, when a dozen French Ninth Hussars attacked. With their scarlet jackets and their drawn swords flashing in the sun, it's a sight I'll not soon forget."

He sipped from his glass and his voice gathered strength. "Since we were surprised and greatly outnumbered, I yelled warning to my companions to see to themselves. I sent a ball from my pistol at the blasted French who were going to ride over me to get to my companions. Thought I'd lost my balance, but in fact they had shot my foot out from under me, and down the bank I tumbled. I was going at such a good rate, I think I would have rolled through the stream and up the other side, except for the hollow oak. I had been looking for a brown and dying tree, but this one looked strong and healthy. Much healthier than I at this point. The hussars gave up on my men and returned to look for me. The tree was hollow on the stream side and not visible to the French, so in I tumbled."

He laughed and drained his glass, "Found Wellington's message and saved my life in that old tree." Matthew appeared to fall asleep, but carried on with his eyes closed.

"As for my short hospital stay, I heard the surgeon saying that it would have to come off. Wasn't sure if he was talking about me or the fellow next to me. Since he suffered from a head injury, I felt it prudent to have a friend make arrangements to rejoin my regiment which had been ordered home."

The doctor bellowed at that and the rest joined in. Matthew, encouraged by the favorable audience, continued. "He slipped me out, and we suffered a beastly wagon ride to the coast, then caught a cutter carrying dispatches to London."

A melancholy sound crept into his voice. "And now they're going to lop it off after all. Don't b'lieve I'll like that at all."

The doctor laughed aloud. "Not at all, m'boy, not at all. Would we be having the ladies in to hold your hand if we were up to such mischief? Not at all."

Matthew quickly pulled up the covers to his chin and said weakly, "Ladies?"

By this time Elizabeth had seated Mariane near Matthew's shoulder and leaned over to whisper in her young cousin's ear. In a daze, Mariane obediently pulled Matthew's hand into hers and smiled bravely at the inebriated young man. Words were obviously beyond her, but the smile that grew between the two young people not only drew a sigh from Elizabeth, but the doctor as well.

Elizabeth and Dr. Cameron moved to the table to wash their hands and cover their clothing with spotless white aprons from the kitchen. It seemed no time at all before the unpleasantness began.

No stranger to carnage in his secret journeys to war-savaged areas over the past years, Hawksley marveled at how deeply emotion burrowed into his heart when people he cared about were involved. Even Mariane, the foolish little gudgeon, touched him when she bowed over Matthew's head, dripping tears that poured over his face and melded with his.

Elizabeth was similarly affected. Even in her intensity to see to her tasks, she wiped her wet eyes against her shoulder at the sight. As her glance swept from the couple to Hawksley, whose job it was to lend his enormous strength to keep Matthew's body immobile, their eyes met and held. In that instant, something sizzled and clanged, and another link between them cooled, hardened, and fell into place. Similar to the fusion that had so touched and confused him near the stream years ago in Paxton, this bond joined the others.

He looked at her dear face, her freckled nose now dotted with tiny drops of perspiration. He wondered if she was privy to his thoughts, for she blushed and looked away.

"Well, aren't we doing just fine, m'boy," Dr. Cameron crowed as he wrapped a bandage around his patient's leg. Since Matthew had long since fallen into blessed unconsciousness, the good doctor needed no answer. He smiled broadly at his confederate whose white face wore a weaker smile than his own. The silence in the room didn't seem to worry him, though, as he stood and stretched, then reached for Matthew's bottle and drained it.

That seemed to break the silence and true smiles broke out on each person's face. The doctor picked up a dish and rattled the bits of metal, saying to Elizabeth, "Put these in a bottle for the boy. He'll want to show them to his grandchildren. Fine specimens of the Frenchies' handiwork."

*   *   *

"Elizabeth."

Hawksley's voice brought her awake. She opened her eyes and saw flickering candlelight. She turned her head just as Hawksley slipped in her room and closed the door behind him. She sat up, instantly worried. "Grandfather? Matthew? What's wrong, Nathan?"

"They're fine, Elizabeth. I need to talk to you before I leave."

She took a hurried appraisal—roughly dressed in dark riding gear, he was obviously just on his way out. She glanced at the mantel clock. It was four in the morning. Her heart began to pound in a heavy, dreading cadence. In her fear, every question spun away, leaving her silent as Hawksley sat on the edge of her bed and spoke.

"The Traitor has struck again. We have just received word that his contacts on the Continent have been systematically killed. He has obviously directed his henchmen to destroy all traces of his spy network and he's preparing to go to ground. Before he does that, we believe he will target his enemies as well."

"Will he try our family again?"

"Grandfather is convinced that he will save him for last, but we leave you heavily guarded. He struck Forster and Wiggel at their country homes today and Woolfe and I are on our way to contact others who are in outlying areas."

As he told the tale, Elizabeth clutched at the counterpane. "Will you take guards, Nathan? What if you meet him and he tries to kill you again?"

Hawksley's voice took on a grim note. "That is exactly what we hope to do, Elizabeth, find him in places where we know he will strike."

She knew that the Traitor was unquestionably, frighteningly in her future, but had somehow thought she would be the one to encounter him—not Nathan. She tried to concentrate, to see if she could sense a vision from her Monster. She opened her mind and waited, sending out searching tendrils. Nothing, no color, no emotion of any kind. She put her next thought into words.

"What can I do?"

Hawksley hesitated, clearly resistant to ask her help. "We haven't talked about your ability to hear people's thoughts."

"Not the most popular topic of conversation between us."

His face relaxed into a smile. "Remember when I asked you to stop delving into other people's minds?"

"Demanded, you mean?" She was stalling, knowing what he meant to ask her.

"Hmmm," he agreed absently. "I suppose you ignored me as usual?"

"Oh, Nathan, this is terrible. You need me to try to find him by listening, and I am not sure I can anymore. I have spent the last four years schooling myself not to."

She could feel his disappointment. Finally, he said, "How on earth did you do it?"

"Concentration—counting, reading, learning difficult things."

"Like medicine," he mused. She nodded, remembering the added difficulty of learning languages.

"Can you revive it? Do you hear nothing at all?"

She was grateful for the dim light, for she could feel a blushing heat glow in her face as she remembered Hawksley's lusty thoughts of her while she danced at the ball. She tried to explain. "Sometimes something will break through. Mostly, it's like music in the background at a party, you don't really hear it."

"Why did you turn it off?" Curiosity edged Hawksley's words.

She hesitated, realizing that the answer was no longer simple. "It distressed me as I grew older and understood more. When I went to Scotland it seemed even more important."

"If it still distresses you, Elizabeth, perhaps I shouldn't ask it of you. However, our situation is crucial."

With a pain in her heart and a sinking dread for her future, she said cheerfully, "Shall I practice on you?"

"No," he growled, a touch of embarrassment in his voice. He stood and paced to her window, then back again. "I don't know how long we shall be gone. If you can revive your skills, it may be our last chance. Tarr has been commissioned to guard you with his life. Keep him with you at all times and in the meantime, see what you can do by practicing on other people. If Woolfe and I cannot find our man in the next few days, we'll come back and tour every social event we can pack into each day. Do whatever you must to get ready for a busy social life."

He sat down again, changing the subject. "If anything happens to me, both Woolfe and Tarr have strict orders to take you and the other ladies to a place of safety. Guards will remain here with

Matthew and Grandfather. You are to forget the Traitor, Elizabeth. Let the others worry about him." When she opened her mouth to object, he said, "I'll have your promise on that, Elizabeth."

Finally she nodded, her mind dwelling in agony on the danger to Hawksley. Her eyes were full of tears and her throat burned with the effort of not weeping.

"There's something remaining for me to say, Elizabeth."

Once more she nodded. It took her a moment to realize he had spoken again. "I would like to hope you could forgive me."

She blinked away her tears, confused at his words. "Forgive you?"

"For sending you to Scotland the way I did with no explanation. If I could undo it, I would, but I'd like to go tonight knowing that you no longer think of me with anger."

"Dear God," she whispered, knowing that forgetting his selfish cruelty was near to impossible. Yet, how could she let him go without some assurance from her? She tried to frame words that would be as honest as possible, carefully not looking at him lest she weaken.

"When you rescued Mariane, I was so grateful that you believed me, that you did not seem to hate me for having that terrible curse in my life. I thought we would be friends, that I wouldn't be so lonely, that I would have someone to talk to—I couldn't have been more mistaken."

He watched her carefully, a frown beginning to tense his features once more. She only wanted to hurry and tell him how she felt.

"What you did was terrible, Nathan. You tore me away from my family. No discussion, no asking if I wanted it. You came, didn't like what you saw, and threw me away."

She rushed to finish. "You didn't have to bring me to London, you could have at least left me in Paxton where I had no chance to shame the family."

There, she had finished spitting out her diatribe, and she was instantly ashamed of herself, to have indulged her anger so. She should have lied and said she forgave him.

When he didn't speak, she looked up at him. She thought she knew all his expressions, but the sorrow she found in his eyes was totally foreign. Finally he spoke, his voice shaken. "I did not throw you away for fear you would shame the family, Elizabeth. I sent you away for fear of your safety."

She straightened up, astonished at his words. He nodded and continued. "You had just proven that your dreams come true—and in your dream about our parents, you attacked the monster. Remember when you described your monster's knife? I recognized it as belonging to my Traitor. I knew you were in danger."

Thoughts tumbled over each other inside her head like little pieces of colored glass. As each new combination of possibilities presented itself, her conception of the last four years took on a different hue. One question took precedence. "Why did you not explain?"

He growled. "I should have told a child that her monster was real and had murdered her parents—that he would cheerfully slit her throat for a moment's entertainment?" His voice softened. "That was one choice. The other was to let you hate me. I chose the one that seemed less traumatic for you."

She looked at him warily. If she let her anger go, she would have to trust him again, to open the possibility of pain from him once more.

He shrugged his enormous shoulders. "In those days, I thought I had the answer to everything, Elizabeth. I was an arrogant young fool. I should have sent your family with you or set a dozen guards on Paxton to safeguard you. Instead I thought it would only be a few weeks before I caught the Traitor and could bring you home"—he laughed cynically—"on a white charger."

He reached for her hands, and when she tried to snatch them away, he held tightly. She was somehow grateful.

His voice was fierce now and dark with an emotion she could not identify. "Elizabeth, tell me what you are thinking. Is there no hope that we can ever be friends? Can you not even trust that I'm telling the truth?"

"Oh, Nathan, how can I explain? You must understand that I have spent the last four years protecting myself against you, building a wall so strong that you could never hurt me again. I trust you with my life—if you blindfolded me near a cliff and told me to walk forward, I would not hesitate. But," she said carefully, "if you promised never to reject me again, I would be afraid to believe you. It's not a lack of trust, Nathan, it's fear."

He sat without moving, as if her words were beyond his understanding. The silence was a living thing, painful to them both.

Then he curved his palm around her cheek, moving it down to lift her chin. He looked deeply into her eyes, and she could only look back helplessly, unable to give him what he wanted.

She knew he sensed that no words could bring her any closer to him, could make the barrier between them any less. She, too, wished he could find the magic words that would bring back the enchantment of Paxton, but he was too wise to try. Instead, he asked for something she could grant him.

"Promise me, Elizabeth, if I return, that you will not leave me until you have given me a chance to make it right. That you will not run away like a child, but that you will stay like the woman, the healer that you are."

He brought her hands to his cheek and she welcomed the caress. It seemed to infuse some new strength and truth into her.

"Perhaps we shall never have more than we have now, my dearest Elizabeth, but what we have is too sweet not to fight for. Will you promise me? A solemn promise?"

She managed a watery smile and made her vow. "A solemn promise."

He stood, letting her hand fall onto the bed. Never taking his eyes from her, he went to the door. "Then, God bless, Elizabeth. I'll—"

She couldn't stand it. She flung back the covers and ran to him. She threw her arms around his solid chest and held him tightly. "I'll have a promise from you now, Nathan. You will not endanger yourself in some heroic attempt to capture the Traitor. I'd rather you fail."

He pulled her arms from around him and her heart fell, sure that he was appalled by her emotional raving. When she saw his face, she changed her mind.

His eyes were dark, almost black, looking at her with a hunger akin to obsession. His mouth moved toward hers as his strong hands slid into her hair and curled around her neck. His lips were warm as they briefly touched hers. A tremor of sensation radiated out from that tentative connection, spreading throughout her body like wildfire while the entire world spun into one aching need for more.

She could have cried with the beauty of his second touch, so hot now, so welcome. His lips molded to hers, moving sensuously, almost tasting her if such a thing was possible. She had always known that mouth, the flavor, the scent of his heated skin.

He buried his face into her hair, then kissed her forehead, her cheeks, then he shifted to seek her lips from another angle, touching, lifting, shifting, and beginning all over again.

"Open," he commanded and she obeyed without really knowing what he asked. His hand moved to hold the back of her head and turned her face to accommodate his new desire. This kiss found its resting place, slanted perfectly to explore and conquer. His tongue touched the corner of her mouth and she felt a lightning bolt shock both of them.

She murmured and he laughed into her mouth and they both moved closer, seeking to renew the warmth. He explored each crevice of her lips, then moved inward, marking every soft curve and hollow as his.

He groaned and one arm curved across her shoulders to pull her closer. She melted into the embrace without a protest, mewling soft whimpers as the world narrowed and centered on the touch and taste of this one man.

She felt his fingers explore her neck and shoulders, slowly as if committing each curve to memory. When his palm curved over her breast, she trembled at the pleasure of it.

He shuddered, then stopped his wonderful foray.

"Madness," he groaned, and withdrew slowly, softening the blow of separation, turning passion into comfort, kisses into an embrace, and ending it as it began, with her tight against his chest.

Her thoughts reeled as she sought to gain control. She could barely open her eyes, so drugged did she feel, so limp with the emotion that she could now identify as passion. Dear God, if this was the weapon used, no wonder so many innocents were ruined.

He picked her up and carried her to the bed, pulling the covers up to her chin in a brisk manner. A smile played around his lips for a moment before he left her with a soft, enigmatic pronouncement. "Know this, Elizabeth. I never throw anything of value away."

As she lay awake, the dreamy side of her brain wondering how soon they could engage in that particularly interesting exercise again while the practical side argued that it had never happened, that she had fallen and hit her head and went a little loony for a moment, she was convinced she would not sleep all night.

In truth, she slept soundly for the first time in days. She awakened refreshed, with the sun streaming into her bedroom as Sally brought her toast and chocolate, clucking about their visitor. "Lady Lowden is here and Marsh is hiding in the kitchen."

Chapter Fifteen

"LADY Lowden is downstairs? Where are Mariane and Eunice? Has the doctor been here this morning?" She pulled back the bedclothes and sat up. "Why did you let me sleep so late?"

Sally looked at her mistress in surprise. Elizabeth knew she was acting like a wind chime in a storm, but it rattled her to awaken completely out of control like this. She wanted desperately to think about Hawksley for a few private moments. She needed to attend Grandfather and Matthew. Moreover, not only must she now look over her shoulder for fear of the Traitor every minute while hurriedly buying a wardrobe, she had to find a way to eavesdrop into other people's minds. She wanted to scream.

Sally handed Elizabeth her cup of chocolate with an admonitorial flourish. Elizabeth obediently took a sip while Sally ticked off her answers. "Mrs. Wydner and Mariane are dressing now to receive Lady Lowden. Tarr took her ladyship to the parlor and I let you sleep late because Lord Hawksley left orders with the footmen downstairs that no one was to disturb you before ten of the clock." At this pronouncement, Sally said in a teasing manner, "Very kind of his lordship to be worrying about your sleeping habits, miss."

Elizabeth's hand froze and the chocolate sloshed in the cup. What was wrong with Hawksley, had he no sense of propriety? Did he not think what the servants would deduct from his too-personal request? By now the entire staff had them engaged—or something less respectable. She lowered her face to hide a heated blush, only to find that she had dripped chocolate on her nightgown. This was not a good morning.

Deliberately ignoring it, she reached for her toast, trying for a casual, unaffected tone. "I must wash quickly, Sally. If Lady Lowden corners Eunice, she will make her miserable."

This time Sally's knowing smile engulfed her face. "His lordship has ordered a bath. As soon as you finish eating, it will be brought in."

Elizabeth moaned and consumed the rest of her breakfast in mortified silence. Just like Hawksley to give such outrageous orders, ignoring completely the embarrassment she would endure.

Thirty minutes later she left her room and hurried down the stairs. Blast Hawksley. Even the footmen were giving her amused looks this morning. She longed for a peaceful moment in which to make her plans; instead, she must deal with Lady Lowden's screeching voice now catapulting from the floor below her.

"What do you mean, the duke is not receiving? I demand you take me to him immediately."

Eunice's soft voice murmured words Elizabeth could not understand. Lady Lowden's voice vaulted upward again. "I do not care if he has cut off both hands and feet. If he has ears to hear me and a tongue to answer, that will be sufficient. He has allowed an innocent girl to be placed in an impossible position right under his nose, and I want it stopped this instant. If he can spend the day talking to you, he can certainly spend a few minutes listening to me."

Upon Elizabeth's entrance into the parlor, Sylvia turned and directed her fury on her. "How dare you put my baby into such a compromising situation? I spent the better part of an hour cooling my heels in this parlor yesterday afternoon while my baby was enduring . . . enduring—"

Elizabeth reeled at the blast of words. She was searching for a rejoinder when Eunice interrupted her sister. "Your baby?"

Lady Lowden's face, glowing with anger, whitened momentarily, but like a maddened bull, she turned to attack Eunice. "I have often wondered why the Lord saw fit to bless you with a beautiful, spirited child like Mariane. You can surely see that she's more like me than you. You only wish to waste your days with flowers and those endless drawings. Why, if you should walk into Almack's, no one there would recall your name."

The sisters looked at each other in silence, Sylvia still indignant and Eunice beautifully calm. Sylvia, sure she had summarily disposed of all objections, lifted her chin and said to Eunice, "Well, sister, take me to him."

Eunice answered her without hesitation, her words uncompromising. "Sylvia, do not ask me again. I will not let you disturb the duke."

Then an expression of compassion for Sylvia flashed briefly across Eunice's sweet face as she spoke to her sister. "As for Mariane, you must remember, Sylvia, that she is my child. I have shared her with you so you might not miss the joy of motherhood. As a result, she is indeed a lot like you—fearless and spirited— and that pleases me. Now, however, she must be left alone to make a decision that will affect her entire life, and neither of us need interfere. Yesterday she had my blessing to attend her betrothed and, save a few understandable tears in the circumstances, she has not been injured by the experience."

Sylvia stared at her, openmouthed. Eunice added a final bit of advice. "As for Elizabeth, she is my brother's child and my beloved niece. I find no fault with her or her actions, nor do Lord Hawksley or His Grace. I am sure this has all been a misunderstanding and we shall forget it."

Elizabeth couldn't believe what she was hearing. Eunice standing firm against Sylvia? She exchanged glances with her aunt, indicating her approval. The interchange gave her the impetus to inform Sylvia of her own plans, for she intended to avail herself of the formidable woman's expertise as fashion adviser no matter that the woman was an *ogre extraordinaire*. Hawksley was counting on her.

"Lady Lowden, I assure you that Mariane can only have benefitted from her kindness to Matthew and at this minute is cheerfully dressing to tour the shops with us."

"Us?" Sylvia shrunk back, her manner appalled.

Elizabeth pressed forward, ignoring Sylvia's reaction. "Mariane wishes me to accompany her in her reentry into society. Indeed, I have relayed the idea to His Grace and to Lord Hawksley and they have been most enthusiastic about how beneficial your mentoring would be. The duke was especially concerned that I commit no *faux pas* to shame the family."

"Surely Mariane will not expect—"

"You may ask her yourself," Elizabeth said, realizing how cleverly Sylvia had pinpointed the weak point of her plan. "However, Lord Hawksley also wishes—"

"Wishes her to be in the forefront of fashion," Eunice said smoothly, "And for that we will be grateful to you, Sylvia."

Mariane's cheerful voice sang out as she sailed through the

door. "Good morning, isn't it a wonderful day?" Oakes trailed behind, obviously not sharing Mariane's enthusiastic mood.

Sylvia turned toward the young girl and a bright smile spread across her face. "Oh, my dear Mariane, how can you be so brave when you have suffered so?"

Mariane looked startled and confused, then realization struck. As with an infant who has fallen softly and doesn't begin crying until she sees the anxious face of her mother, so with Mariane. A mask of martyrdom furrowed her brow and puckered her perfect mouth.

Elizabeth knew not whether to laugh or cry, but it was clear that Eunice's warning had not penetrated, and the battle was on. Elizabeth turned slightly away from the others to speak privately to Mariane. "Whatever you do, don't give Lady Lowden any details or we'll spend the morning burning feathers under her nose."

Mariane blinked at Elizabeth, then giggled, losing her tragic slump in an instant. Elizabeth reached up to Mariane's brow as if to straighten a strand of hair and said sotto voice, "Behave, you scamp."

Perplexed, Sylvia watched the interchange with her mouth open in mid-word, then looked to Oakes who seemed equally uneasy.

Only momentarily thwarted, Sylvia proceeded to disentangle Elizabeth from the morning's activities. "Mariane, Oakes and I have planned quite a limited shopping expedition this morning. Elizabeth has offered to join us, but do you not feel that—"

Eunice interrupted her sister's flow of words. "Sylvia, if you feel that the burden of dressing two girls is too difficult, I shall be happy to take them myself."

The room fell silent. Had Eunice begun frothing at the mouth, no one could have been more surprised. Mariane recovered first and turned her enthusiasm toward Eunice. "Oh, pooh, Aunt Sylvia could dress ten girls without thinking about it. But, Mother, come with us anyway. It would be marvelous fun and you could buy something for yourself. It has been ages since you shopped."

Elizabeth joined in. "Do come, Auntie. I'll have Sally look after the duke and Matthew."

Eunice dithered and protested, but in the end she relented. When all was resolved and the group congregated in the ground floor hall, Sylvia cut her losses with a toss of her head and led the way to the waiting carriage—where another surprise awaited her.

Pulled up behind Sylvia's barouche stood the duke's enormous coach. Tarr stood at attention near the coach door and two guards stood alertly on the platform board over the hind axle tree. "Miss Elizabeth," he said, "Lord Hawksley left orders for your transportation."

Alert to a strange tone in Tarr's voice, she looked closer at the faithful guard. Tarr's mobile face gleamed with amusement. Elizabeth quickly glanced at the two guards whose faces wore the solemnity due their stations but whose eyes echoed the merriment in Tarr's.

Be calm, Elizabeth, she told herself. This is serious business and you must accept the security with gratitude. However, she argued, Hawksley's new overconcern for her needs had provided the servants with a little too much entertainment for her comfort.

As Tarr ushered the three older ladies into the coach, Elizabeth asked Mariane, "Do you think your mother has felt left out before but wouldn't admit it, Mariane? It was very rag mannered of us to have left her home on our last outing. We should have overcome her objections then."

"Oh, Elizabeth, I'm surprised she even came today. She is having a wonderful time with His Grace and Dr. Cameron. They are both flirting outrageously and Matthew has adopted her. You know she loves to fuss over people. She's going to spoil our children excessively."

Elizabeth held her breath, wondering if Mariane realized what she had just said. She laughed softly, she couldn't help it. "Mariane, admit it, we'll have to drag you both out of the nursery to come to meals."

After they were all seated and the four horses began trotting down the cobbled street, Elizabeth initiated her plan. "Now, Mariane, you and Lady Lowden need to educate me on the dos and don'ts of London society."

I need a tally stick, Elizabeth thought, or a clerk to keep an account of who is winning in this verbal deluge. All I did was proclaim my ignorance of fashion and manners and now I am drowning in a sea of advice.

"Please, Miss Wydner, stand still. For the warm days, the chemise in fine cotton and when the chill is in the air, the flannel." The modiste's assistant pulled the almost sheer, low-necked garment over her head. "Just so," she said, straightening it at the knees.

"One does not speak of legs." Oakes interrupted as if no one else was speaking. "If one must, the word 'limbs' may be used." Aunt Sylvia had circumvented having anything to do with Elizabeth by allowing Oakes to tutor the upstart, and this after a heated interchange while huddled in the anteroom of Madame Bernice's establishment.

Mariane took up where Oakes left off, choosing her own cheerful subject. "The gentlemen who dance with you will send flowers and come calling the next morning."

"Stays," the seamstress announced, as if Elizabeth had never heard of them. Elizabeth did find, however, that the London stays were more comfortable and designed to enhance rather than simply hold firm. "Here, we push up without wadding, for miss's bosom is bountiful. At the waist we pull tight, and lower we must decide yes or no to padding, for the hips are too slender. Next, petticoats, then we begin."

Elizabeth moaned inwardly. "Next we begin?" When was she ever to try out her mind-reading skills? With all this chaos, how was she to concentrate on the Traitor? The man could walk by the shop and she wouldn't notice him with all the clucking going on. Of course, with three hulking guards obviously dogging their every step, the Traitor would soon scuttle off looking for weaker prey.

Oakes ignored the modiste and persisted, obviously relishing the opportunity to reveal Elizabeth's ignorance. "One, dancing with a man more than twice in an evening is tantamount to being considered fast or a signal of an impending betrothal."

Elizabeth looked to Mariane to verify this and Mariane nodded and sent back a look that said, "now you know what I went through when I made my come out."

Oakes continued. "Two, one goes nowhere without a chaperone. Three, a lady does not really eat in public. Instead, she may daintily pick at small portions. And, four, a lady does not discuss topics outside her own realm lest she be condemned as a bluestocking."

So much for her studies of language and science, Elizabeth thought, and murmured to Mariane, "Which part of midwifing do you suppose my admirers would enjoy discussing?"

Mariane exclaimed, "Elizabeth!" and quickly turned away, her shoulders shaking as she appeared utterly absorbed in a copy of *The Lady's Magazine*.

Elizabeth and Eunice deferred to Mariane's opinions when choosing, thereby gathering back to them some of the closeness they had enjoyed years ago when the girls had planned to take London by storm. Hope for Mariane rose within Elizabeth as they trudged from shop to shop, Mariane excitedly suggesting items and Elizabeth gratefully agreeing. Challenged to include some color to counter the requisite white that Sylvia and Oakes insisted unmarried girls wore, they found breathtaking blends of colors in Norwich and paisley shawls, ribands in every shade, and outrageous hats that brought more giggles from Mariane and dark looks from their chaperones.

An uneasy feeling came over Elizabeth as they approached Gunter's, where Mariane promised Elizabeth "the most heavenly ices and pastries." As they alighted from the coach at the sign of the pineapple that signified a confectioner's shop, she looked quickly around—no sinister-looking characters followed them, no other coaches stopped nearby.

Perhaps it was a feeling emanating from her two antagonists. Upon examination, she realized they were tense and edgy, yet pleased with themselves. Sylvia's expression reeked anticipation. What could she be planning? She followed Sylvia's glance over the crowd outside the shop and found only lighthearted customers who loitered while waiters rushed back and forth taking orders. Young men lounged against railings entertaining young misses who smiled sweetly in open carriages. It was a pretty, cheerful sight, not unlike a picnic.

Mariane's enthusiastic chatter carried them up to the door of the shop where, indeed, they enjoyed the wonderful aroma of the promised pastries. The ducal coach had garnered instant attention and they were ushered to a table near a window. As they gave their delectable choices to the waiter, Elizabeth decided that she had delayed far too long in opening up her mind.

Using the strength of will she had developed to close the images and sounds in Scotland, she concentrated and bid her mental barriers open. Praying she would have the courage to withstand it all again, she shuddered nervously as the flow began.

It was like turning on the spigot at a pump, spitting and choking at first, then bursting out in a hurried rush. A painful experience, she thought, how did I ever stand it.? Not only could she hear the vocal sounds, but overlaid were the private noises—the former assaulting her ears and the latter laying siege to her brain.

Desperately, she started counting. Six chairs at the table, nine panes in the window, twenty-six letters in the advertisement overhead, four spots of something orange on the waiter's apron. Gradually she could begin to think coherently.

This was not going to work. Not at this rate, and not if she could not devise some method of filtering. Hesitantly, she turned the noise back on and tried to concentrate only on one person's thoughts.

She chose as target the two gentlemen at a neighboring table and was amazed at what she heard. A distinguished older man had graciously accepted the younger gentleman's refusal of his invitation to join him at Scott's Gaming Establishment. Inwardly, however, he was furious and determined to convince him. The older man was in trouble with the money lenders and needed the fee he earned by bringing gullible customers there to gamble. The urge to lean over and warn the young man was so strong she had to grip the edge of the table to restrain herself.

No matter how distressing what she heard might be, she told herself, it was working. Encouraged, she looked to the other side and heard the trembling excitement of a woman who had just learned she was *enceinte*. The woman was silent, but terrified. Elizabeth's heart softened and she turned to Mariane. "Who is that lady in the green sprigged muslin dress?"

Mariane followed her gaze, thought for a second, then said, "That's Lord Copley's youngest. This is her first season."

"She is not married or betrothed?"

Mariane shook her head and said, "Have you met, does she look familiar?" Elizabeth shook her head, swallowing hard, fighting an ache of sadness for the young woman.

Just then another jolt of emotion broke through from another source. Startled, she looked at Sylvia.

Sylvia had almost risen from her seat in excitement as she looked out of the window. She glanced at Oakes who in turn found something of great interest outside. A picture from Sylvia came into Elizabeth's thought, that of Lord Stanley, the obnoxious gentleman they had come to London to avoid, Mariane's unwelcome suitor from Paxton.

Lord Stanley? Sylvia knew him?

A large group entered Gunter's just then. Elizabeth was not

surprised to see Lord Stanley emerge from among them. The plot became clearer when an older lady of the group hurried to Lady Lowden and gushed, "What a surprise it is to find you here!"

She leaned closer to Eunice and murmured, "Watch, Auntie. Sylvia and Lord Stanley's mother are bosom beaus and have obviously cooked up this entire scheme to unite the children."

It was like watching your favorite hat blow away, Elizabeth thought with dismay, hopping and jumping at the whim of the erratic, fickle gusts of air. Mariane was soon enveloped by Lord Stanley and his entourage, the young elite of the *ton*. Made over and puffed up by all the attention, she couldn't resist. Soon invitations were issued, plans were made, and Eunice and Elizabeth were skillfully culled from the crowd by Lady Lowden and sent to their coach with the day's purchases.

In a fit of temper, Elizabeth marched back into the shop, minced over to the young man who was about to be fleeced by his companion, and said in a simper, "My dear, I thought it was you." When the young man turned red and tried to place her, she leaned forward and said into his ear, "I was so impressed by your cleverness in saying no to your companion. A friend of mine with far less town bronze than you lost his entire quarter's allowance before he found that this villain is paid to bring young men to Scott's." She curtseyed and said, "Give my love to your mother." She glanced at the young lady in regret, her inventive mind already concocting a scheme of assistance.

Later at home, Elizabeth defended her cousin. "Give Mariane credit, Auntie, the poor beleaguered girl tried to include us, but she was no match for Lord Stanley's mother and Sylvia."

Eunice added, "Nor were we."

"What shall we do, Auntie? We were thoroughly routed."

Eunice seemed to gather herself together, like a boxing champion Elizabeth had once watched. "First of all, I shall cease feeling sorry for my childless sister and giving her carte blanche with Mariane. Then I suppose we should use our own weapon."

At Elizabeth's curious stare, Eunice explained. "Matthew. We shall give her a good healthy dose of love."

Chapter Sixteen

EARLY-MORNING light filtered into the room as Sally opened the curtains. "Good morning, Miss Elizabeth, did you sleep well?"

Elizabeth stirred, tried to lift her head from the pillow, and fell back in defeat. She was losing her mind. There was no other explanation.

"I'll just leave the tray, miss, and be back with your bath." The teasing smile she was beginning to hate lingered on Sally's pert lips. Blast Nathan. Blast the Traitor. Blast Lord Stanley. Blast all men. And especially blast her dream lover.

A phantom figure had come to her two nights ago in the middle of the night. He sat and watched her sleep, occasionally touching her hair or kissing her brow. Last night he had lain beside her, caressing her until he began to take liberties that had awakened her instantly.

Both times she had quickly searched the room, sure a real person had visited her. The second night she had taken the precaution of locking her door, and when she later looked for the culprit, she found her key still in the lock. It couldn't have been Hawksley, her first suspect, for not only would that gentleman have scorned anonymity, he probably would have slammed the door on his way out. Well, never again, she vowed, if she must stay awake for the rest of her life!

Not that it was easy to fall asleep. Somehow during the active part of the day, it was easier to keep the fear for Nathan at arm's length. Dear Eleanore cleverly organized an agenda that Mariane found irresistible. They toured the newly opened Egyptian Hall, then jaunted off to view the Elgin Marbles. Mariane's open delight in Astley's Amphitheater was fun to watch. Indeed, they were all enthralled with the enormous arena filled with hilarious clowns and amazing feats of horsemanship.

However, at night when Elizabeth tried to compose herself for sleep, her toes wiggling in tune to her unleashed thoughts, every possible danger to Hawksley grew in her imagination. She wanted to force Tarr to take every man in the house to go safeguard him, not that Tarr would admit he knew where Nathan had gone. Lying safely in her bed at night was the hardest work she had ever done.

Woolfe had returned last night, frightening her speechless until he explained that the plan had always been that he and Nathan would split up into two groups, the better to cover a larger area. He retired, grim-lipped, refusing to discuss anything else with her until Nathan's return.

Even listening to the emotional outpourings of strangers was maddening. She could not seem to find a *steady* method to listening to her neighbors' thoughts. At first she smugly assumed she was in control of whose thoughts she heard, turning her attention here and there at will. As a refining process emerged, she realized that she might concentrate her power toward one person with great success, yet toward another and hear only silence.

So what good would she be to Nathan when he returned? She might stand shoulder-to-shoulder with the Traitor and not know it. For this vital job she must be able to hold the reins of her power with a delicate touch, with the finesse of a glass blower and the power of a blacksmith.

Only two things had the power to distract her. Watching Mariane bounce back and forth between Matthew and Lord Stanley and the hilarious courting of Aunt Eunice by Dr. Cameron and the duke. There, she thought, just what she needed this morning, a distraction.

She made short work of her morning ablutions and went in search of a little entertainment. A moment later she opened Matthew's door a crack and said, "Hello. May I come in?"

Dr. Cameron's voice boomed out, "Come in, come in. Just in time to see our boy take his maiden voyage, so to speak."

Elizabeth cried out in alarm when she took in the scene. Matthew was standing, one arm around the doctor's shoulders and the other on his cane. In an enveloping dressing gown that must belong to the duke or Hawksley, he looked thinner than ever, and certainly unfit for such an adventure.

"Do not worry, dear lady, the boy insists we get him up and moving. Says he saw too many men lie down and die, whereas the ones who kept going fared better." He winked at her and she relaxed.

Matthew stepped forward, carefully using his injured leg as he leaned heavily on the cane. Steadily he went, wincing with every step. Sweat broke out on his face, but he reached the window where he rested his forehead against the cool glass, then he turned and rested again.

"Stop if you are in such pain," Elizabeth begged him.

He grinned at her and said, "It's not my leg so much, Miss Wydner, I've a terrible head from the doctor's Scotch whisky." Then, to the sound of the doctor's chuckles, he traversed the room back again.

He had almost reached the bed when the door creaked open and Mariane slipped into the room. "Mother said that Matthew had been asking for me—" Her eyes opened wide at the scene before her.

"Oh," she said angrily to the doctor, "how could you be so cruel? Let him back in bed this instant!"

Every eyebrow in the room raised in surprise, but the doctor recovered first, saying in a servile voice, "Yes, miss, as you wish."

Matthew was right behind him in cleverness, and moaned pitifully as the doctor arranged him beneath the covers. As Mariane flew to Matthew's bedside, Dr. Cameron winked once more at Elizabeth.

Elizabeth was slow to recover from the shock of what she had witnessed. She had seen Mariane play the virago many times in Paxton, but then only in her own selfish interests. She was further shocked when Mariane flung an order at her. "Elizabeth, watch the stairs and warn me if Oakes comes up. I'll love you forever if you can send her on some lengthy errand and keep her out of my way."

Elizabeth sent Oakes to Hatchard's with instructions to purchase a twenty-two-year-old book, *Vindication of the Rights of Woman*, insinuating that the request came from Lady Lowden. As she walked back toward her room, she heard giggling down the hall. Curious, she followed the sound to one of the back bedrooms. There, leaning against the two windows that overlooked the back garden, were three maids, Tarr, and a footman. They turned at her entrance and scattered, curtsying and begging her pardon. All save Tarr who motioned her forward to look for herself.

"This is better than a play, miss. You'll not want to miss it."

She looked downward into the garden. Her attention was drawn to the espaliered fruit trees covering the garden walls and the hedges of lilac. Her eyes followed a path to where she finally found two people sitting near a round pool in the center of the garden. "Dr. Cameron and my aunt in the garden?"

"Yes, miss. Well, the real problem is not the doctor and Mrs. Wydner in the garden. It's His Grace, the duke. You know how the doctor has been getting him up every day to walk to the water closet?"

"I expect the entire house has heard his bellowing objections."

"Doesn't it strike you as curious that the duke would want to be lying about, him being so proud of his energy and strength?"

"I'm afraid I haven't been around him for the past few years, Tarr."

"He's playing possum, miss. To get Mrs. Wydner to sit with him and fuss, so to speak."

"He's malingering?"

"I don't know about that, miss, but he's strong as a workhorse and has been keeping Mrs. Wydner from going out with the doctor by his goings on."

"I see. And what is it we are looking at now?"

"Dr. Cameron has finally convinced Mrs. Wydner to show him the garden, her loving flowers like she does. When the duke found out, he got up out of bed and stomped down the stairs to break it up."

"Oh, no. We must stop him." She turned to run to the duke's aid.

Tarr's amused voice stopped her. "Easy, miss, here he comes now. See if you think he needs someone."

She turned back to the window and looked down. The duke strode heartily down the stairs and around the graveled path until he spotted the errant couple. When Eunice saw him and rushed forward, he slowed and reached for her as if he needed help.

Elizabeth said in amazement. "The old faker." A smile spread across her face and a laugh rose up to join it.

"Never a dull moment here, miss."

They laughed together. Elizabeth felt better already.

Her dream lover lowered himself to the edge of her bed, his black velvet dressing gown a shocking contrast against her lace coverlet. Making no effort to move closer, he reached across the expanse between them and stroked her loose hair. Down his fingers slid, letting her tangled locks fall across the back of his strong fingers, down still further until they came to her shoulder. His warm hand curved around her neck and slipped under her loose bed gown, then across her back and around her shoulder, forcing the gown to give way to his direction.

He smiled at her as her breathing quickened, and without freeing her gaze from his, his clever fingers pulled at the ties that held the front of her gown together.

Once more his hand began a slow exploration, this time torturing her as his fingers moved across her breast, lightly marking his claim. Then he stopped as he reached the peak to capture the sensitive flesh between two fingers and tugged, as if bidding her surrender to him. A cry escaped her lips, for she could not give herself to him, and yet she longed to . . .

She awoke with a start, crossing her arms protectively across her bosom. "Oh, no," she cried, "not again." She leapt from the warm bed, hurried to the open window that overlooked the street, breathing deeply. She had fallen into her bed, exhausted, the evening before, forgetting to be wary of such an occurrence disturbing her again.

Energetically, she began her ablutions. Scrubbing hard enough to wake herself, she vowed that tonight she would give herself strict orders. No admittance to the stranger of her dreams. No more soft caresses and no more responses from her.

She realized after a few moments that she was pacing the floor, wondering as always where Nathan was. She felt like a northern wind was coming, so twitchy did she feel. She knew what it meant, this anxiety. Something was about to happen and as yet she did not know what it was. She searched her mind for an answer, but it remained stubbornly silent.

She knocked at the duke's door a moment later, a smile hovering upon her lips as she remembered the duke's roguery of the previous day. When he bid her enter, she opened the door cheerfully, hoping he could banish her fidgets. Half expecting Eunice to be in attendance, she stopped short when she saw Woolfe and the duke sitting at a table near the fireplace. Torn between wanting to know what they talked about and the distinct feeling that she was intruding, she hesitated. "Shall I return later?"

Woolfe stood and said, "I'll come back, Your Grace. I'll send the messages we discussed and we can talk afterwards." He nodded to Elizabeth and departed.

"Are you sure?" Elizabeth still felt awkward.

"Come in, m'girl. Sit down and tell me what you and m'grandson are up to. Woolfe tells me that Nathan is out chasing the Traitor."

"They did not tell you of their plans?"

"You're not the only one who's been feeding me pap, m'girl."

"Well, you were injured and we were all so worried."

"I'm up now, and let's have no more nonsense. What have you and Nathan been planning?"

"Very well. Mr. Woolfe has no doubt told you about the Traitor eliminating the people who know him."

The duke waved the information away with his hand. "Yes, and I'm not surprised. The damned villain did it once before and I thought he had died. Didn't hear from him for over a year. Wily bastard, if you'll forgive my bad language."

"What you don't know then is that if Nathan cannot find the Traitor, we intend to use my powers to search for him among the *ton.*"

"About time. I told him to do that a week ago, but the young fool keeps thinking he has to protect you. You're just like my Victoria and Lord knows she didn't need anyone to carry her parasol."

Elizabeth smiled. "You were happy together, weren't you?"

The duke nodded, a soft expression around his eyes. "Yes, she was one of a kind."

They sat quietly for a moment and then the duke spoke. "How's my grandson treating you, missy? Still bumbling around in the dark like a blind man or has he figured out that you're the gel for him?"

"What . . . what do you mean?" The question was so surprising she wondered if she had heard him aright. One glance at the knowing look on his face and she realized what the old rascal was up to. "Have you been matchmaking all along, Grandfather?"

"To be truthful, missy, it was my Victoria's idea. Always thought you two would strike sparks off each other."

Elizabeth laughed nervously. "I do not think we are suited, sir. He'd hate my hearing his thoughts."

The duke rubbed his chin as he pondered. "That so? Well, well . . . I shall have to think what Victoria would say to that."

He stood, still a strong figure at his age. He watched her face with pure glee as he spoke. "The boy sent word that he's on his way home, so don't go out today."

He nodded in satisfaction as her face lit up, then chuckled as she unsuccessfully assumed a serious expression and excused herself. She was boiling inside, tamping down the pure joy and relief the duke's announcement evoked while she worried over how Hawksley would act when first they met again. What had his kisses meant? How did he view her for allowing such liberties? Would he ignore her—or snatch her in his arms? Oh, how could she stand this agonizing feeling? He was safe. He was coming home. She couldn't help it, she let the joy loose.

She fairly danced up the stairs and into the ballroom, feeling as if she could float on the sunbeams of light coming through the high windows of the elegant room. Silk-covered chairs lined the parameter and cozy table arrangements softened the corners. Silk inserts adorned the walls while figurines danced in niches between the rosewood panels. Fairyland clusters of crystals formed chandeliers in midair while light from the many windows transformed itself into colors as it flew though the transparent prisms.

Mariane's friends were due any minute for their day's activities, this morning a waltzing practice. Elizabeth hoped they would be late for she wanted a moment alone to celebrate. Holding her arms out to her imaginary dancing partner, she hummed to herself. "Dum, dum, da da . . . " Had life ever held a happier moment? Round and round she went, dipping and twirling, soaring with her wonderful thoughts.

She calmed herself when she heard their boisterous voices echo up the stairs and wondered once again what was in her cousin's mind. Under normal circumstances, no one in the house would be in doubt what Mariane's pleasures and unhappinesses were. Since Matthew had returned, Mariane had gained a quieter, more composed demeanor, and neither she nor Eunice knew what her thoughts were.

As Mariane's friends trooped in, Elizabeth greeted them politely, intending to escape as soon as it was polite to do so. She looked toward the door and found Woolfe leaning against the wall. He smiled hesitantly at her, then crossed to her side and bowed. "My apologies, Miss Wydner, I have been brusque with you since my return. Might I beg pardon as we dance?"

The pianoforte plunked out a lilting waltz and he swept her into the dance position.

Hawksley slowed as he and his entourage of guards approached the stables. He was anxious over Elizabeth's foray to purchase her fripperies and worried about the two invalids' health. He was also impatient to confer with Woolfe. He hated to involve Elizabeth, but after following the crafty Traitor and finding nothing except his destructive trail, he had no choice. Woolfe must be pacing the floor, waiting for him. As for Elizabeth, she had seldom left his thoughts, and he was looking only for her sweet smile.

The stable boy ran forward to take the reins the minute he dismounted. He strode briskly up the path through the garden and stopped short at the sight before him. The duke and Eunice were hurrying toward him with welcoming smiles.

"Welcome home, m'boy. You had us all worried until we got your message. Woolfe's filled me in on your mission, and after you get settled, we'll confer in the library. That all right with you?"

"What are you doing out of bed?"

"It's a miracle, m'boy. I woke up yesterday and there I was, fit as a fiddle."

What could he say? He felt like he'd blinked and awakened a year later. He clasped Eunice's hand. "I believe we both know where the credit lies, dear lady. In the caring hands of his nurse."

Eunice blushed and the duke waved him away. Hawksley escaped before he burst into laughter. The duke's fist had been full of flowers.

He took the stairs to the back door in twos. Anxious to rid himself of his travel dirt, he hurried to his room. By the time he was clean and comfortable once more, he'd begun to wonder why he hadn't seen Elizabeth. She knew he was coming, didn't she? He'd hurried past Mariane's clutch of friends on his way up, not wishing to become immersed in their greetings. Perhaps she had not been so lucky and needed to be rescued.

He followed the sound of the music to the ballroom. He stopped at the door and watched the pleasant sight. It was like a field of half-opened flowers with an awkward wind blowing as the couples hesitantly followed the directions of the dance instructor. Off to the far side danced one couple who had obviously mastered the steps. Ah, Woolfe had found one flower who could match his long stride, a daffodil in a yellow dress. They turned and he felt a shock go through him. The dancer was Elizabeth. He didn't know which emotion was the stronger, the jealous urge to toss Woolfe out the ballroom window or the itch to turn Elizabeth over his knee.

He strode forward and pulled Elizabeth into his arms. Her squeal of delight upon seeing him mollified him somewhat, but he was burning with anger. Woolfe retired to the doorway with a quizzical expression, then left the room.

Dancing being the last thing on his mind, he pulled her along behind him, growling, "Let's get out of here."

"Hawksley, I am trying to concentrate, but I am presently far more terrified of this phaeton than I am of our enemy." She clung simultaneously to the railing with one hand and his coat with the other as they went around the corner on what seemed to be two wheels.

"And furthermore, were you utterly devoid of common sense when you ordered not only that I be allowed to sleep late, but that a bath be sent to my room?"

He looked surprised. "Were you not pleased?"

She hesitated, for to Hawksley it was probably the equivalent of sending flowers. She gentled her tone. "I was touched, truly I was. It was . . . exactly what I wanted. Only—"

"Well then," he said, dismissing the rest, "that is what I intended."

So much for the raking down she had planned. Indeed, with Hawksley, she might have to take his tenders of affection in whatever form he offered them. She risked a glance at him as they sped along, wondering what was truly on his mind. His only answer to her anxious questions about his trip had been an abrupt directive to come out and show him what she had accomplished while he was gone.

She was miffed that he had ruined their wonderful reunion with his abrupt manner. Even his terrible disappointment of not catching the Traitor did not excuse his manners, especially after how they had parted. Besides, she had never been to the park and wanted to enjoy it, despite the cold air that had already chilled her ears and, she was sure, reddened her nose.

To her everlasting gratefulness, and probably that of the contingent of guards behind them, they slowed as they entered Hyde

Park. They joined what seemed to be a large equestrian promenade traveling on a course around the enormous grounds. She marveled at the throngs of people, beautifully dressed, and all nodding and waving to each other. In what seemed to be terrible travel manners, some stopped to speak to a party passing in the opposite direction, effectively stopping those behind them. Even more surprising was that no one seemed to mind.

She found herself distracted by the speaking looks Hawksley received from the ladies. From old to young, from ladies of disputable morals driving their own equipages to innocent misses hiding behind fans, they all responded to his masculine appeal. Face it, she admitted, I am jealous. Hawksley took in their admiring glances with an aplomb that infuriated her even more.

"What do you hear?" Hawksley's voice broke into her thoughts.

"The same thing you do," she snapped, "women swooning at the sight of you. I cannot imagine why."

Hawksley threw his head back and laughed heartily. He wiped his eyes and asked, "Anything else?"

She looked around and tried to activate her power. She received an occasional jolt of pleasure emanating from people seeing a friend or an occasional unspoken swear word at an unruly horse, but nothing else. "Drat," she moaned. After some measure of success, albeit erratic, while he was away, she wasn't about to admit her failure while he was in this mood.

Bubbles of rebellion and retribution floated noisily to her consciousness. Enervated by such allies, she mutinied. Why should I suffer an explanation at all, she decided, when I am perfectly capable of improvising and giving Hawksley what he wants without actually probing anyone's mind? She looked around and chose as her victim a beautiful woman who was sending Hawksley a much too obvious invitation.

"The woman in burgundy with the French boas?"

"Yes?" She hated the way his eyes traveled over the woman in indisputable pleasure. "She is wishing the wig she wears had been deloused this morning and is dying to dig at her scalp."

He turned to her, startled at the revelation. "That's a wig?"

"Ummm," she lied, biting back a satisfied smile. "She wonders who you are and how much money you have."

She delighted at his disgust. She was rather good at this, she thought with glee, and it was far more fun than the real thing.

"The two women ahead of us? Do you know them?"

He shook his head so she continued, free to improvise at her own pleasure. "The one in blue. She wishes she was home." She paused, her fertile mind choosing a benign vice for the woman. "She craves her sweetmeats and has a novel hidden under her pillow. The woman with her is not very pleasant and makes her long to be home reading about dangerous villains and screaming heroines."

"This is better than an opera, Elizabeth."

She smiled, then realized that she was suddenly hearing the real thing. She looked around to find the originator and spotted a man on a horse drawing near. Pleased by her find, she said, "And the very young military gentleman on the black horse coming toward us?"

"I see him."

"He borrowed it from a friend and hates it immensely. It has bitten him twice this morning and once in a place that hurts when he bounces. He daren't get off and walk for fear it will bite again and yet dreads the long ride ahead of him."

They shared an enjoyable laugh, and she was suddenly very glad they had come out this afternoon. She relaxed and told him all that had happened while he was gone, and they laughed once again at the antics of the house's inhabitants.

Hawksley said, "Would you object if I offered to help you persuade Mariane toward Matthew?"

"Heavens, no. I would be grateful. Do you have a plan?"

"Let's say I am willing to join forces with you on this. I believe Mariane owes me a victory."

"But you were the victor when you saved her life."

"And I damned near coughed my teeth out with the inflammation I contracted after spending the afternoon in that freezing stream."

She laughed. "I would have liked to have taken that thought with me to Scotland." He looked quickly at her, then smiled in relief at her teasing expression.

Hawksley, encouraged by her peaceful look, became lost in his own thoughts. He was still dazed at the sudden outpouring of emotion the sight of her had evoked upon his arrival home. After breaking her away from Woolfe's clutches, all he really wanted was her undivided attention. All she had wanted was to discuss the Traitor and where Hawksley had gone. He needed to forget the Traitor for a time and just be with her, to reaffirm she was real, not something he had dreamt. But it wasn't enough, he wanted to hold her.

When he realized where he was, locked into the trail with hordes of people around, he couldn't believe what he had done. At the first break, he turned out of the park and headed home. He needed to be alone with her, if only driving down a street full of strangers.

As he watched her laughing face, all the reflections and confusion of the past few days coalesced into a moment of discovery. Elizabeth, his exasperating, irritating Elizabeth—she was a kite on a string in a high wind, a puppy chasing a butterfly, a grass fire streaking across a meadow. And he wanted her with a passion that bordered on dementia.

She fired his imagination with visions of her with his babe in arms. He wanted that woman strength and tenderness for his own. He wanted to sink his strength into hers, to bring forth children stronger than them both. He wanted their children to love life as she did, to fill their home with noise and confusion.

He wanted her mischief to cheer him, her unruliness to challenge and jolt him from his unrelenting sense of duty. He wanted to wake each morning with her in his arms. He wanted to be the one who made her happy, to be the one she danced with.

There must be an answer to their dilemma, a weapon against the two-headed beast who fought against their happiness. His agile mind flew, choosing and discarding, drawing on all his resources to form a plan, to do what he did best—to outwit and prepare for all contingencies. Seconds later, everything clicked into place. No matter what measures were necessary, he knew what he must do to ensure her serenity and his own. He cracked his whip in the air to hurry the horses.

Elizabeth was stunned at the change in Hawksley's demeanor. All at once, in the middle of the park, he had looked at her as if he had never seen her before, then granted her a touch of heaven. The look in his eyes was like a welcome home.

Hawksley jumped down, abandoning the phaeton to the care of a hurrying footman, and reached for her. She leaned forward to accept his assistance and reeled, nearly falling as a river of swirling red terror flowed through her.

Chapter Seventeen

AT first Hawksley thought she had slipped, but when he caught a glimpse of her white face, he quickly lifted her up into his arms and hurried toward the house. "Marsh!" he roared as a footman opened the heavy double doors.

He carried her into the hall and tenderly placed her in the nearest chair. Kneeling, he rubbed her hands, concern furrowing his brow as he felt the chill of her skin. He turned to the footman and ordered, "Find Marsh and a shawl for Miss Wydner. And hurry." He leaned back to examine her face, but Elizabeth clutched his arm. He quickly knelt back at her side, surprised as she wrapped her arms around his neck and pulled herself tightly into his embrace.

"Oh, God, Nathan, it's back."

"What, sweetheart, did you see your monster again?" He held her close, finding her unusual dependence on him endearing.

"No, just the rage and swirling red color."

"Could you tell where it came from?"

"No, I never can, it just overwhelms me."

Tarr rushed into the hall. Hawksley barked, "Go and get a blanket."

"Yes, sir. Is she going to be all right?"

Elizabeth's muffled voice gave the anxious man his answer. "I am fine, Tarr. I became faint for a moment and it worried Lord Hawksley." She held herself back and with a slight blush staining her previously pale cheeks, she reluctantly slipped her arms from Hawksley's neck and looked directly into his eyes, adding, "And I am not the least bit cold or in need of a blanket."

I cannot believe it, Hawksley thought, the little minx is flirting with me. He pulled over a nearby chair and sat next to her, wishing once more they were alone. He asked impatiently, "I called for Marsh, where is he?" Tarr's worried face broke into a mischievous grin. The ex-soldier turned-footman held a running battle with the unyielding Marsh and delighted in his discomfiture, no matter what its source. "He's at sixes and sevens today, my lord, with all the company in the house."

"Company?" Hawksley and Elizabeth chimed together.

"The War Office crowd in the library, smoking up the draperies with their tobacco-pipes and cigars. Then there's the young crowd in the parlor, eating everything Cook can prepare, and—"

Tarr paused, as if hesitating to say more. Hawksley impatiently waved him on. "Go on."

Tarr was clearly happy to add to his tale. "Cook is singing at the top of his voice, he's so happy doing for a mob of youngsters, but some of the staff are in revolt at the extra work on their half-day and one of the serving girls said an old gentleman visiting the duke pinched her and she refuses to return."

Tarr paused to catch his breath. "And Miss Mariane slipped away from her company to see to the boy upstairs. Marsh wouldn't let her in and she was dressing him down when Lady Lowden and her crony, Oakes, caught her. Such a to-do you never heard, my lord. They marched her back to the parlor in a hurry, but we've not seen the last of that yet, if the look on young Miss Mariane's face means anything."

Elizabeth's smile grew and Hawksley had to agree with her obvious sentiment. If the silly miss could find the gumption to defy the two old battle-axes, she might make Matthew a good wife after all.

Elizabeth asked, "And my aunt, Mrs. Wydner?"

Tarr's pleasure dimmed as he replied. "She got the megrim after the duke's friends arrived, I'm sorry to say. Such a sweet lady." The grin returned as he continued. "Dr. Cameron dosed her and is sitting with her. Wait till His Grace hears about that."

Hawksley frowned, then sighed. "So that is all?"

"Oh, yes, sir, unless you want to count the flowers that have been arriving in a stream for two days for Miss Wydner."

Hawksley nodded absently and said to Elizabeth, "Very nice, Mariane is no doubt in alt over the attention."

"Oh, not for her"—Tarr corrected Hawksley—"for our Miss Elizabeth. They're all for her. We've denied the young men admittance just as your lordship ordered, but they left their cards and promised to return." Tarr turned to Elizabeth and executed a smooth military bow. "Honors the house, miss, to have the florist cart coming every hour."

"Thank you, Tarr," Hawksley said through gritted teeth, resisting the urge to stuff his neckcloth into the man's mouth. What's more, Elizabeth needn't look so happy by such frivolous news while still faint from her vision and while conflagrations leapt to life all over the house.

As the library door opened and Woolfe slipped out of the room, Elizabeth stood and gasped. Hawksley immediately rose and turned to look at her. She wavered, her face ashen as she stared at Woolfe. Hawksley reached for her and followed her gaze, wondering why the sight of Woolfe should disturb her so. Directly upon his thought, she said, "It's Woolfe, the Traitor is furious with Woolfe." She rubbed her hands back and forth across her temples. "Oh, Nathan, will it never end?"

He pulled her into his arms, and tucked her head against his shoulder. How could he answer her? He couldn't promise her protection from the unknown, but he could ensure that she was never alone again, that she was protected from those around her—and from her own impulsive actions.

Nathan watched Woolfe's progress to Elizabeth's side. He had never seen Woolfe's affection captured by a woman before and could not deny a sense of jealousy as he watched the two of them together. Woolfe would protect her, Hawksley knew, but he could not allow that friendship to blossom into anything else. Only he could understand the complexity of her needs and see to her happiness.

Woolfe said, "Miss Elizabeth, I hate to see you so upset on my behalf." Elizabeth reached out a hand and touched Woolfe's sleeve.

Hawksley snapped, "Woolfe, from this moment on, I don't want you out of my sight."

Offended, Woolfe said stiffly, "I can take care of myself."

"That was an official order, Woolfe. If there is something you must do important enough to risk your life, tell me now."

"My cousin, Geoffrey, expects me to dine with him tomorrow night." He brandished a note clutched in his hand.

"Send your regrets."

Woolfe looked to Elizabeth's concerned face then back to Hawksley. He sighed deeply. "Very well." Then his voice lightened and he ventured, "Can we not use that information to trap the Traitor? Use me as bait and draw him out of hiding?"

"No!" Elizabeth said. "Absolutely not!"

Woolfe and Hawksley looked at her strangely, but she insisted. "If you persist in putting Woolfe's life in danger, then I will never tell either of you anything again." She paused, then in an unyielding voice, "I mean what I say, gentlemen. Do not put me to the test."

Hawksley frowned, wishing Woolfe had not blurted out his proposal in front of Elizabeth, for the plan had some merit. Wanting to save her distress, yet at the same time knowing he must go forward quickly to stop the Traitor, he turned to Woolfe. "We will give Elizabeth a few days, trying to find him through the social circuit. If that fails, we shall forfeit her good wishes, peg you out as a bleating lamb, and wait for the wild animal to come after you."

He turned to Elizabeth and hardened his heart against her dismay. "He's in danger in either case, my dear. We must find the Traitor before he goes into hiding again."

Before she could respond, the sound of cheerful revelry emanated from the direction of the parlor and moved down the stairs. At the same time, voices rose inside the library, signaling the imminent departure of the duke's guests. Woolfe quickly listed the visitors for Hawksley. "Stafford, Burns, Montesford, and Darlington. Burns and Montesford huffed and snorted about things not being what they used to be and Stafford and Darlington wanted to know each and every detail. Of course, they heard only what the duke wanted them to know."

By the time the duke and his visitors came through the library door, Elizabeth had composed herself. Hawksley watched her reaction to them, wondering if she would see them as he did. Burns was clearly too advanced in years and Montesford leaned heavily on a cane, the result of a crippling inflammation of his joints. Stafford was fit enough and Hawksley didn't care for Darlington as a suspect, for the man spent more time with his tailor than in serving his country. However, the Traitor had fooled them for so long that no one rose above suspicion.

Lord Stafford's eyes lit up at seeing Elizabeth and he stopped to greet her. Hawksley tried to ignore the jealousy that arose as the two chatted. By this time, Mariane's crowd had reached the bottom of the stairs and greetings were bounced around between the two groups. Two of the younger men spotted Elizabeth and once more Hawksley's impatience surfaced as they rushed to speak with her.

Telling himself that jealousy in no way accelerated his actions, he decided this was the ideal opportunity to launch the strategy he had formulated in the park. The first step was to immediately attach Elizabeth firmly to him. He raised his voice above the din. "Darling, I don't believe you know these gentlemen. May I present Lords Darlington, Montesford, and Burns. Gentlemen, my betrothed, Elizabeth Wydner."

Silence struck the room. He watched only Elizabeth's face, vitally concerned by her first reaction. First he saw disbelief, then a bright burst of joy that was so fleeting he might have missed it had it not been the one important nuance he looked for. It was enough, this trace of hope. Of course, her anger followed, then a dignified acceptance. Retaliation, he knew would be forthcoming.

The duke stood silent, a strange look on his face as the others expressed their good wishes. Mariane was quiet at first, which was unusual for her, but rose to the occasion by announcing, "You shall make her happy, Nathan." It was not a question.

Woolfe silently watched Elizabeth. His words were all that was proper, but his approval was reserved. Finally the duke came forward to gruffly offer his blessings. After the guests left, the duke murmured quietly to Nathan, "A wonderful maneuver, m'boy. We'll speak later."

The duke then turned to Elizabeth, and grasping her elbow, led her away from the others. "I know Hawksley's done it again, Elizabeth, used the finesse of an overgrown bear to handle a delicate task. You are not constrained to accept, but if you do, give him a chance to make it right."

Elizabeth answered, a stiff dignity in her brisk words. "I am sure he has his own reasons, no matter that he has not seen fit to share them with me. These are difficult times and I am as dedicated to stopping the Traitor as he is. In the meantime, I assure you I shall do my part and parade around on Hawksley's arm as the besotted fiancé."

The duke nodded thoughtfully, then changed the subject. "I do not mean to leave you out of the proceedings now, Elizabeth, but I cannot see any benefit to your hearing the details of Nathan's and Woolfe's reports. The Traitor has eluded us and it's best left at that. Try not to let this upset you. I need you to concentrate on the preparations for the upcoming social events. Which reminds me, have your gowns been delivered yet?"

"A few day dresses only, Grandfather."

"Send a note in my name saying they must be here by tomorrow. We have no time to waste."

She awakened slowly, opening her eyes in time to see the last flickering light of the candle she had left burning. She sat upright and replaced it with a fresh one, not that it had kept her wraith away from a midnight sojourn. Her dream lover had made his usual visit, disturbed her exhausted sleep, and now she was angry. She had enough mystery surrounding her without this complication.

If life had taught her anything, it was to look at a problem straight in the face, solve it quickly, and go on. And she intended to solve this one now. She rose and donned her wrapper, then went to Hawksley's room, candle in hand. She slipped in the door and placed the candle on his bedside table.

Hawksley looked exhausted. Even in his sleep, dark circles underlined his eyes. He and Woolfe had left the house this afternoon, directly after their discussion with the duke, and she had heard them come home less than two hours ago. She felt a little niggling of guilt at her intrusion. What if he was not her dream lover? How embarrassing.

He stirred, moving the bedcovers, and her guilt fizzled and disappeared in the heat of her anger as she beheld the proof of his culpability. There it was, lying sprawled across the end of Hawksley's bed, the very same black velvet dressing gown worn by her wretched phantom.

She should have guessed sooner. In Paxton, his thoughts had risen above all else, and at Eleanore's dance, they had penetrated her four-year barrier with seeming ease. Indeed, since she had reactivated her power, deflecting the emanations coming from him had been a constant struggle. She had fought against listening to him, though, desiring above all else to grant him the privacy he so coveted.

Now she wanted the same courtesy granted to her. She had taught herself to block his thoughts—he could now exert a little effort and cease invading her privacy.

She whispered, "Nathan, wake up."

He didn't budge. Perhaps a little more volume. She raised her voice to a murmur. "Nathan, wake up." He stirred somewhat, but merely wrapped his arm around a pillow and pulled it closer to join the one his smiling face rested upon. The motion renewed her anger—who was he dreaming of now? She walked to his window and stood fuming in the darkness. The longer she stood thus, impotent against all the worries in her life, the hotter her anger grew. The emotion she had held in check during these last dreadful days erupted and burst forth. She marched back to his bedside, stopping to lift a pitcher of water from the fluted bowl it stood in, and flung the contents upon Hawksley's head.

"What—?" he spluttered and sat up. Wet covers fell halfway down his chest, and the attractiveness of his bare torso made her even angrier than before. Saying the first thing that came to mind, she hissed: "Lecher! How dare you invade my dreams?"

"Elizabeth? What are you doing in my room?" He wiped the water from his eyes and stared at the pitcher in her hand. "Did you do this to me?" Water dripped from the thick mane at his forehead. He lifted the edge of the wet sheet and rubbed it across his face and hair. "Ugh. I hate cold water."

"Good. I hope you get the ague. Perhaps that will cool your ardor and keep you out of my dreams."

"What are you talking about?"

She banged the pitcher down on the table, wincing at the loud noise it made. "Listen, Nathan. Every night you dream about me, right?"

He stopped his ministrations and looked warily at her. "You are asking about my dreams?"

"Yes, and every night they come creeping into my head and wake me up. I am dreaming those dreams with you and I want it stopped this instant!"

It took him a second to assimilate her words. His face flushed, but a smile danced around the corners of his mouth. "You've been dreaming my dreams with me?" When she nodded stiffly, he took a deep breath and assumed a concerned expression. "I am sorry, Elizabeth, but how can I stop it?"

"I spend all day blocking out your thoughts; you can return the favor during the night."

Then he lost all composure. He laughed. The laughter stopped and started again, only harder. Through gasps, he said weakly, "Oh, Elizabeth, you should see your face." Then he closed his mouth tightly, taking deep breaths, trying unsuccessfully to stem his mirth.

That was the end of coherency for Elizabeth. She leaned forward and brought her face near his. "How dare you make light of this? I believed you sent me away because of my ability to hear thoughts. I suffered for years, blaming myself for my own banishment. You'll never know how hard I had to work to bring this power under control—just to please you. And now that you are guilty of invading my thoughts, you laugh!"

The smile vanished from his face. "You did all that to *please me?*"

"Yes, for all the good that it did me. It's only a joke to you."

"Why did you think you had to stop it to please me?" She simply glared at him, so he rephrased his question. "What did I ever say to make you think you must stop it for *me?*"

"You cannot remember, can you? You said how could my grandfather stand it. You said nothing could be worse than having a wife who could read his mind. No privacy, you said, no control."

His eyes narrowed. A thoughtful expression dominated his features. Finally, he said, "Surely you must have realized when I announced our betrothal today that I am no longer concerned with that nonsense."

"Heavens, Nathan. Your announcement told me nothing at all, only that you had your own reasons and, as usual, I was not taken into your confidence. You have not changed at all."

He ran his hand through his wet hair, frustration in his voice. "When could we have spoken privately? The situation we were in forced me to act quickly—and you were asleep when I returned home."

She straightened up and folded her arms. "I am here now."

He sighed, obviously stalling for time while he decided which particle of the truth he wished to feed her. He reached for his robe and said, "Turn around."

She turned quickly. The rustle of cloth behind her was unnerving, signaling his intention to leave his bed. Finally, he said, "Come here, Elizabeth." When she turned, she found him before the fireplace, adding wood to the banked fire. He pulled a pair of chairs close to the blaze and bid her sit. She hesitated a moment, then acquiesced and crossed to the chair. She curled into the cushioned chair, tucking her gown over her cold feet. Her heart pounded now in tune to her panicky thoughts. Did she truly want to hear this? Nervously, she broke the silence. "It should be interesting to see what reason you choose to excuse that lunacy of this afternoon."

She could tell he did not like her attack. He raised his eyebrow at her sarcasm and smiled. "Well, then you may pick your own. How about that it was necessary that we become betrothed, and we don't have time for all the courtship rites. We had a formidable audience and it was an opportune time."

"We *must* be betrothed, Nathan? Why? It makes no sense."

"I compromised you by coming to your room the other night."

"Nonsense. Nothing happened and I shall never tell."

He smiled, clearly enjoying himself now. "You have compromised me tonight. I could yell for help."

"Go ahead. We are already betrothed. What is one more compromise?"

He saluted her and grinned. "Well then, I have another choice for you. I need you close to me in the coming days, and only betrothed couples stay together at social events. I cannot have you spending time on the dance floor with your eager young swains."

"Since when did the rules of the *ton* govern you?" she snapped, rising from the chair and shaking the folds of her clothes into place. "I should have known better than to hope you would deal honestly with me, Nathan. Good night."

"Tough lady." He laughed, reaching out to grasp her dressing gown. "She wants the truth."

She stilled, looking pointedly at his restraining hand.

His voice softened. "How about the fact that I love you and don't want to chance losing you?"

She couldn't speak, she trembled so. She searched his face, looking for some indication that he was serious. It was terrible to wish so badly that your most coveted desire was near, yet might be snatched back before it became real. She blurted out the truth. "I don't know if I can believe that, Nathan."

He took a deep breath and rose. "I know." He placed a kiss on her brow and draped his arm around her shoulders. "It's time you went back to your own room before we are discovered."

She balked. How could he dismiss the entire matter so easily? If his avowal of love was serious, why did he not argue, try to convince her? Then she remembered something else. She had come here to demand he stay out of her dreams, and now he was ousting her. "Not so fast, Nathan. What about your dreams? I want them stopped."

He frowned as if searching for a solution, then reflected aloud, "Can you govern your dreams, Elizabeth? I do not think it is possible." He did not expect an answer, but his thoughtful musing continued for a moment while a mischievous smile crept slowly forth. "I never thought about turning this thing around and projecting my thoughts outward toward you."

"You wouldn't."

She knew her protest was pointless before she had finished uttering it. She squirmed out from under his arm and backed to the door. "Before you embark on this further insanity, there is something you should know. I have no right to tell you, but ask your grandfather about Victoria's attitude toward a gift like mine and the difficulties it presents."

He walked to his bed table and retrieved her candle. "More mysteries, Elizabeth?" He shrugged. "I shall ask him if you wish." She nodded and held her hand out for her candle.

He reached around her and twisted the door handle. "I'll walk you back." He followed her into her room, lifted her covers and waited until she crawled in. He covered her to her chin and placed the candle back on her table. Then, pushing loose tendrils of hair off her cheek, he said, "Perhaps we have time for your courtship, after all, Elizabeth. A bit unorthodox, but it might get the job done."

The miserable scoundrel—he did intend to deliberately invade her mind! He smiled at her mutinous expression and said, "We have the rest of our lives to fight over this, little tiger. Go to sleep."

All day, Elizabeth's puzzling words about his grandmother had not only piqued his curiosity, but had made him uneasy. Even more disturbing had been her disbelieving stance against his declaration of love. He and his grandfather had not been given the opportunity for a private discussion yesterday and he viewed this conversation with mixed emotions.

He hurried past the guards and entered the library. The old man began his assault immediately upon his entrance. "What idiocy have you committed now, m'boy? Never hoped to see Elizabeth almost in tears at announcing your betrothal."

The assault was a relief. He grinned at his grandfather. "Not you too."

"What in hades are you talking about?"

"From your comment, I must assume that you, like Elizabeth, feel my proposal was not sincere."

"Strangest bit of romancing I ever heard."

"Just what I wanted to discuss with you, sir. Nice that I never have to go roundabout with you."

"Impertinent boy."

"Yes, sir." He went directly to the point. "I need your advice in convincing Elizabeth."

"You're in trouble if you cannot handle that alone, m'boy."

Chagrined, Hawksley nodded. "I suppose you're right about that."

"Humph."

"Elizabeth said I should ask you about Victoria's opinion of a gift like hers."

"Haven't a clue what she means, Nathan. It seems a simple thing to become accustomed to after you get the knack of keeping them out of your mind."

"Elizabeth's grandmother listened to your thoughts?"

"Hell, boy, the whole clan of 'em did and Elizabeth's grandmother, Georgia, tormented me from the moment we met. Wouldn't have stayed within a mile of her if not for my Victoria"—he slowed and smiled at some private jest—"but I didn't mind when she did it. Made my courtship a lot easier. I could never find the right words, but with her helping herself to my thoughts, we got through all the balderdash in a hurry."

Hawksley sat heavily in a chair. *"Good grief, my own grandmother had the gift as well as Elizabeth's grandmother?"*

"Always was sorry you didn't inherit it, Nathan. You would have been a better match for Elizabeth. On the other hand, Victoria always said you were perfect for each other just the way you were."

"Oh, my God. I've been such an ass with her, and all the time my own grandmother . . . " Stunned, Hawksley asked, "You planned all this?"

"By 'all this,' Nathan, can I take it to mean that you have fallen in love with the girl?"

"How could I not, considering all the planning that evidently went into it?"

"Don't blame me for the idea. Not me, m'boy, never had a way with romance. Now, Victoria, she and her cousins were always cooking up some pot of mischief."

After the moment of shock passed, Hawksley said, "Elizabeth said you would explain how difficult it was, having this gift."

"Ha!" The duke broke into laughter. "It wasn't hard for my Victoria. She always had more fun than anyone, and passed it on to me." He paused, then said seriously, "And that's the secret, m'boy."

Hawksley gave his grandfather a questioning glance.

"Show her the light side of it, Nathan. She's only seen it from the view of a frightened child."

She overslept and awakened in a frenzy. After thinking of Nathan for hours last night, she had vowed to put it out of her mind until the Traitor was caught, and that was exactly what she was going to do. Appalled that the morning was half gone, she washed quickly and rang for Sally to assist with the many buttons that ran down the back of her dress. After several moments passed without Sally making an appearance, Elizabeth decided in her impatience to make up for the hours lost sleeping and go in search of her aunt or Mariane. She stuck her head out the door and was immediately assailed by Mariane's excited exclamation.

"Elizabeth, wait until you see! Our clothes have arrived. I cannot believe such speed. Oakes says one mention of Lord Standbridge's name and everyone jumps to serve him. I have tried all mine on and they are wonderful."

Mariane was just what she needed. Her jubilation was a perfect foil to the lingering memories of the night. She smiled at Mariane's enthralled expression and attempted to calm her a bit by asking, "Have you talked to your mother yet, Mariane? Is her headache gone?"

Mariane's face softened in a sweet smile. "Yes, and we have been in to see Matthew. You could see them together. He is so gallant with her. You can tell she should have had a flock of children because she already loves him."

Elizabeth's heart took a little dip at her words. Did Mariane then think of Matthew as a brother?

"Oakes"—the younger girl called to the woman exiting Mariane's bedroom—"tell the servants to bring Elizabeth's parcels at once."

Oakes stopped short, obviously insulted to be asked to serve Elizabeth. She turned quickly and marched away, her back ruler-straight. Mariane shrugged and turned back to Elizabeth.

Elizabeth turned her back to Mariane and said, "Fasten my dress, please, Mariane. I am undone in back."

"Oh pooh, Elizabeth, just sit in a chair until they are gone. I shall have to undo it in a minute anyway." Mariane went to the door, practically bouncing in her excitement as Elizabeth obeyed her and sat. When Oakes returned, she and Mariane began opening the packages.

Elizabeth watched them for a moment, then realized that she wanted to enjoy this rite without Oakes's oppressive presence. This was a day she and Mariane had anticipated during their girlish plan-making and she did not want to share it with anyone except Mariane. She caught Mariane's eye and looked pointedly at Oakes, then nodded her head toward the door. Mariane caught on immediately and said, "You may go now, Oakes. I shall play maid for my cousin."

Clearly surprised at her charge's firm direction, the older woman stilled in her efforts, looked toward her charge, and then shot a deadly look at Elizabeth. Elizabeth, determined to avoid another confrontation with Oakes, looked away as if not noticing.

After Oakes lifted her chin and left, Elizabeth confided to Mariane. "She'll go directly to her room and write a scathing note to your Aunt Sylvia."

Mariane quickly looked at the closed door as if to see what Oakes was truly up to. She frowned for a few seconds, then shrugged her shapely shoulders. Tossing Elizabeth a parcel with a devilish look, she said, "Let's play."

Mariane was a genius, Elizabeth thought after an hour of playing dress-up. How fortunate that she had deferred to her cousin's judgment. She admired her reflection in the pier glass, and marveled at how the right colors seemed to wage less of a war with her brilliant coloring. She ran her hands over the knotted cream silk shawl. How she loved the feel of silk.

Dresses lay strewn across the bed and even more hung in the wardrobe in a profusion of colors. Had she let Mariane order all these gowns? Instead of stark white that drained all the color from her face, Mariane had insisted on velvety creams enhanced by the addition of soft apricots, warm pinks, iridescent greens and blues. The clever cut of the Pomona-green velvet riding habit with fur trimming made her less conscious of her too slim hips and generous bosom. She donned a warm pink gown and turned, admiring the flattering drape of the empire line.

A soft scratching on the door announced Oakes once more. "Lord Stanley is here, Miss Wydner. He's in the parlor, waiting for you."

Elizabeth's heart hit bottom as Mariane promptly jumped up, preened before the mirror, and left the room. Elizabeth panicked. What could she possibly do to stave off the seemingly inevitable victory Lady Lowden had so cunningly staged? Then the answer hit her—Hawksley!

This time when she went searching for him, she bypassed the wasted effort of looking into empty rooms. At the first floor, she leaned over the stair railing and bellowed, "Hawksley!" in the Standbridge-Hawksley proven method of communication.

It was rather like watching an ant family. The front hall filled with swarms of people—servants, Marsh, Woolfe, Mariane, and Lord Stanley. Last came Hawksley himself, fiercely frowning, and moving fast. He was halfway up the stairs when he spotted her standing serenely above him. He stopped short, his massive chest heaving as he deliberately calmed himself. He sent his searching glance over every inch of her, and his eyes narrowed as he walked purposefully toward her. By this time, the humor of using Hawksley's own system against him had faded and she moved prudently backward until the wall halted her retreat. When he reached the top, his eyes continued to search, this time peering down the hallway in an attempt to discover anyone who might be posing a threat to her. He gave one command to the now edgy footmen. "Leave us." They raced for the back staircase and disappeared.

Her voice came out in a whisper. "I needed your help."

His face did not move a muscle as he walked up to her. Slowly, his arm wrapped around her waist and pulled her to him. He spread his fingers at the nape of her neck and pulled her mouth to his, then proceeded to kiss her senseless. All the while his hands took possession of her, moving across her back as if to ensure himself that she was all there, safely in his arms.

Then he lifted his head and released her, bracing his hands on the wall to either side of her head. "You have my complete attention, Elizabeth."

It took her a moment to find her voice. Finally she said, "Lord Stanley's here."

"I know."

Her words flew, tumbling over each other. "I thought Mariane was still in love with Matthew and felt so smug about how my plan had worked. She was visiting him against Sylvia and Oakes's disparagement of him and it seemed as though she was making her own decisions. Then this morning she talked about Matthew as if he was a brother and when Lord Stanley came, she ran down with her eyes all lit up with I don't know what."

When Hawksley didn't answer, she wailed, "You said you would help."

"I did. I invited Lord Stanley to dinner."

Chapter Eighteen

"YOU traitor, you Judas, you . . . " Elizabeth sputtered as she pushed against his chest with all her strength. To her surprise, he stepped back. She paced away a few steps, then turned back to face him again.

"I thought better of you, Nathan. I thought Matthew was your friend. Or do you think Mariane would make him such a poor wife that you can just toss her away to Lord Stanley? You said you would help. In fact, Nathan, you *offered* to help!"

He grinned, totally unmoved by her tirade. "Sweetheart," he said, placing his palm over his heart, feigning a mortal wound, "don't you trust me?"

"Trust you?" she hissed, "I trust actions, not words! How is keeping that miserable fop around going to get Matthew and Mariane together? And don't call me sweetheart."

"But, darling, are you sure they should be together?"

"Of course. I certainly do not want her aligned with Lord Stanley—or his conniving mother, who, in case you did not already know, is Sylvia Lowden's best friend. He's not near good enough for Mariane. And I am not your darling."

"Ah, but is Mariane good enough for Matthew?"

"What?!"

"Calm down, Elizabeth, and hear me out."

She took a deep breath. "I am trying my level best, even in the face of your meaningless endearments."

Now his grin disappeared. His black eyes looked deeply into hers. "Do not ever think my endearments are meaningless, Elizabeth. As for Mariane, do you honestly think I would deliberately hurt her?"

She sighed resignedly. "No, of course not, Nathan."

"So, that leaves us with an obvious plan of attack."

"Which is . . . ?"

"Trust me."

*   *   *

It had been a strange few days, Elizabeth thought, as she dressed for dinner some days later. Mariane cheerfully enjoying Lord Stanley's morning visits, then whisking herself upstairs to spend time with her mother and Matthew. Matthew determinedly getting up and walking the minute Mariane left, healing himself as if by pure willpower. Eunice feeding Mariane a steady dose of Matthew while Hawksley gave her a surfeit of Lord Stanley.

Grandfather directing the search for the Traitor with the manner of an overlord, then turning meek as a lamb when Eunice entered the room. Evenings with the unwieldy group of Hawksley and Tarr and Mariane's crowd attending whatever invitations Hawksley decided were de rigueur. She had faithfully opened herself to any visions, but the Traitor remained ominously silent. The men never mentioned their timetable for using Woolfe as bait, and was it not for the stalking danger, she could have been lulled into thinking all was well.

Yet she knew they were in that deceptively motionless time before a raging storm, for she felt a breathless anxiety building in her—and she knew it was going to be calamitous. Lest this apprehension dominate her every thought, she kept busy, for the fear clouded her mind and made her want to hide under the bed.

Speaking of bed, she thought, hers was beginning to resemble a battlefield. Each evening she gave strict orders to whatever part of her mind reigned during those sleeping hours, demanding she be granted dreamless sleep. Early each night she awakened to enticements so foreign to her experience that she would have marched into Hawksley's bedchamber and beat him into wakefulness, except she worried that would only initiate a new level of seduction.

The wretch had begun sending her mental pictures during the day as well, startling her in the middle of her more mundane tasks, during meals and in the company with others—pictures that flushed her face bright red and made her forget whatever she was about at the moment. With each mental encounter he took more liberties and she battled for her virtue without Hawksley more than lifting his wicked eyebrow.

And tonight, as if she hadn't enough to aggravate her, she must face one more dinner with the ultimate popinjay, Lord Stanley. To be precise, Lord Stanley and friends. Each morning the parlor filled with young visitors. Each evening the guest list increased, thanks to Lord Hawksley's sudden questionable affinity for so-

:ializing. Oh, yes, one would think it spring with the hibernating bear coming out of his cave eager to play.

Woolfe stayed away from the whole, save watching the gaming rooms under the guise of gambling with his cousin, Geoffrey.

She tugged upward once more on the neckline of the gold and cream gown she and Mariane had chosen for the evening's festivities, a rout at the home of the beautiful Emily, Lady Cowper.

"It really is too bad of you, Elizabeth, to refuse to have your, mm, bosom 'up' as is the fashion."

"Mariane, if I was pushed up any further, with the size of my bosom, my chin would be resting upon it. Whoever dreamed of such a ridiculous fashion? Some lady with an affinity for pouter pigeons?"

Mariane's giggle followed her as she gathered up her silk shawl and moved toward the door.

Hawksley and Woolfe glanced up as Mariane and Elizabeth gracefully descended the stairs in all their finery. Elizabeth felt anything but graceful as her knees turned to water at the very sight of Hawksley in evening dress. Though far from handsome, he took her breath away. As usual, he wore a black coat and breeches, which contrasted with his white linen shirt and waistcoat, making his penetrating eyes seem even darker and more dangerous. Like now as his gaze strolled leisurely over her, stopping at the shawl as if it presented no barriers to him. Indeed, before she could count the places she would like to send him, he had undressed her down to her shift!

She deliberately looked away, turning her attention to Woolfe who was dressed in dark blue. Somehow in evening gear, his limness seemed less accented since his wide shoulders and long legs filled out the frame of his clothing without padding. His habitual laconic speech and idle stance disappeared when they entered the room, which she found endearing and flattering. Her terrible concern for his safety only added to the bond of friendship that was growing between them.

He bowed deeply as they reached the ground floor, stepping in front of Hawksley to take her elbow. She glanced quickly at Hawksley, wondering what retaliation he would take in the unspoken rivalry between the two. Although his thoughts were at the moment unavailable to her, she recognized his look, the one that said this was his idea.

Mariane and Hawksley followed them into the parlor. As usual, Tarr's soldier-footmen stood unobtrusively about the elegant room, watching the guests while keeping one eye on the pretty serving girls.

The cheerful babble ceased upon their entrance, then a soft feminine whispering ensued. Elizabeth bit back a smile as Lord Stanley, in a lemon-yellow wasp-waisted coat, frowned at seeing Mariane's hand on Hawksley's arm and came forward immediately. The danger he put the seams of his coat in by such imprudent speed and action betrayed his apprehension at losing his prize. Or at least, she thought, the prize his mother and Lady Lowden had awarded to him.

Mariane seemed in no hurry to give up the picture she made with the marquess in tow, and instead greeted the guests with her arm firmly in place. Elizabeth squelched the tiny demon of jealousy that prodded her at how beautiful Hawksley and Mariane looked together, and proceeded to introduce Woolfe to the others whom he didn't know.

The younger crowd seemed fascinated with Woolfe. A tall, unusual-looking gentleman who counted Lord Hawksley as friend and host and Geoffrey, the Earl of Kingsford, as cousin, was worth cultivating. Woolfe accepted the attention with amusement, unlike Hawksley who, although he hid it well, would rather have been elsewhere. The duke and Eunice Wydner came forward to greet them.

Since it seemed all the guests were present, Elizabeth wondered why neither the duke nor Hawksley seemed in any hurry to lead the guests into dinner. Hawksley instead followed her talkative cousin in supposed contentment, accepting effusive compliments unto himself and issuing polite responses in turn. Then the door opened and Hawksley's face broke into an unfeigned smile.

Marsh announced "Lieutenant Matthew Stephens of the Ninth Light Dragoons" as he might royalty, and in her delight to see her patient so well treated, Elizabeth immediately forgave the stiff, unyielding butler all his slights to her.

Mariane's smile, too, spoke of a real affection, no matter if she thought of him as friend or betrothed. Hawksley led her to her intended and Matthew bent over her hand with a grace hard-earned in his forays back and forth across the room upstairs. He carried his cane and only rested upon it lightly. The barber had been visiting, and his tailor had replaced Matthew's ragged uniform with a resplendent new one. More than one young lady sighed at seeing Matthew's handsome face and military bearing, much to Mariane's delight.

The duke insisted the couple lead the group into dinner, no matter the rank of the company. Dinner was served and all seemed favorable until during the second course Lord Stanley went on the attack. "Mr. Stephens, I understand you farm."

Matthew looked quickly across the table at the young lord, surprise in his expression. Although the gatherings had taken on a relaxed and casual air with only twenty in company, it was still a duke's table and Lord Stanley was not usually one to break a rule as ingrained as not speaking across the table.

"When we have won the war, then, yes, I will be once more a landowner who produces crops."

"You have been away for over two years. Surely if you can be absent for that length of time it must be a simple task for your agent to manage."

"I must confess, Lord Stanley, that I have put the worry quite out of my mind in my concern for my military duties."

"Perhaps there will be nothing left to worry about when you return. Agents are ever an unpredictable lot, are they not?"

Matthew laughed aloud. "Actually, I retired mine shortly before I left and turned over the entire lot to my neighbor's care."

Looks of pity rested upon Mariane and she squirmed in discomfort. Elizabeth thought at first that her cousin's discomfiture came from the embarrassment of having been deemed not only pitiful in marrying a mere untitled landowner, but perhaps an impoverished one as well. On second glance she realized that her cousin looked ready to engage in fisticuffs instead. Matthew leaned close and spoke in her ear and Mariane relaxed and attended to the next remove.

Elizabeth was happily eating her pheasant and green peas when once again Lord Stanley broke the pleasant tenor of the room.

"I see you have received an unfortunate wound that requires you to walk with assistance."

Elizabeth caught her breath and quickly looked at Mariane to see her reaction to such effrontery. Mariane looked surprised, but calmly turned to hear Matthew's rebuttal.

Matthew's biting tone reflected his experience as an officer dealing with inferiors. "Surely such a discussion is not fit for either the ladies' ears nor does it aid digestion, Lord Stanley." He looked away from Lord Stanley as if that should suffice. Elizabeth couldn't believe it when Lord Stanley persisted.

"I am sure the ladies will forgive me if I end their suspense in wondering whether you will be able to give them the pleasure of dancing with you, Lieutenant."

Matthew stopped with his wineglass in the air. "Alas, at the present time, the only boon they might ask of me would be to sit out the dance. And unless they plan to drag me to Almack's for stale cake and weak lemonade, I could offer them the delight of excellent refreshments while I tell them some humorous stories about Wellington." He smiled, shrugged his shoulders, and said, "Unless they wished to discuss sailing, of course, in which case I would decant. I hate sailing," he explained with a lopsided grin.

Several of the young ladies laughed at that, making Lord Stanley even more determined. He bided his time until after the next remove.

Elizabeth's spoonful of plum pudding was halfway to her mouth when Lord Stanley casually brought the conversation back to Matthew. "Perhaps, Mr. Stephens, you might begin refilling your coffers by selling your commission. Miss Wydner cannot be expected to follow the drum, nor can you expect her to wait another several years for you to retire. She might begin looking around in greener pastures, but then as a farmer, you would understand that."

Hawksley's burst of laughter shocked the entire table to silence. "Should Lieutenant Stephens wish to fill his coffers any fuller, he has only to allow me the privilege of buying a strip of pasture that marches alongside Standbridge. We have been haggling over it since childhood."

At the questioning looks from around the table, he went on to explain, "The stream that runs through it holds the finest fish in England. It meanders back and forth on both our properties, but the best fishing hole is on Matthew's side."

He laughed and turned to Matthew. "Do you remember the time you had me arrested for trespassing when we were in a race to catch the biggest trout?"

"Arrested? The duke's son?" several people protested.

"Oh, you would never know him in the country," Matthew told them, "or His Grace for that matter. They dress like impoverished gypsies."

Lord Stanley opened his mouth to speak again when Marianne

stopped him with an angry wave of impatience. "Matthew would like your attention for a moment before we leave for Lady Cowper's."

Matthew rose to his feet, a little clumsily, but with a beaming smile. "As some of you may know, my regiment has returned to England and I am transferring to the War Office as Lord Hawksley's aide. Not that he needs my help, but he wishes to begin battering my ears with pleas for my fishing hole."

He drew his betrothed's hand into his and continued. "We have given the tidings to Mrs. Wydner and His Grace earlier, but you may all now share in our good news." Looking directly at Lord Stanley, he announced, "As you know, Mariane has graciously consented to be my wife, and we have chosen mid-June for the happy occasion. We shall announce it formally at the ball where the duke and Mrs. Wydner shall join us."

This was greeted with a mixed response, but Matthew forged on. He turned to look at Elizabeth. "My apologies to Miss Elizabeth Wydner, but Mariane wished to surprise her and, as you can see by her expression, we have succeeded admirably."

Elizabeth rose to engage the happy couple in joyful hugs and kisses. In the noisy celebration that followed, Hawksley murmured in her ear, "I told you to trust me, Elizabeth."

When Elizabeth gave him a questioning look, he explained, "Mariane had to decide for herself. I only gave her the opportunity to make a close comparison between the two men." They shared a silent victory when they saw Lord Stanley excuse himself from the room.

The presence of the Prince Regent sealed Lady Cowper's affair as the premier event of the season. Her satin-draped ballroom resembled clouds with replicas of the vastly popular hot air balloons hanging from the ceiling. Greenery abounded throughout the room to complete the illusion of the outdoors.

Woolfe wandered off to seek his cousin, Geoffrey, in the card room as was his usual practice, and Matthew and Mariane settled the duke and Eunice comfortably in chairs and wandered the room, spreading their good news to everyone. When Lord Stafford approached Elizabeth for a dance, she looked to Hawksley for permission since he had been so adamant about her remaining close. He shrugged and gave his permission. His offhand manner infuriated her, so she extended the dance to include a stroll to the punch bowl before returning. When they arrived at the precise spot she had last seen him, it was to find Hawksley on the dance floor—with the woman from the park whose hair she had so badly maligned.

She waited angrily, foot tapping, for his dance to finish. He bowed so gallantly in response to his partner's bosom-revealing curtsy, that she wanted to pull the woman's hair out, alleged livestock and all.

Hawksley returned to Elizabeth's side with a smug look, murmuring, "Tit for tat, my dear," as he guided her resisting body onto the floor for a waltz.

"Lecher."

He laughed, and pulling her close, whirled her around the room until she was dizzy. As the last strings of the music ended, the breathless couple walked off the dance floor in harmony. They veered toward the buffet table along the wall and saw Woolfe before them. Woolfe piled his plate high with lobster patties and said, "Thought I'd eat now since Geoffrey is late tonight."

And then the nightmare began, the familiar storm she had anticipated. A red mist swirled before her eyes, completely blinding her to the room for a brief second, while half revealing a scene that frightened her more because of its incompleteness. Immediately she searched her vision for some familiar room or piece of furniture for fear she would see her loved ones in this hellish scene, but nothing looked familiar.

Then she saw him, her illusive monster. He was turned slightly away from her, making it impossible for her to see his face. She watched in horror as he leaned forward with a swinging motion of his hand. Then he straightened and laughed, a silent, macabre grimace. The red mist began swirling faster then, and she saw his victim in flashes as the mist crossed his face. It was the face of Woolfe, fading away as the white cloud came to close the scene.

She clutched Hawksley's hand as her knees weakened. Hawksley exchanged a worried look with Woolfe and immediately curved his arm around her to stop her from falling. No one seemed to notice the quick interchange as he steered her into a hall and quickly found an empty room. Woolfe followed them in and closed the door. Hawksley guided her to a settee and sat beside her. "My God, Elizabeth, what is it?"

She looked past him to the other man. "Oh, Woolfe, it was horrible. I saw my monster killing you."

Woolfe stiffened and said urgently, "Are you sure it was me?"

"It was you but the room is one I have never seen before."

The two men quickly looked at each other and Woolfe's face turned stark white. He said in a deadly calm voice, "Describe the room."

It took her a moment to tear her eyes from his face before she could think. "It was a billiards room. The walls were paneled and there were huge paintings of ships and scenes of the sea. One painting had a lighthouse in it with a red roof. Then there was—"

She stopped as Hawksley stood and crossed to his friend who had leaned back against the door and closed his eyes in terrible agony. "That's Geoffrey's home, isn't it? Woolfe, I'm sorry."

Woolfe stood up straight again and said in an urgent tone, "I need to go, maybe he's not dead. Maybe if we sent for a doctor—" He started to turn back toward the door, but Hawksley's superior strength held him fast.

"You know that is not very likely, Woolfe, but we'll go immediately. First we need to be sure we are prepared for all eventualities and see that Elizabeth is safe."

Woolfe nodded, but Elizabeth could see that he was in a fever to leave. She said to Hawksley, "I saw his cousin, Geoffrey?"

Hawksley nodded. "Geoffrey and Woolfe look very much alike."

She wiped away tears that threatened to fall and stood. "Walk me to the duke's side. I shall explain the tragedy to him after you leave lest he insist on going with you. But, first, you must give me your oath that you take plenty of guards with you."

Hawksley quickly reassured her and they hurried back to the ballroom. As soon as they reached the duke's side, Hawksley whispered into his grandfather's ear. As the men turned to leave, Elizabeth had a terrible thought. She reached out to touch Hawksley's arm. "What if this is a trap to capture you both?"

Hawksley growled, "I hope to God it is." They hurried away.

A few moments later, Tarr and another guard brought Matthew and Mariane to join the duke's party, then moved into place along the wall, standing at attention just as if no guests were openly gawking at Standbridge footmen in the Cowpers' ballroom. Two more appeared, one at each door, one at the balcony, and one at the entrance leading to the stairs. Such outrageous behavior initiated excited whispers.

Lady Barton and her husband stopped to pay their respects to

the duke and Eunice. Soon, the corner where the duke's party sat
looked like a beehive with visitors swarming round, eager to
gather enough information to feed the next morning's social
rounds. Dignitaries came and went, pleasing Elizabeth with the
genuine respect shown the duke. Lords Stafford and Montesford
also came by to speak to His Grace.

Elizabeth's sympathies were evoked by Lord Montesford's
difficulty in moving through the crowd. As he turned to leave,
she walked alongside him, unobtrusively opening a path for his
ease in maneuvering back out of the crowd. He smiled know-
ingly at her and said, "You're a sweet girl, Miss Wydner." He offered his unhindered arm. "Lord Hawksley is a fortunate man.
Might I beg the pleasure of offering you a glass of champagne
punch?"

Oh dear, this was awkward. The refreshment table sat across
the room and she would have to accompany him rather than let
him hobble across the room and back again with her punch.
"That's kind of you, Lord Montesford, first let me just tell my
aunt where I am going."

He looked pointedly at the crowd around her family. His unspoken intimation was correct, it would take forever to ease her
way through and back again while Lord Montesford stood waiting. She was indecisive for a moment, not wanting her family to
worry if she moved away, yet not wanting to hurt the poor crippled man's feelings either.

"Hawksley bid me wait for him here," she explained, "and I
must give Tarr my direction so Hawksley can find me."

"Well, then, that's perfect. I left a message at the door for
Hawksley to meet me on the balcony, so we can procure our
drinks and go out where it's cool to wait for him."

She had visions of Hawksley's reaction should she go out on
the balcony under the circumstances, and had no intention of
doing so, but decided she would go as far as the punch table in
order not to offend Montesford. She motioned to Tarr that she
was going. He nodded and surprised her by leaving the duke's
corner to follow along the wall as she and Montesford slowly
made their way around the dancers.

Montesford watched Tarr with amusement. "Are you certain
you want to ally yourself with a man so possessive that he sends
someone to watch your every move?"

"Oh, my dear Lord Montesford, that is the way of the Stand-bridge family, I'm afraid. They're rather feudal, you know."

When they reached the buffet, she acquired their drinks while he leaned heavily on his cane. He nodded his thanks and turned to go toward the balcony. She quickly forestalled him. "Lord Montesford, I don't wish to go outside. May we not sit here?" She indicated a grouping of chairs that had just been vacated.

His face fell in perfect imitation of regret, but her heart chilled as she suddenly saw into his mind—a scene where four men waited near the balcony to capture Hawksley. Then she saw Montesford's diabolical pleasure in anticipating Hawksley's demise at his own hand.

She quickly closed her eyes to hide her reaction from Montesford. She needed to steady herself and try to make sense of her vision. Montesford was crippled. He could barely walk, let alone be the graceful knife wielder she saw attack the duke.

And why did she not sense the red haze, the rage that always accompanied him?

"Are you all right, my dear? It's very warm in here." Her eyes flew open as his hand grasped her arm. It felt like a spider crawling on her skin. "Let me assist you to the balcony where you might rest for a moment in the fresh air. Hawksley can retrieve you there, so you won't miss him after all." His hand was very strong.

Her mind flew. She was at a disadvantage with both her hands holding their champagne and Montesford pulling her along beside him at an amazing rate. However, she could feign a faint and drop at his feet or simply stand here and scream Tarr to her side; indeed, she was in no real danger yet. But Nathan—he might actually go to the balcony before she could stop him.

Then as if she had conjured him, Nathan appeared at the ballroom's entrance with Woolfe beside him. He glanced first at the corner where the congenial party still stood around the duke, then at the paper in his hand. He motioned Woolfe to go to the family while he headed for the balcony. At the speed he was moving, he would reach the balcony long before she could stop him, with or without Montesford's propelling hand.

Montesford's voice purred beside her, "Here's your betrothed now, my dear, and just in time. We'll have you together at last."

It was then that she finally felt Montesford's red rage engulf her, almost choking her in its intensity as it swirled violently in a

thick spiral. Montesford's rage, like a stalking jackal, fed itself
with satisfaction as he looked upon his enemy and indulged in anticipating the pain of his hated foe, the duke. She couldn't see
past it—she was helpless, blinded by his rage.

She did the only thing she could think of. She threw the glasses
of punch on the floor with all her might, breaking them with a
wonderful crashing sound. Cold liquid splashed on her feet, and
from the protesting sounds around her, she surmised on others as
well. She could feel cool air on her cheeks as they backed away
from the wet floor and shattered crystal, leaving her and Montesford to stand isolated from the crowd.

Montesford's hand fell from her arm and he swore under his
breath. She could see the red swirl thinning as he drew back his
rage in order to think clearly, containing it with marvelous control. Through the dissipating haze, she could see him turn to look
toward the balcony, indecisive and anxious. He wanted to ensure
that Nathan was taken more than he wanted her. He finally decided to try for them both. He pulled her forward, saying in a conciliatory tone, "I'll take you to your betrothed and we shall
summon a servant to tidy you."

"No," she insisted, afraid now. His strength was amazing and
she could not escape from his arm. She glanced at his cane and
realized that if she could cause him to fall, all the better. In her
struggle to move away from him, she reached out a toe and
kicked at his cane.

She would never forget the sight that followed. Like a circus
performer, he moved with the fall, twisted and landed erect a few
feet from her, without losing his breath. Oh, Lord, he was no crip-
ple at all.

He dismissed her with an ironic bow, promising retribution
with his cold eyes and evil smile. He was going after Hawksley,
and now he was angry. He thought he had them both together and
she had ruined his plan. The red haze intensified briefly then disappeared as he turned toward the balcony.

Oh, no. How could she stop him?

"Lord Montesford"—she screeched at the top of her voice—
"you are a villain!" She saw him stop and turn to stare at her,
completely dumbfounded at her audacity. No lady would ever
make a scene like this at Lady Cowper's ball, especially with the
Prince Regent in attendance.

The sound of conversation had changed, as word of the spectacle spread and people turned to see what she would do next. Her frantic warning to Hawksley fell into a silently waiting room.

"You attacked the Duke of Standbridge in the streets of Grosvenor Square and killed his footman. Even now you have your henchmen waiting in the garden to attack Lord Hawksley."

A flurry of movement near the balcony ensued as some people scrambled away from the balcony door and others peered outward to see the villains themselves. She could see Hawksley now. At his direction, Tarr quickly gathered his men and darted out. Hawksley himself turned and began moving urgently through the thick crowd toward her.

Montesford, careful to keep himself aloof from any taint, said to her, "My dear child, I believe you are overset. Let me get someone to take you home." He started toward her. She moved back, frantically wondering how she was going to escape from what she had started.

"Here now, watch what you say about Lord Montesford. Who are you to tell lies like that?" This from a dissipated man to her left whose love of port wrote its own story on his red-veined nose.

What should she do now? If people began jeering at her, Montesford would escape to again be a menace to her family. She had no proof, nor did Nathan. On the other hand, she had all the proof she needed sitting handily in Montesford's mind. And this night he had given her the key to opening his mind. He, like all the others whose minds she had been able to see into, had projected them forward with the thrust of strong emotion. She had only to jolt him, then follow his own deadly trail.

For now, though, she must respond to the dissenter on her left in a way that would give her words power and believability.

She hesitated on the brink of disaster. If she showed the world her power, she would be forever banished from Hawksley's world. No matter that he might stand by her, she would not allow it. On the other hand, if she did not use her power, the Traitor would win and Hawksley's life would be once more in jeopardy. It was no choice at all.

"I can read minds, especially minds full of evil deeds." She tuned out the new wave of whispers calling her deranged and concentrated on her task at hand. She turned her power toward the protesting gentleman with the red nose. "You have a secret." A jolt of fear followed by a picture came pouring out from the man and she relayed it to the room. "You have taken up with an actress and you do not want your father-in-law to know since he holds the strings to your money." The man sputtered and protested, guilt flushing his face. The crowd grew uneasy.

Standing near her was the young *enceinte* girl from Gunter's, holding the hand of a distinguished young man. She said to him, "Come close and I will whisper your secret." He hesitated and she prodded him. "Or I can speak it aloud." Without losing his dignity, he let her whisper into his ear, "Your feelings for Miss Copley . . ." She paused. He revealed that he loved the girl and had taken advantage of her . . . "the girl is expecting your child and is terrified to tell you. Will you do the right thing?" He stiffened for a second, then a tender look briefly crossed his face. Instantly dignified again, he bowed respectfully to her and said aloud, "I believe this woman tells the truth." He returned to Miss Copley, clutching her hand with a new possessiveness.

She turned back to Lord Montesford, who stared in amazement at her. She streaked into his mind for information. "You are a smuggler and a spy for France." She could feel his mind opening as his emotion rose. "You do it for revenge and the money, money you have hidden"—she could see a room in his house and—"in a secret trapdoor under a chair in your bedchamber."

Now Montesford was moving toward her and his eyes were wild. She started to speak, then saw Woolfe edging his way through the crowd that had gathered about them. Montesford saw him too and a dark look of enjoyment passed briefly across his features.

Elizabeth caught a glimpse of his thoughts and recoiled. "Your latest deed, Lord Montesford, is grisly indeed." Tears fell down her cheeks. "Tonight you murdered Lord Geoffrey Kingsford." Woolfe's tormented face told her that he had indeed found his cousin murdered. Her heart broke for him.

The pain Elizabeth felt as the crowd's reaction to her registered was surprisingly difficult to bear, indeed, it was everything Hawksley had foretold. But it was nothing to the hurt she felt as she looked into Hawksley's eyes across the room. He was horrified by her actions. She told herself it was worth it if she could save him from the agony Lord Montesford had planned for him this evening. The thought steadied her and she concentrated on her enemy, who had stopped a few feet away from her.

"Lord Montesford, I am walking through your mind, opening doors even as I speak. What an evil mind it is, full of grisly deeds you have committed. You have tortured brave English men who were gathering information against France. You enjoyed doing it. And then you brought them home and discarded them on England's shore to show your arrogance."

By now the duke and his followers had gathered around. The duke's cronies' faces were shocked but not sure what to believe. Montesford hobbled closer and people moved back from him, not believing her, but not trusting him either. Elizabeth backed away from Montesford, taunting him once more as she toured his evil mind.

"Would you like these good people to know the worst thing you have ever done?" Like a torrent racing down a river, she followed his thoughts as they streamed toward a ghastly scene. She gasped out in disbelief, "You murdered your own father?"

Hawksley had finally reached the edge of the circle with Woolfe at his side. A commotion from the balcony ensued and Tarr and his men dragged Montesford's henchmen to stand before Hawksley. Hawksley spoke to Woolfe. "The night that you were attacked so many months ago, were any of these men present?" Woolfe pulled the largest man out of Tarr's grip, forced him to his knees, and snarled, "Take your choice. Either confess and receive a fair trail or remain silent and my pistol will end your miserable life here and now."

The kneeling henchman hesitated until he heard the pistol being cocked, then blubbered out a confession. "It were him, Lord Montesford, what told us what to do. But he said we was killing traitors to the crown."

In a nightmarish flurry of motion, Montesford's rage burst forth, pinpointing itself at his betrayer. He drew his knife from the handle of the cane and slew his own man, toppling him backward into Woolfe. Hawksley leapt forward and grabbed Montesford's wrist and twisted, forcing him to release the knife. Montesford swung his cane viciously onto Hawksley's head, dropping him to the floor. Forgetting Montesford completely, Elizabeth fell to her knees at Nathan's side. An enraged snarl erupted behind her as Montesford retrieved his fallen knife and pulled her off her feet in one sweeping motion. He held her imprisoned, his knife at her throat.

No one dared move. The duke stepped forward and Elizabeth

could hear the duke's inner thoughts and knew that his intention was to risk himself to save her if necessary. Elizabeth was terrified. Montesford's rage burned hot, terrible in its intensity. The ballroom fell to deathly silence.

"Montesford."

Everyone gasped as they looked toward the new voice. Hawksley, now on his knees, looked at the Traitor with an arrogance that sent an aching thrill of pride through Elizabeth.

"I see you're still preying on people weaker than you," Hawksley taunted. "You are impotent, though, when matched against me. You have tried to kill me more than once and have failed. You have lost all your power and will never have your final revenge against the duke."

Montesford's arm tightened against her in his excitement and she saw his grisly plan—he was going to kill her and attack Hawksley. As his energy rose, she twisted her head and bit him on the knife hand. Furious, he flung her across the floor, then dove toward Hawksley.

Hawksley twisted as Montesford lunged, leaving the monster off balance as he slashed at nothing but air. As Montesford fell awkwardly downward toward his prey, Hawksley heaved himself up to meet his attacker and with powerful strength, catapulted the killer into the air. Montesford landed hard, crumpled on the ballroom floor. With a groan, he slowly rolled over onto his back, and his bloody fingers slid from the handle of the knife embedded in his chest.

With a venomous look of hatred at the duke, he said, "I had to kill my father, Standbridge, and it was all your fault. When you destroyed my smuggling operation, he found out about it. He said he was going to disinherit me, turn me out, and never call me son again." Montesford's breathing accelerated and his voice rose hysterically, "I loved my father, and you made me kill him." He struggled to rise, then fell back, vengeance indelibly etched on his still face.

The duke pushed his way through to Hawksley and helped him to his feet. "Elizabeth," Hawksley croaked, and staggered to her side. He knelt beside her and pulled her into his arms. "Oh, sweetheart, you brave little fool. You had to attack him, didn't you?"

She stirred and opened her eyes. She reached up to touch his face. "You're safe?" Tears fell on her cheeks. "I am sorry I was forced to shame you after all, but I couldn't let the monster get you."

Hawksley smiled at her worry for him and sought a way to prove his love to her. Looking at the hovering crowd, he said, "Have you all had the pleasure of meeting my betrothed?"

Chapter Nineteen

HAWKSLEY stood back from the study window lest Woolfe and Elizabeth spot him watching them. These days it was impossible to find Elizabeth alone to have that final discussion she promised, and here she was tonight at the front door of the town house, standing under the light meant to welcome the guests coming to Mariane's engagement party, bidding an extended fond farewell—or was it just *adieu*—to Woolfe. He clenched his teeth and told himself he would let her make her own decision, and he would honor it no matter what her answer might be.

Hawksley stiffened as Woolfe leaned forward and kissed Elizabeth. Perhaps, after all, he would not fight fair.

"Woolfe!" Elizabeth said. "What on earth are you doing?"

"Just seeing if you might like to take me up on the offer I made a few days ago."

"Be serious, Woolfe. One fiancé is really quite enough, thank you."

"I am serious, Elizabeth. And I wholeheartedly agree, one is quite enough. Since you haven't said yes to Hawksley, why don't you look into your crystal ball and see if that one should not be me?"

She smiled back and said, "You know I cannot do that on command, I just have to wait—oh, no . . . how can this be?" She touched his sleeve to steady herself and looked into her vision. "Oh, Woolfe, I do see you . . . and there is someone else with you . . . she has the most incredible silver hair."

Woolfe stiffened and involuntarily whispered the name, "Taryn? But this is impossible, she has already chosen someone else."

"Oh, Woolfe, I see trouble . . . you must hurry." She blinked, focusing once again on Woolfe. "If you want her, she can be your future, dear Woolfe."

Woolfe looked in thoughtful wonder at Elizabeth's serene face. "And you, Elizabeth, what does the future hold for you?"

"I would that I could know mine as clearly as I just looked into yours."

Woolfe motioned toward the house behind them. "Perhaps your future has been standing in front of you all along, and you need only acknowledge it."

"If only it were that simple. You see . . . oh, no!" She closed her eyes while a red blush crept up her neck and into her face. She rubbed her fingers across her forehead, trying to oust the picture that moved so lazily into her thoughts. Finally she looked back at the study window, the promise of retribution in her eyes. "Oh, that wretch, that low . . . " She grabbed Woolfe's shoulders and kissed him right on the mouth. "Go with God, dear friend. Bring your sweetheart back to see us when you have her right and tight." She glared at the now empty window and marched back into the house.

She opened the door herself just as Tarr leaned forward to do the office for her. She glared at him and said, "Where is Hawksley?"

"He said he would be in the garden, miss."

"Fine." She slammed the door behind her with all her might.

Tarr turned to Marsh and, eyes sparkling, said, "Just think of the children we'll be having here." Marsh shuddered.

Elizabeth found Hawksley sitting calmly on a bench, and went immediately on attack. "What was that outrageous maneuver you orchestrated just now? I told you not to send any more provocative thoughts my way, and what do you fill my head with? Us kissing in the nursery, and the study, and in the ballroom—Nathan, that was the most—"

He looked at her innocently. "I thought you might wish to compare my courting technique with Woolfe's. And since you find time for him and not for me, I was forced to resort to the only tactic available."

"You know we have been getting ready for Mariane's wedding."

"I find it is the most amazing thing, Elizabeth. After all the squabbling between the Lowden household and ours, the minute a wedding was mentioned, all was forgotten and you ladies have been working together like an assaulting army. And with all those busy hands, you still have no time for me."

He raised an eyebrow. "How can Eunice find time for Grandfather and you cannot for me? You have not seen any grass grow under her feet since he asked for her hand, have you? Face it, Elizabeth, you have been avoiding me, or more specifically, avoiding the issue."

"I told you, Nathan, that I wanted to see the impact of my actions at Lady Cowper's ball, that I was not going to burden you with a woman labeled as a lunatic."

"And I told you that I do not care what anyone thinks. Why, the only one who tried to publicly stir up any trouble was Lord Stanley and a few of his cronies." Hawksley chuckled. "After Grandfather offered to help him air out his financial status, Lord Stanley decided that an indefinite stay at the seaside was what his empty pockets needed."

A smile touched the corners of her mouth. Hawksley continued, "And in case you are still concerned, let me share with you what is being said. Each paper carries a different story and the satirists are making a fortune. Cruikshank has dubbed his caricature, *The Villain and the Gypsy.*"

Hawksley grinned. "The most popular opinion, and my personal favorite, is that I planned the entire thing, put the words into your mouth, and am the most brilliant spy—ah—War Office negotiator His Majesty has ever employed." Then he teased, "Unfortunately, the critics rate your performance as mediocre at best. Too dramatic, they say."

She laughed softly, then released a sigh and strolled to the rock-garden waterfall, soaking her slippers in the damp grass. He followed along a few steps behind her, and at long last pulled her back into his embrace. She felt his arms come round her, one at her waist and one at her shoulders. His warm mouth nuzzled the nape of her neck and his teeth nipped a soft command of surrender. Her heart pounded as the fragrance of roses completed the magic picture. *It was her vision, the one she saw in Paxton.*

"So, Elizabeth, what is your excuse now?"

She could not have answered if she tried, for before her enfolded a vision of their future together. Oh, she breathed, there are girls . . . twins? And the boys, what a rowdy mob they are . . . and they look exactly like . . . Nathan. She hugged the secret to her. If someday a little resentment against him rose, she would simply think of those little boys who were going to be all the reprisal she would ever need.

Hawksley slipped a ring off the tip of his little finger and held it up to the light shining down from the tall windows of the house. Green lights flashed through the emerald stone of the ring.

Filled with the euphoria of her vision, she could hardly speak. Oh, life with him would be perfect . . . except for . . . she straightened up as she remembered the one problem they had not solved, her ability to read his thoughts.

He forestalled her last objection with a teasing threat. "I shall keep sending you messages until you say yes, you know."

She burst into laughter, realizing how ridiculous all her worries and obstacles were. She had seen the future and had no wish to change it. Indeed, the challenge of outwitting him for years to come was something she heartily looked forward to.

She joined in the fun. "Naughty pictures, you mean. You should be ashamed, Nathan."

"It's my weapon against your nosy mind, Elizabeth. I have just been practicing."

"What do you mean?" She frowned, the light of suspicion dawning.

"Every time you take a little trip into my mind, I shall send you back a love letter to counteract it. I do believe we are rather evenly matched."

"You wouldn't."

"I already have. Perhaps you would like to bargain. Wear my ring or think my thoughts."

"You scoundrel." She held out her hand.

"Incorrigible brat." He slid the ring home.

"I love you, Elizabeth. Will you marry me?"

She leaned her head back against his shoulder. "I do not think I can resist the challenge, Nathan. Who else would take on a bad-tempered man whose idea of courting is to blackmail the woman he loves?"

He caressed his cheek against hers. "Probably the woman who thinks nothing of delivering babies, stitching knife wounds, or chasing fearlessly across the street at midnight to accost her most deadly enemy."

She looked up at him, a twinkle in her eye, and sighed, "A perfect match."

Epilogue

"A RE you sure you want to try this, Nathan?"

"Of course, my grandmother had the gift too."

"All right, then. Concentrate your mind on where I want those clever fingers of yours."

"Here?"

"Try harder."

"Here. I'm sure this is it."

"Ummm, I believe you are just a little bit gifted too, Nathan."

"And you want a kiss . . . right here, correct?"

"Oh, my—"

Just then a cry rang out, one that brought both participants upright and scrambling into their robes. They rushed down to the end of the hall and hurried into the bedroom. Two tousled girls sat in a bed. One held her blanket to her ear and a thumb firmly in her mouth. Her charcoal eyes were filled with tears.

The other girl tossed her red hair at their entrance as if to say it was about time. "She wants you."

Hawksley knelt beside the bed. "What, darling? What does she want?"

The red-haired child rolled her bright green eyes in impatience. Then she turned to the first child and looked at her intently. Turning back to her father, she said, "She wants a drink."

The dark-haired child took her thumb from her mouth and clarified her request. "Chocolate, please." Then she looked at the red-haired child and smiled. "Sister wants lemonade."